A collecti...
the world...

Two books from international bestselling author of more than ninety novels

EMMA DARCY

"*The Marriage Risk* by Emma Darcy sizzles with...hot scenes, enjoyable characters and interesting story development."
—*Romantic Times*

"Emma Darcy's *The Hot-Blooded Groom* is a daring tale filled with sensational characters and red-hot tension."
—*Romantic Times*

EMMA DARCY

Hot-Blooded Affairs

Containing

**The Marriage Risk
& The Hot-Blooded Groom**

*All the characters in this book have no existence outside the
imagination of the author, and have no relation whatsoever to anyone
bearing the same name or names. They are not even distantly inspired
by any individual known or unknown to the author, and all the
incidents are pure invention.*

*M&B™ and M&B™ with the Rose Device
are trademarks of the publisher.
Harlequin Mills & Boon Limited, Eton House,
18-24 Paradise Road,
Richmond, Surrey TW9 1SR*

Hot-Blooded Affairs © by Harlequin Books S.A. 2007

The Marriage Risk and *The Hot-Blooded Groom* were
first published in Great Britain by Harlequin Mills & Boon
Limited in separate, single volumes.

The Marriage Risk © Emma Darcy 2000
The Hot-Blooded Groom © Emma Darcy 2001

ISBN: 978 0 263 85554 8

010-0407

*Printed and bound in Spain
by Litografia Rosés S.A., Barcelona*

The Marriage Risk

EMMA DARCY

Initially a French/English teacher, **Emma Darcy** changed careers to computer programming before the happy demands of marriage and motherhood. Very much a people person, and always interested in relationships, she finds the world of romantic fiction a thrilling one and the challenge of creating her own cast of characters very addictive.

Look for Emma Darcy's latest novel
The Billionaire's Scandalous Marriage
**coming in May 2007 from Mills & Boon
Modern Romance®.**

CHAPTER ONE

'AND how is my ever delightful and worthy Miss Worthington this morning?'

Lucy gritted her teeth against a seething wave of resentment, almost hating the man who clearly had no idea how such blithely tossed off words lacerated her heart.

The breezy greeting from her boss probably meant he'd spent a highly pleasurable night with his latest woman. His voice lilted with macho smugness, a sure sign of sexual satisfaction, and his playful play on her surname accentuated the fact that Lucy wasn't the type he'd toss in his bed, however delightful she might be to work with. *Worthy* women didn't excite him.

Though if her breasts were big enough to fill and overflow a D-cup bra, he might consider her more *bed*-worthy, Lucy thought caustically, ungritting her teeth and turning from the filing cabinet to direct a bland smile at the sexy wolf who employed her as his sensible secretary.

'Good morning, sir,' she piped sweetly.

James Hancock was the classic tall dark and handsome prototype, with the potent addition of a shrewd business brain and the kind of charm that won friends and influenced all the *right* people. He was thirty-four, in the prime of life, had the well-earned reputation of being a dynamic agent in the entertainment field, which helped make him an A-list bachelor in Sydney society, and he was definitely exuding an air of being on top of his world.

His rakish black eyebrows lifted. 'Sir?'

She cocked her head on one side, returning his quizzical look. 'Weren't you cueing me to greet you formally with *your* Miss Worthington?'

He laughed, his blue eyes twinkling devilish delight. 'The comeback queen strikes again. What would I do without you to entertain me, Lucy?'

Resentment crawled down her spine and loosened her tongue. 'I imagine you'd quickly find someone else to score off.'

'Score off?' he repeated incredulously. 'My dear Lucy, the scoring honours invariably go to you.'

'Really? I hadn't noticed.'

She picked up the files she'd extracted from the cabinet and carried them to her desk, ready to hand them over to him.

'It comes naturally to you,' he assured her, grinning from ear to ear. 'One of the joys of office hours, hearing your salty down-to-earth comments. They invariably reduce all the hype in this business to what's real and what isn't. An invaluable talent.'

'Invaluable enough to be *worth* a raise in salary?'

'Ouch!' He mockingly slapped a hand against his forehead. 'She strikes again.'

'Pure logic, James,' she pointed out with limpid innocence while savagely wanting him to pay for seeing her as nothing but a bottom line sounding board when it came to dealing with his high-flying clients. 'You'll need to check these files while answering this morning's e-mails. Is there anything else you need from me right now?' she asked, pressing for him to enter his own office and leave her alone to get over the frustrations he aroused in her.

He ignored the files, shaking an admonishing finger at her. 'You're a money-grubber, Lucy Worthington.'

She shrugged. 'A woman has to look out for herself these days. I just don't believe in free meal-tickets.' Which was a neat little jibe at the women he favoured, women who traded on lush physical assets to get where they wanted.

'Ha!' James crowed. 'I gave you free tickets to tonight's charity bash.'

'Oh?' Lucy viewed him with sceptical eyes. 'You're not expecting anything of me, like being conveniently on hand to fix up some last-minute hitch with the program?'

'Completely free,' he insisted loftily.

'How novel!' She smiled. 'I might just keep you to that, James.'

'A reward for all the good work you've done in putting the program together.'

Since the tickets were a thousand dollars each and her salary was already generous, Lucy couldn't, in all conscience, imply she wasn't well rewarded for the job she did. 'Thank you. I shall look forward to relaxing and enjoying myself tonight,' she said dis-

missively while still doubting the tickets were entirely free of obligation.

*Why would he give them to her if he didn't want
her there for some reason?*

His eyes twinkled. 'It will be my pleasure to see
you enjoying yourself, Lucy.'

He did have a motive. She could feel it in her
bones.

'Who are you bringing?' he tossed at her as he
finally picked up the files she'd supplied.

'A friend.'

One eyebrow lifted teasingly. 'A male friend?'

Did he think her so sexless she couldn't have one?
Lucy struggled to maintain a calm demeanour. 'Yes.
Is that a problem for you?' The challenge slid off
her tongue before she could stop it.

'Not at all. Glad to hear it.'

He went off smiling, carrying the files he needed,
leaving the door between their two offices open so
he could call out to her when he wanted to.

Lucy sagged onto the chair behind her desk,
shaken by the thought his last words had conjured
up. Had he suspected she only had female friends?
That she might even be a lesbian, because she didn't
openly adore *him* like all the other women who
came through these offices?

A wave of wretched misery churned through her
stomach. She should get herself out of this job. It
was eating up any kind of normal life she might
have, being with James Hancock every working day,

constantly wanting him, being jealous of every woman who took his eye.

He was never going to view her as anything other than an efficient secretary. Eight months she'd been with him—eight months of a helpless sexual awareness she couldn't control or even dampen. Lust at first sight, she now thought with sick irony, and it hadn't worn off.

No other man had ever drawn such a strong physical response from her. In fact, she had never really understood why other women got themselves in such a mess over men, losing all perspective and self-respect, too, when they were badly let down. *Being sensible* had been Lucy's long-held belief on how one should conduct one's life. Indeed, her mother had drilled it into her from early childhood and Lucy had come to see it saved her from a lot of grief.

But *being sensible* couldn't seem to override what James Hancock made her feel. Over the years she had admired the physiques of other men, but it wasn't just physique with James. Somehow he emanated a sexual energy that was quintessentially male, and as much as she'd tried to block it out, it always got to her, stirring up a hornet's nest of hormones.

Despairingly she propped her elbows on the desk and rested her head in her hands. The truth was, she didn't feel she really belonged to herself any more, and she didn't like the person she was becoming. What right did she have to think bitchy thoughts about women she didn't know, just because James favoured them over her? It was pure sour grapes and if she didn't stop it, she'd end up sour all through.

She should move on. Give in her notice and go.

It was the sensible thing to do.

Today was Friday. First thing Monday morning her resignation would be on his desk.

No doubt James would have his latest gorgeous model on his arm tonight at the charity ball for the Starwish Foundation, and no doubt it would ram home to her how hopeless it was to spend any more time craving what would never be available to her.

Come Monday she would definitely have screwed herself up to hand in her notice and put James Hancock behind her. For good!

So…she was bringing a man. Interesting to see what kind of man Lucy favoured, James told himself as he settled at his desk and switched on the computer. She never chatted about her private life and he couldn't deny he was curious. Most women opened up to him but not Lucy.

She was one very buttoned up lady who never lost her head over anything. Which made her the perfect assistant in his line of work, with half his clients all too ready to throw a fit of temperament if any little upset occurred. Put Lucy in the eye of a storm and she could ground everyone in no time flat by coming up with the most sensible response to the situation.

An accountant he decided. That was the kind of

man Lucy would approve of—a nice, safe accountant, solid and dependable, someone who'd never broken a law in his life and never would, a nine-to-five man, regular in his habits, serious-minded, considerate of her needs, probably wore spectacles with fine gold rims and very conservative clothes. That was Lucy's taste—neat and conservative.

James nodded to himself as he brought up the e-mail inbox on the monitor screen. He was sure he was right but Lucy had been with him eight months and all that time there'd been an elusive quality about her that nagged at him. More so, the longer they'd been together. It was worth giving her the tickets to get those tantalising flashes of something else brooding behind Lucy Worthington's buttoned up exterior sorted out in his mind.

He'd even started thinking about her when he was with other women, missing her sharp wit, wondering what she might be like in bed. And that had to be stopped. He was not going to mess with the best secretary he'd ever had. Besides which, Lucy would probably be horrified at some of the thoughts he'd been harbouring lately. Seeing her with a man of her choice—almost certainly an accountant—would definitely affirm her not-to-be-played-with status.

The telephone rang. He picked up the receiver.

'Buffy Tanner for you on line one,' Lucy stated crisply.

'Thank you.' He smiled as he pressed the button to take the the call. Nothing hidden about Buffy. She let it all hang out. And that was fine by him. Very relaxing.

'Hi, Buffy,' he said warmly, bringing her lush curves to mind.

'James darling, I'm sorry to be calling you in business hours, but I might not be able to catch you later. What time did you tell me I have to be ready by for tonight?'

He winced. Punctuality was not Buffy's strong point. 'Seven-thirty. And we must leave on the dot. I did warn you.'

She sighed. 'I have a long shooting schedule to-day. A new swimwear range at Bondi Beach. I'll be a mess. Will it matter if we're a bit late?'

'Yes, it will matter. It's my people doing the show tonight. I have to be on hand. If you want to cry off…'

'No, of course I don't.'

He could hear her pouting. A very sexy pout it was, too, but right now he felt impatient with it.

'Seven-thirty, Buffy. Be ready or I'll go without you,' he said irritably and cut the connection, thinking Lucy wouldn't keep her man waiting. She was a very precise time-keeper, always ensuring that appointments were kept.

With a niggling sense of discontent, James applied himself to answering the e-mails that required an immediate response. He worked through them, adding the printouts to the files, making notes of things for Lucy to check. She never slipped up on details, which was another thing he liked about her.

He could count on Lucy getting things right. No
excuses. Meticulous attention to detail.

He called her into his office, his instructions already clipped onto the files for her attention. He
smiled over his own judgement of her as she walked
in, wearing her all-purpose navy suit, smart, classic,
timeless, typical of what a sensible career woman
would buy. It would take her anywhere and never
go out of fashion.

The skirt ended modestly, just above her knees.
No micro-minis for Lucy. Yet what could be seen
of her legs—nicely shaped calves and fine ankles—
suggested the full length of them could form quite
a distracting sight. Just as well they weren't on
show, James told himself, mentally approving her
choice of apparel which neatly skimmed her cute
little figure.

Being below average height, Lucy could never be
called statuesque, but she was certainly built in
pleasing proportion, and the way she twitched her
pert bottom at times was definitely distracting. And
tempting. James stifled these wayward thoughts and
fixed his gaze on her face.

It was a finely boned face, not strikingly pretty,
though if all the make-up tricks of a beautician were
applied to it, James fancied it could look quite stunning. It, also, was perfectly proportioned, though the
spectacles she wore gave it a prim look, which was
accentuated by the way her hair was pulled back and
pinned into a chignon from which no tendrils *ever*
escaped.

The thought of unpinning what was obviously a wealth of soft brown hair presented a tantalising prospect. Would Lucy come undone in other ways? And if he took her spectacles off, what would he see in her eyes?

As it was, all he saw was a bright intelligence looking at him expectantly, nothing but business on *her* mind.

Piqued by her apparent indifference to what many other women considered his attractions, James found himself blurting out, 'Is he an accountant?' and could have instantly kicked himself for letting her get under his skin to this extent.

Her smooth creamy forehead creased as her eyebrows lifted above the colourless rims of her spectacles. 'To whom are you referring?'

Instead of dismissing the slip—the only prudent thing to do at this point—James lost his head completely to a potent mixture of compelling curiosity and a rebellious rush of seriously displaced hormones.

'Your partner for the ball tonight,' he shot at her.

She looked incredulous. 'You want to know if he's an accountant?'

'Is he?'

'Do you need an accountant on hand for some reason?'

'No, I don't *need* one.'

Her eyes narrowed in suspicion. 'Then why are you asking?'

Why, indeed? James gritted his teeth. He was getting no satisfaction here and was fast making himself look foolish. His mind zapped through possible escape routes.

'Conversation always goes more smoothly if I'm prepared with a knowledge of people's backgrounds. Your partner is the only one I won't know at our table.'

She stared at him. Her chin took on a mulish tilt. Her shoulders visibly squared. In fact, her whole body took on a tense rigidity. Even her hands clenched. James had the wild notion she was barely stopping herself from stepping forward and hitting him. Which, of course was ridiculous! He'd made a reasonable statement. He *did* like to be prepared with background information before meeting anyone. She knew that.

Though he had to concede this was more personal than professional ground. Her private partner wasn't exactly his business. Maybe it was simply the effect of the glass lenses but her eyes looked very glittery and he was definitely sensing some dagger-like thoughts being directed very sharply at him. But dammit all! He was going to meet the guy tonight so what was she getting so uptight about?

'Why do you think my escort for the ball is an accountant, James?' she bit out, her voice dripping with icicles.

'Well, is he?' he persisted, frustrated by her evasive tactics.

'Generally speaking, people consider accountants

boring,' she stated, once again denying him an answer.

'Not at all. Obviously they're very intelligent, very clever, very astute,' he put in quickly.

'Boring,' she repeated as though she was drilling a hole in his head. 'Boringly worthy for Lucy Worthington.'

Uh-oh! James saw the red rag waving. He instantly gestured appeasement. 'Now, Lucy, I have never thought you boring. You know that,' he pressed earnestly. 'And I can't imagine you tolerating a boring man. You're taking this the wrong way. I was merely wondering…'

'What kind of man I'd bring.'

The intense focus of her eyes was like an electric drill, sparks flying as it kept tunneling into his brain to the true core of his question. James shifted uncomfortably. He didn't like the sense of her seeing right through him. No doubt about it—he'd dug himself a hole and somehow he had to climb out of it with some fast face-saving.

'It would be helpful if you'd give me his name, Lucy,' he said reasonably, dropping the background issue which had stirred her into this totally unacceptable attack. 'It would save any slip-up with introductions.'

Her mouth thinned. Her eyes glittered even more sharply. He sensed her fierce urge to cut him to ribbons and perversely enough—given the tricky situation he'd brought upon himself—he felt quite pumped up by the passion she was emitting. Nothing

cool and collected about *this* Lucy. Clearly he'd
tapped into the real flesh and blood woman beneath
the navy suit and James found himself actually getting excited—aroused by the prospect of the inner
Lucy emerging. If she did step forward to tangle
with him physically…

'Josh Rogan,' she said.

'What?'

'You asked for his name,' she tersely reminded
him.

James gave himself a swift mental shake as de-
flation set in. The navy suit had won again, damn
it! The Lucy he'd wanted to experience was in full
retreat. Which was just as well, he told himself,
quelling the madness of imagining her sprawled
across his desk while he satisfied a rampant desire
for the most intimate knowledge of her. It was absurd to have this sudden burst of sexual fantasies
about his secretary when he had Buffy Tanner more
than willing to satisfy his carnal needs.

'Josh Rogan,' he repeated, grateful that Lucy had
her head on straight and was heeding what was appropriate in the work-place between boss and secretary. However, something about the name she'd
given niggled him. 'Isn't there a lamb curry called
Josh Rogan?'

He was almost sure of it, the suspicion instantly
growing that Lucy was paying him back by giving
a false name that would embarrass him when he
used it tonight.

'No,' she said with a fine edge of scorn. 'The curry is called Rogan Josh.'

'Oh!' He frowned. Was she playing him up or not?

Her mouth softened and curled. 'Actually, I don't think Josh would mind your confusing him with the curry.' Her hips gave a wicked little wiggle as she added, 'He is hot stuff.'

Hot stuff? Lucy with *hot stuff?* Unaccountably James felt his temperature rising. 'I'll keep that in mind,' he snapped. 'You can take these files now. I've made notes for you.'

'Fine!'

She smiled at him as she stepped forward and scooped them up from the desk. Then she sashayed out of his office with all the feline grace of a cat, waving its tail in his face.

James sat brooding over this aspect of Lucy Worthington for some time. He was definitely right about her. There was much more to Lucy than met the eye. The navy suit was nothing but a front, designed to put him off seeking the real truth about the kind of woman who burned inside it.

Good thing he'd given her those free tickets. It was going to be interesting—illuminating—to see how she behaved with her *hot stuff* tonight. Hair down, sexy dress, full make-up on, no spectacles…if her Josh Rogan was truly *hot stuff,* he'd expect that of her.

A zing of anticipation tingled through James. It had nothing to do with looking forward to having

Buffy Tanner on his arm tonight. He didn't even think of the swimsuit model with the lush curves and sexy pout.

Tonight he was going to see the unbuttoned Lucy Worthington in action!

CHAPTER TWO

LUCY was still boiling mad as she stomped up the stairs to her first-floor apartment in Bellevue Hill at six o'clock that evening.

An accountant!

A boring old accountant!

O-o-o-o-h, she wanted to punch James Hancock's lights out with Josh tonight. She wanted to see him sitting at their table, looking like a stunned mullet as *her* partner outshone him, which Josh was perfectly capable of doing, the ultimate party guy when he was in brilliant form—huge charisma, pouring out his energy in bursts of winning charm. *And* he was as handsome as sin.

It was handy that he lived right next door to her in this old apartment block. All she had to do was ask and either Josh or his partner, Larry Berger, would help her with anything she needed help with. *Gay* men, she had decided long ago, could make the very best friends for a woman.

Even before she had known Josh was *gay,* back in their school days, she had really liked him as a person and they'd been good friends. He was kind and sensitive and supportive, as well as being great fun.

She had been grateful to have him as her boy-

friend then, being able to go out as a couple without
any of the hassle of being pressured to have sex.
Some boys could get mean and nasty in pushing
their wants. Some men, too, she'd found in later
years. Even the few relationships she'd enjoyed for
a while had lost their shine with the build-up of
selfish demands. On the whole, her mother was
right. Men wanted women on their own terms and
being fair didn't come into the equation.

Josh was always sweet relief from all that. His
company had no price-tag on it. He was safe and
safe was good. She couldn't get into any trouble
with Josh Rogan. He didn't feel any sexual desire
for her and she didn't feel any for him. In fact, he
was the perfect foil to her ungovernable feelings
towards James Hancock, whom, in her wilder fantasies, she'd like to handcuff to her bed and watch
him go mad with lust for her.

Which she knew was absurd!

James Hancock was never going to see her as
anything but his *worthy* secretary. But no way was
she going to let him think the only man she could
attract was a boring accountant!

Having emerged from the stairwell, she bypassed
her apartment door and strode straight to Josh's,
ringing his doorbell with an emphatic need for a
swift response.

He was satisfyingly prompt in opening the door.
'Lucy love!' His eyebrows arched over merry brown
eyes. 'A change in plan?'

'Yes,' she snarled as a fresh rush of venom spilled

onto her tongue. 'My beastly employer thinks my escort this evening will be an accountant.'

'Like…boring?'

Very quick on the uptake was Josh. 'Exactly,' she confirmed. 'In retaliation I told him you were *hot stuff*.'

'Absolutely! When I'm hot I literally sizzle with high octane energy. You want me to sizzle?'

'I want you to burn him up. And Josh, wear that gorgeous metallic waistcoast and the blue silk tie.'

'A touch of flamboyance with the formal suit?'

'Shining is the order of the night.'

'Lucy love, I shall glitter for you.'

'Not too much,' she warned. 'You're not to let anyone guess you're gay.'

'Totally straight behaviour, I promise.'

She heaved a sigh to relieve all the horrid pent-up feelings James Hancock had left her with today. 'I need to get that guy, Josh.'

'In more ways than one I gather.'

She eyed him wryly. 'Hopeless case, I'm afraid.'

'Oh, little miracles can happen.' He grinned, gleeful mischief twinkling in his eyes. 'Trust me. We'll make the man see you in a different light tonight.'

'I'll still be me, Josh.'

'And so you should be. It's his vision at fault, Lucy love, not you,' he assured her. 'Now go and put your glitter gear on and practice some sultry looks in the mirror. If I sizzle and you simmer…'

Despite the dejection that had suddenly overtaken her anger, she laughed at the picture he painted. 'I'm not exactly a sex-pot and *he'll* be with one. Buffy Tanner, the swimsuit model with the overflowing D-cup.'

Josh gestured an airy dismissal. 'You're fixated on big boobs. Superficial padding.'

'Padding or not, I wish mine were bigger.'

'*Sexy* is more in the attitude than the equipment,' came the knowing advice. 'And one other thing. Best to turn up late.'

'I'm never late. I don't like being late,' she protested.

Sheer wickedness sparkled back at her. 'But I'm hot stuff, Lucy love, and you just couldn't resist having me. Punctuality shot to hell!'

She couldn't help laughing again. 'I doubt he'd even notice, Josh.'

'Oh, he'll notice all right.' He waggled his eyebrows as he elaborated. 'His predictable little secretary suddenly not fitting the frame he's put her in. Believe me. He'll notice.'

'Well, I don't actually *need* to be there on time,' she argued to her obsession for punctuality. 'He did say the tickets were free, no work-strings attached.'

'There you are then,' Josh asserted triumphantly. 'Off you go. I'll bring you a gin cocktail at seven-thirty. Some Mother's Ruin to put you in the right party mood.'

They should be leaving at seven-thirty, her time-keeping brain dictated. It would take half an hour to get from Bellevue Hill to Darling Harbour, park Josh's car, walk to the Sydney Convention Centre where the fund-raising ball was being held in the main auditorium. Cocktails in the foyer from eight o'clock the tickets read.

But so what if she had a cocktail here? The world would not come to an end if she didn't turn up on the dot of eight o'clock. Why not be unpredictable for once?

'Okay. And thanks, Josh.' She flashed him an appreciative smile. 'A friend in need is a friend indeed.'

The very best of friends, she thought warmly as she left him and let herself into her own apartment. Even this place, which was now hers—with a hefty mortgage—Josh had advised her was a good buy, if she could scrape up the money. The previous owners, now a divorced couple, had wanted a quick sale, and Lucy had stepped into a bargain, considering the real estate values in this location, midway between the inner city and Bondi Beach.

Walking into her very own space always gave her spirits a lift. James Hancock could call her a money-grubber as much as he liked. At least she didn't have to depend on a man to provide her with the security of a home, which wasn't secure at all if there was a divorce. Her careful savings over the years had added up to a solid down payment on this apartment. She was now a woman of property and she'd achieved it by herself.

Her mother was definitely right.

Being sensible did bring its own rewards.

Yet as Lucy headed for her bedroom, she wished

she had splashed out and bought a glamorous gown for tonight. Although her one little black dress was perfectly adequate for any evening engagement, it was...*boring*. Not that it really mattered, she told herself. It was still a classy dress, bought cheaply from a secondhand designer boutique, and it would do...once again. She couldn't compete with Buffy Tanner anyway. No point in trying. And the money saved would go towards buying the furniture she wanted.

All the same, she felt vaguely disgruntled with her basic common sense as she set about getting ready for the charity ball. It would undoubtedly give her considerable satisfaction to flaunt a flamboyant Josh as her partner tonight, hopefully delivering a metaphorical slap in the face to James Hancock and his opinion of her private life. But the truth was she never did do anything wildly exciting. Perhaps she was overly careful in her weighing up of whether a step was worth taking or not.

The worthy Miss Worthington...

The words stung.

The urge to act in a totally unworthy and outrageous way suddenly held a highly tempting attraction. Especially in front of James Hancock. Free tickets meant free from any responsibility. She could play as fast and as loose as she liked with Josh, knowing there'd be no nasty consequences from him, and if she was going to hand in her notice and find another job, why not do and say anything that came into her head. Puncturing James Hancock's complacent judgement of her would go a long way towards salving her pride. And hurt.

Lawless Lucy…

She chuckled over the name that had slid into her mind.

Why not?

She stopped burning and started simmering. *Attitude,* Josh had said. Never mind her clothes or anything else. It was all in the attitude.

It wasn't like Lucy to be late.

James Hancock couldn't stop himself from glancing at his Rolex watch yet again. Another few minutes and the crowd of guests enjoying cocktails in the foyer would be moving into the auditorium. She should have been here at least half an hour ago. While he'd been waiting for her to arrive, he'd greeted an endless stream of the beautiful people and he could feel his smile getting very stiff. Damn the woman! Where was she?

His buoyant anticipation had slid through a frazzle of frustration at her continued non-appearance and was now descending into nagging worry. Had there been an accident? Lucy didn't drive, didn't own a car—too penny-pinching to buy one—but he knew nothing about this Josh Rogan who was bringing her here tonight. If he was *hot stuff* behind a wheel and had involved Lucy in a smash…no, surely she was too level-headed to go out with a speed-jerk.

But what was keeping her?

'Wow! *Who* is *that?*' Buffy breathed, her sexual interest obviously stirred.

James snapped out of his introspection, his male ego somewhat piqued. While Buffy might still be a bit miffed about his lack of appreciation for how long it took to look her fabulous best for him, drooling over other men was hardly designed to win his favour. It was as rude as unpunctuality, another black mark against continuing the relationship.

With a jaundiced eye, he looked where she was looking and was instantly jolted into electric attention. Lucy! Hanging onto the arm of a guy who could be cast as the romantic lead in a movie, and probably *was!*

He had a matinee idol face framed by a riot of black curls, a smile a dentist would be proud of, and he certainly didn't mind drawing attention to what was obviously a gym-toned body, wearing a flashy waistcoat with an over-lustrous coloured tie which mocked the regular black bow-ties most of the other male guests, including himself, had automatically used.

A young trendy show-off, James was telling himself, just as Buffy heaved a sigh that undoubtedly set her opulent breasts aquiver for the approaching sex symbol to notice. His teeth grated together as he switched his attention to Lucy, who, he was suddenly pleased to see looked her normal self—hair neatly tucked up, glasses on, the same little black cocktail dress she invariably wore when called upon to attend an evening function.

Except there was something different about her—
a jaunty self-satisfied sway to her hips—which
struck him as decidedly un-prim. Her mouth, too,
seemed to have a more sensual purse to her lips as
she gazed up at the self-styled *hot stuff,* who was
apparently amusing her with his playboy patter.

In fact, James began to feel that Lucy's prim facade was more innately provocative than Buffy's in-
your-face femininity. It was certainly tantalising,
posed next to the party guy who was parading her
towards the group in which James and Buffy stood,
waiting to be joined by these two last table com-
panions.

Waiting, James thought irritably, able to dismiss
his concern over Lucy's absence now. No doubt it
was the star act she had in tow who had kept them
waiting. He struggled to adopt an affable manner for
performing introductions, hoping Buffy would stop
ogling and have the decency to remember who her
escort was.

'Ah!' he drawled with a bright, welcoming smile.
'Here you are! We're about to go into the auditorium,' he couldn't resist adding to point out their
lateness.

'But there's time for introductions,' Buffy pressed
eagerly, positively jiggling with eagerness.

'Lucy…' James invited, keeping his teeth
clamped in a smile.

'James Hancock, Josh Rogan,' Lucy obliged with
commendable economy.

James braced himself to return a macho handshake but apparently the younger man felt no need to prove himself stronger than Lucy's employer. He simply radiated self-assurance, his dark eyes twinkling the kind of focused interest that made people feel at ease and pleased by the interest. James recognised the ploy. He used it himself. Josh Rogan was clearly an accomplished salesman.

'A pleasure, having you with us,' James rolled out, containing his curiosity while he did the honours. With a sweep of his hand encompassing the group around him, he went on, 'I think you're all acquainted with my punctilious secretary, Lucy Worthington.' *Although she had certainly not been punctilious tonight!* 'Josh, this is Buffy Tanner...'

Buffy leaned over as she took Josh Rogan's hand, giving him an eyeful, but unlike most men who would find the view irresistible, Josh smiled into her face and repeated her name with a happy lilt that could have been applied to a Matilda or a Beatrice. If he was receiving Buffy's signals, he had no intention of answering them.

The other three couples in their group were given the same treatment by Josh Rogan as he was introduced to them. James could find no fault in his manner. The response to him was instinctively positive, an attractive person putting out pleasant vibrations and getting them back.

'What business are you in, Josh?' Hank Gidley, the last one to be introduced, inquired with keen interest.

'Fine wines. Import and export,' came the answer

that allowed James to slot him into place, though it wasn't the place he'd first imagined. However, it did explain the polished savoire-faire displayed so far. Josh Rogan was used to dealing with customers who could afford to buy fine wines and he probably charmed them into buying whatever he wanted to sell.

'Oh, I thought you'd be in modelling like me,' Buffy gushed.

The dark eyes twinkled at her wickedly. 'Like everyone else, I admire external beauty, Buffy, but I'm really into tasting superb content.' And he swung his gaze to Lucy as though she provided the taste he most relished.

She grinned at him—grinned like a Cheshire cat who'd just been fed lashings of cream—and James felt his stomach clenching with outrage. Here he'd been worrying about her, while she had been revelling in being tasted by this wine buff, no doubt with much sensual appreciation. Which explained why her hips had been swaying with that smirk of satisfaction about them.

'Time to go in to our table,' he announced tersely, and wrapped Buffy's arm around his to lead off their little procession.

Nothing was going to plan this evening.

Nothing!

And he didn't like it one bit.

CHAPTER THREE

As THEY followed James and Buffy into the auditorium, Lucy was still laughing inside at the way Josh had complimented her *content*. It was all she could do not to burst out in spluttering amusement. James had been positively tight-faced about Josh preferring her to *his* trophy woman, and Buffy Tanner's jaw had literally dropped at being so cavalierly dismissed in favour of Lucy Worthington.

A double blow to ego, she thought sweetly, and it served them both right—James for calling her his punctilious secretary on what was supposedly her night off, and Buffy Tanner for thinking she could vamp Josh right under Lucy's nose.

However, her amusement didn't last long. As they trailed after the leading couple towards their designated table, Lucy had to concede Buffy looked absolutely stunning, even the back view of her which she was swishing in front of Josh right now. The white beaded evening dress she barely wore was cut almost to her free-flowing buttocks, leaving a lovely curve of naked spine on display, and her shining mane of black ringlets dangled to just below her shoulder-blades, tempting touch.

The gleaming expanse of naked skin was without blemish, and Lucy couldn't really bring herself to

believe there was any cellulite hidden under the
clingy fabric that moved so enticingly with every
step forward. It was all very well to feel smugly
pleased that Buffy couldn't hook Josh with her seductive padding, but she did have James securely at
her side.

With so much femininity on display and available
to him, why would James even bother to look at his
commonplace secretary in a different light? It wasn't
really feasible, Lucy decided, although Josh had certainly delivered a surprise impact out there in the
foyer. That, in itself, was some balm to her wounded
pride.

She told herself to be content with it because miracles were not about to happen on her behalf tonight. Better to concentrate on enjoying herself with
Josh than burn herself up, hankering after what was
never going to be with James Hancock.

The auditorium seemed vast—a sea of tables for
ten set around a dance-floor. Four hundred guests
were pouring in, settling around the starched white
table-cloths which added the required class to the
gleaming cutlery and glasses and the centre-pieces
of angel candles set in clusters of perfect camellias.
Countless silver stars hung from the ceiling, a reminder that this ball was being held by the Starwish
Foundation to raise funds for children with cancer.

James had organised the entertainment, free of
charge, and a young, up-and-coming band was on
stage, enthusiastically playing a jazzy number to get
everyone in a party mood. Behind the musicians on

an elevated platform was a gleaming red convertible, an Alpha Spider sports car which was to be raffled tonight, a prize to promote the idea that in every heart is a hope for something special to magically happen to them.

A wish come true was the theme of the charity ball, but Lucy couldn't, in all honesty, believe her wish that James could suddenly find her desirable had any possibility of coming true. He might wonder how a man like Josh could find her attractive, but why would that niggle of curiosity alter what he felt—or rather, didn't feel—towards his secretary?

Sex appeal was a chemistry thing and Lucy just didn't have the right elements to spark that kind of interest from him. Eight months of purely platonic treatment should have drummed that into her.

Ahead of them, James ushered Buffy to a chair at a table which had a direct view of centre-stage, one row back from the dance-floor. A prime position, Lucy thought, which, of course, James was adept at manoeuvring for himself.

'You next to me, Lucy,' he directed, nodding to his left, having already seated Buffy on his right.

Lucy was dumbstruck and instantly agitated by having to be so close to him all night. It would be sheer torture for her, almost touching, forced to hear how he spoke to Buffy, made excruciatingly aware of the contrast in his manner towards herself.

She had expected him to give his friends the more favoured places facing the stage. She was, after all, only his secretary. However, no-one protested as he organised the rest of the seating and Josh led her around to their designated chairs, murmuring in her ear, 'Guests of honour, Lucy love. Score one to us.'

Lucy couldn't accept that highly hopeful interpretation. It was too far out of step with the all too painful truth of what she *knew*. She suspected a purpose that had nothing to do with any newly noticed womanly charms. The moment James settled on the chair beside her she muttered to him, 'Why did you put me here?'

His blue eyes sliced to her with a glittering intent that cut into her heart. 'Why not?'

'You said I wasn't wanted for work tonight.'

'You aren't.'

'You've placed me on hand, right next to you.'

One eyebrow lifted in mocking challenge. 'Is that offensive to you?'

'No, of course not,' she quickly denied, although she hated—violently hated—being trapped in this position.

'Is it beyond the realms of your imagination that I might enjoy your company outside of work?'

Lucy flushed, intensely embarrassed by a directness that hit on her own secret desires. 'You've got company,' she pointed out, nodding to Buffy who was busy eyeing Josh with rapt admiration.

'I'm greedy,' James replied, totally unabashed at admitting to wanting both women to entertain him. 'It's my table, Lucy. I'm entitled to arrange it how I like.'

'What? Beauty on one side and brains on the other?' she couldn't stop herself from sniping.

His mouth curled. 'I wouldn't put it quite like that.'

'How would you put it?' she challenged fiercely, completely losing her cool as resentment of his selfish decision raged through her.

His gaze flicked to Josh, then back to her. 'Interesting to think of what caused you to be late, Lucy,' he drawled. 'Somehow I doubt it was intellectual conversation.'

Shock zapped her mind for several seconds. Then a wild welling of triumphant glee billowed over the shock. It had worked! Bringing Josh and being late *was* making James see her differently. At the very least he no longer had her pigeon-holed as his worthy secretary. She was now an interesting woman!

A smile tugged at her lips and broke into a full-blown grin. 'It's such a pleasure to feel free of responsibility, I just let my head go,' she airily explained.

'Heady stuff…wine-tasting,' he remarked sardonically.

Another jolt as Lucy realised he was actually thinking *sexual* tasting. Which was hilarious in one sense, given Josh's inclinations, yet deliciously satisfying in another, given the erotic images James was now applying to her.

She giggled. It was the wrong thing to do. She should have simmered. Josh's advice had been spot on so far. If she was to strengthen the result that had been attained, she had to project a sexy attitude. To cover the sensuality gaffe, she snatched up the glass of champagne a circling waiter had poured and lifted it in a toast.

'To tasting more of the best,' she cried recklessly.

He picked up his glass and she could have sworn his eyes simmered as he said, 'Perhaps the best is yet to come. One has to taste a range of bottles to know which gives the ultimate pleasure.'

'I'm sure that's true,' she agreed, her fantasy world swiftly building a line of gorgeous men with James placing himself at the end of it, ready and willing to show her he was the best.

'What's true?' Buffy interjected.

Lucy's fevered mind snapped back to sober reality. Seeing her differently didn't mean that James found her any more attractive. He might be intrigued by the light Josh had supposedly shed on her private life, but Buffy was his choice for *his* private life. She scrambled for a sensible answer to the question asked.

'You need to sample a lot of different wines before judging which pleases the palate most,' she eventually managed, turning to Josh for his support, wanting him to carry the conversation while she recovered some equilibrium. 'Isn't that so, Josh?'

'Absolutely,' he chimed in. 'Though I must say the very finest do stand out, once tasted.' He slid Lucy a mischievously intimate glance. 'Unforgettable.'

The urge to giggle again almost made her choke

on her champagne. Josh had obviously been eaves-
dropping on her conversation with James and was
deliberately stirring the hot-pot, being wickedly suggestive. She controlled herself enough to sip the
champagne, pretending nothing of any great note
had been said.

'Do you do wine-tasting too, Lucy?' Buffy asked.

She constructed a gently dismissive smile. 'Not
really. Josh occasionally shares his experience with
me.'

That should have been an end to it. However, her
partner in pretence decided he'd been thrown the
ball and it was his job to run with it as provocatively
as he could.

'Lucy uses me shamelessly, Buffy,' he declared.
'As far as she's concerned, I'm on call to deliver—'
he paused to slide Lucy a salacious look '—anything
she wants...when she wants it.'

Lucy kicked him under the table. He was exag-
gerating their relationship and making 'the wants'
sound far from innocent.

'And do you?' James asked somewhat dryly.

'If it's humanly possible,' came Josh's fervent reply. 'An invitation to be with Lucy is a gold-card
guarantee of pleasure.' He sighed and shook his
head at her as he added, 'I wish she didn't keep
herself to herself as much as she does.'

She kicked him again, forcefully warning him he
was overplaying his hand, but his eyes were dancing
merrily and she knew he was having too much fun
to desist.

'So Lucy calls the shots in your relationship,' James commented.

'Very strong-minded lady,' Josh confided. 'When Lucy sets her mind on a path, you either fall in with her or get off.'

'Now come on, Josh,' she chided, feeling she had to scale down his assertions about her. 'I'm not that inconsiderate of you.'

His hands lifted in an eloquent gesture of appeal. 'Lucy love, I wasn't complaining. I wouldn't miss falling in with you for anything!' He laid one hand over his heart. 'Here I am, your willing slave for the night, your pleasure my pleasure.'

'A willing slave,' Buffy repeated, as though that was her idea of heaven, and if only Josh would offer such slavery to her she'd snap it up.

Things were definitely getting out of control here, Lucy thought, but didn't know what to do about it. She'd brought it upon herself, agreeing to Josh's plan, but now she wasn't sure it was leading to anywhere she wanted to be. If James started thinking she was using Josh as a toy-boy...

'I didn't know you had dominatrix tendencies, Buffy,' James drawled, an edgy note in his voice.

'What?' Clearly she was attempting a mental shake as she switched her attention to him, but her big amber eyes looked empty of any understanding as they appealed for him to explain himself.

Lucy's mind was reeling, too. *A dominatrix?* Was that how he was now seeing her...in tight leather

gear with a whip in hand, forcing men to perform
to her will? She almost died on the spot!

Buffy's blankness forced James to speak again.
'Never mind,' he said bruskly. 'What do you think
of the band?' He gestured to the musicians on stage
to redirect her attention.

'Oh!' She obediently looked and listened.
'They've got a good beat. Is this the band you think
may do as well as Silverchair?'

James pursued the conversation with Buffy, much
to Lucy's relief. She needed some breathing space
to assess what had happened, to get her thoughts
into some kind of order for handling the rest of the
night which now stretched ahead, loaded with per-
ilous double meanings to everything!

'He's hooked,' Josh whispered triumphantly.

She looked askance at him. 'He's taken the bait
but he doesn't like it.'

'And doesn't that say something? No indifference
there, Lucy love. The man is wriggling beautifully.'

'But I don't want him to think I'm a dominatrix.'
She was horrified by the image. Even more so, because she had actually fantasised him being hand-
cuffed to her bed! But that was only a mad dream
borne out of frustration, she assured herself. She'd
never really do it. What she dearly, truly wanted was
utterly breath-taking mutual desire.

'Challenges his manhood,' Josh murmured knowingly. 'He'll be thinking about how much he'd like
to dominate you.'

She frowned at him. 'Do you realise you've made yourself out to be my toy-boy?'

He grinned. 'So what? You think Buffy is anything more than a toy-girl to him? What's good for the goose is good for the gander. Makes you more of a match for him.'

She shook her head. 'I doubt he'll think that.'

'Give him time. He might not realise it yet but that guy is possessive of you, Lucy, and right now he's as jealous as hell of me. Why do you think he seated you next to him? To compete for your attention, that's why.'

Could it be so? Lucy found it difficult to believe, yet Josh was no fool in his perceptions of people. And the miserable truth was, James had never sought her company on a personal basis before. Outside of work, he'd been perfectly content with the Buffys of this world.

Until now.

All the same, company in public and company in private were still two different things. Josh could very well be right in that he'd hit some competitive nerve in James. However, that didn't mean she was actually desirable to him, not in the sense she craved. This was probably dog in the manger stuff. He didn't want her himself but he didn't like the idea of someone else having her.

Besides, what was the point in planting false images of her in his mind? What would it win her in the end? She wanted to be wanted for herself, not fancied as some kind of sexual contestant.

'I'm *me* and I'm not going to pretend to be anything else,' she stated emphatically.

'Neither you should,' Josh agreed. 'Being you is perfect.'

'Perfect for what?' she demanded suspiciously.

'Titillating him to death.' He gave her a smugly satisfied look. 'You did want him to burn, Lucy love. If nothing else, we have achieved that objective.'

True, she told herself.

Let him burn.

He'd made her burn all day.

Vengeance was sweet.

She could hand in her notice with the sense she'd had the last word with James Hancock. He'd be left thinking he'd missed out on something. And he had. She *was* worth more than the label of secretary.

CHAPTER FOUR

JAMES was not enjoying himself.

He couldn't fault the food served. It was gourmet standard. Yet he found himself irritated by the bits of decorative garnishes that were so artistically arranged on each plate. Pretentious garbage. He had a perverse desire for something plain and solid, like sausages and mash. But he made all the right noises, joining in the general chorus of approval.

Adding to his irritation was Buffy's vapid conversation. She was just like the gourmet food—pretty to look at, no substance. And her gaze kept sliding to Josh Rogan, who was clearly enjoying himself immensely, the life of the party, happily making everyone else happy, and dominating Lucy's attention.

Not that she hung on his every word. Surprisingly enough, she seemed to be her usual contained self, playing the straight woman to her lover's sparkle. Except on the dance-floor. She certainly wasn't *straight* there. She melted into the music, revealing a sensual suppleness that obviously reflected what she was like in bed, since she had a guy like Josh Rogan coming back for more and more whenever she wanted him.

She was a tantalising mix, and most irritating of

all was her prickly coolness to him. Each time he'd
tried to engage her in conversation, she gave a few
polite replies—the absolute minimum without being
rude—then turned her attention to whatever else was
being said around the table.

Paying him back for sitting her next to him, he'd
concluded, her resentment at being reminded of
work on her night off made very plain. It hadn't
exactly been tactful of him to call her his punctilious
secretary in front of everyone. He suspected it had
put her off-side with him in more ways than one.

Even when he'd casually touched her she'd removed the contact as though he were a poisonous
snake, a fierce rejection coming at him in tumultu-
ous waves. Plus the accompanying look at Buffy, as
if to say, 'There's your touchable doll. Paw her, not
me, thank you.'

The more he thought about it, the more he decided Lucy Worthington was a control junkie. She
remained on top of every situation at work. She had
Josh Rogan on a string which she pulled in whenever it suited her. And she was very tight with
money. In fact, the only time he'd ever seen her part
with unnecessary dollars was when he'd hassled her
into buying tickets in tonight's raffle—probably the
first and only raffle tickets she'd ever bought.

'For the children, not the car,' she'd said, scorn-
ing his sales patter.

No doubt Lucy considered an Alpha Spider sports
car a frivolous impracticality. Since she couldn't
control the weather, a convertible would never be

her pick for day-to-day travelling. If she chose to acquire a car at all, it would be a reliable hard-top with low fuel consumption.

James was sinking into a morose mood when one of the band members came to him, asking to have a private word. He quickly excused himself from the table, grateful to seize any diversion from the problem he had with Lucy. Besides, not involving her in any work-related issue demonstrated he was true to his word about leaving her free to enjoy herself tonight. Maybe she wouldn't be quite so prickly with him when he came back.

Lucy watched him go and hoped he'd never come back. He stirred so much tension in her, it was impossible to relax and enjoy herself. She took a long deep breath, trying to loosen up as she slowly released it, only to be then landed with Buffy Tanner who slid onto the chair James had vacated, determined on having a woman-to-woman chat.

'I love your boyfriend,' she purred into Lucy's ear. 'Where did you find such a gorgeous hunk?'

'Oh, I've known Josh for years,' she answered, not wanting to get specific.

'Why haven't you married him then?'

Lucy allowed herself a dry smile. 'That wouldn't suit either of us.'

Satisfaction oozed from Buffy. 'You mean he likes to stay free-wheeling.'

'We simply respect each other's life-style, Buffy.'

She nodded happily. 'I like that. James is such a

grump about punctuality. He doesn't make any concessions.'

'A flaw in paradise?'

'What?'

'I mean…everything isn't rosy in your relationship with James.'

She shrugged. 'Oh, he's so high-powered all the time. You must know what he's like, working for him. Always thinking about what's got to be done. Pressure, pressure, pressure.'

'Mmmh…that's probably what makes him successful.'

'I guess so.' Buffy didn't seem sure that success was worth so much attention. 'He is good at sex,' she added as though that was some compensation. Then leaning forward confidentially, 'I bet Josh is, too.'

'Mmmh,' Lucy agreed out of pride.

'Is he really built?'

'What?'

Buffy wrinkled her nose. 'You know. Some guys can have a great-looking physique, but when you get them down to the buff…very disappointing.'

Not knowing how to answer, Lucy blurted out, 'I take it James isn't disappointing.'

'Not in that area. He's big. And a real pistol. He can go on and on and on,' Buffy assured her, rolling her eyes appreciatively. 'What about Josh?'

Lucy took another deep breath, desperate to somehow get this conversation steered onto other ground. As it was, she didn't know how she was going to control her thoughts once James returned to his chair.

'Josh has never disappointed me,' she said truthfully, though the claim had nothing to do with sex. She turned curiously to Buffy. 'Do you always rate men on how they perform in bed?'

'Well, it is a big thing, isn't it?' Buffy reasoned. 'After all, it's what they want us for, so it's a dumb deal if *we* don't get satisfaction.'

'What about a sense of companionship? Enjoying other things together?'

'Huh! In my experience, men only put up with what I want to do, to get what's coming at the end of it. Sex is our bargaining chip, and I, for one, am not going to be a loser.'

Lucy had never thought of the relationship between men and women in such stark trading terms and it set her wondering how true Buffy's vision was. She didn't like it. She wanted to believe that one day she might have the best of both worlds, the kind of companionship she shared with Josh, plus the passionate sexual desire she wished she could share with James.

The band started playing again so whatever problem had arisen was apparently resolved. Her gaze fastened on James, striding back towards their table, and before she could stop the downward slide, she found herself staring at the movement of his thighs and thinking of what Buffy had said. Which so appalled her, a tide of heat burned up her neck and scorched her cheeks.

She snatched up her glass of champagne—assiduously re-filled by their waiter whenever the content lowered—and tried to bury her shame in it. Buffy, having also noticed James' approach, leapt to her feet, skirted Lucy's chair, and accosted Josh, leaning invitingly over his shoulder.

'Come dance with me, Josh. I can kidnap you from Lucy for one little dance, can't it?' she pressed with a pretty pout at both of them.

'Now that would be leaving my partner alone,' Josh chided charmingly.

'James is coming. He'll look after her,' Buffy quickly pointed out. 'He *loves* Lucy.'

'Well, should I or should I not stand in the path of true love?' he tossed at Lucy, his eyes dancing wickedly.

'Oh, go on. I'll manage,' she urged, wanting Buffy out of her hair before she said something awful in front of James, dragging her into even worse embarrassment.

'I am commanded,' Josh said, letting it be known it was not his preference before going off with Buffy, who didn't care as long as she was getting her own way. Though she was careful to avoid confronting James with her choice, deliberately not crossing paths with him as she led Josh to the dance-floor.

Of course, James noticed. He looked at them, looked at Lucy, and she felt herself bristling at what he probably thought—Buffy snagging the prize and Lucy left sitting like a shag on a rock. She glared defiantly at him as he pursued his own purposeful approach to the table.

His chair was still pushed back, where Buffy had left it, and instead of pulling it forward and sitting down, he stood in the empty space, making his close presence overwhelmingly felt. Lucy sipped some more champagne, doing her utmost to ignore him while every nerve in her body twanged with awareness.

'I see your partner has gone off with mine,' he remarked.

'Yes. Buffy was panting to dance with him so I let him indulge her.' That should set him back in his tracks, Lucy thought savagely.

'Will you indulge me?'

Her mind jammed, unable to follow his line of logic. She tried a lofty glance at him. 'I beg your pardon?'

His mouth curled into a wry smile, but his eyes were simmering with a very personal challenge. 'Would it be too much of a hardship for you to dance with me?'

Doubt and desire did a violent tango. 'If this is a courtesy...'

'It's not. I *want* to dance with you.'

Unable to believe it, Lucy expostulated, 'There's really no need to feel obliged...'

'I've wanted to dance with you all night,' he broke in, a note of ferocity in his voice. 'If you hadn't been so damned snappy at me, I would have

asked you before this. Just say yes or no, Lucy. I'm
not going to grovel.'

Grovel? The heat started a rush up her throat
again at the reminder of the *dominatrix* tag.
Compelled to deny both the idea he had of her, and
the mess she was in at the thought of dancing with
him, she pushed back her chair and stood up, driven
to affirmative action.

'Let's dance,' she said with as much aplomb as
she could muster.

His eyes flared with triumph as though he'd won
a battle. He took her arm and tucked it around his,
which was totally unnecessary for the short walk to
the dance floor. Masterful, possessive...the words
skidded wildly through Lucy's mind. Was Josh
right? Had she suddenly become a sexual challenge
to her boss?

It was just as well he had taken her arm because
her legs turned to water at the thought of James
Hancock actually lusting after an opportunity to
show her what it would be like sharing a bed with
him...all hot and hard and control-shattering, and
never in a million years stooping to grovel for anything he wanted.

Her stomach contracted in a spasm of sheer nervous excitement. It was awful, reacting like this to
the madness in her mind. It was even more awful
when he whirled her onto the dance-floor, releasing
her to start a face-to-face sequence of rock steps and
she stumbled. Having frantically caught her balance
and fiercely willed her legs to behave themselves,

she tried to focus on the beat of the music, wanting to match his movements.

But it was so distracting watching him, the glide and stamp of his powerful legs, the sway of his snaky-lean hips, the bump and grind that seemed so overtly suggestive. She got hopelessly out of time, her own movements stiff and jerky, not in tune at all with what she should be doing.

'Now you just quit that right now, Lucy,' James growled at her, his expression thunderous.

'Quit what?' she babbled, utterly helpless to correct the havoc he stirred.

'This perverse resistance you're going on with.' He literally glowered with ferocity. 'I saw you dancing with Josh. Pretending you're some awkward amateur is a really petty insult.'

'I'm used to dancing with Josh,' she protested, hunting for some inoffensive excuse for being out of kilter. 'I'm comfortable with him. He's not my boss.'

'This is not the office,' he argued.

'You're still my boss,' she insisted.

His eyes flashed blue lightning. 'Time you stopped putting your life into neat little pockets. Forget playing safe. Take a risk.'

He caught her totally off-guard, grabbing her and hauling her in to him with a thump that left her breathless. Or maybe it was the impact of feeling a vital wall of muscle connected to her wobbly frame that stole her ability to breathe. His arms wound around her back, holding her intimately pinned to him. Her arms had nowhere to go except up on his shoulders and they just slid naturally around his neck.

'Now melt,' he commanded gruffly.

And Lucy melted.

Her breasts seemed glued to the heat of his chest. Her stomach quivered mushily with the awareness of what it was pressed against. Her thighs clung to the strength of his. And her feet…her feet followed his as though it was what they were born to do. The only thing that didn't melt was her heart. It was going nineteen to the dozen, super-energised by the volatile energy flowing from him.

'That's better,' he muttered, satisfaction coating his voice.

Lucy kept her mouth shut. It wasn't actually a conscious decision not to answer him. She was speechless as well as breathless at what was happening. James Hancock had her clamped in the kind of embrace she had dreamed about and there was nothing the least bit platonic about the way he was dancing with her. She was in seventh heaven.

She had no idea if this was some exhibition of macho manhood that demanded he get the better of her. Right at this moment, she didn't care. She was revelling in the sense of having him where she wanted him. Well, not exactly *where,* but it was close. It was certainly an exhilarating taste of the sexual power he exerted.

And he was not unmoved by her, either. She could definitely feel his arousal. Amazingly he didn't seem at all concerned about removing himself to a discreet distance. Was *he* revelling in feeling her pliant softness, imagining what it might be like to move what was currently outside her, *inside?*

That thought melted her even further, reducing her to a state of feverish mindlessness. Breathless, speechless, mindless, her treacherous body just kept on responding to wherever he led, circling the dance-floor as one, moving with a continually pressing sensuality, the physical friction becoming so acute, Lucy felt herself on the verge of climax.

The music stopped. It took Lucy a few moments to understand why James was no longer moving her around. Her ears finally registered that the band had finished playing. It struck her that, despite their mutual arousal, he had been more aware of external things than she had, which instantly cooled her brain.

Had he been on some sexual ego-trip, flagrantly demonstrating how much of a *pistol* he was…better than Josh? Lucy's excitement died on the spot. She started shrivelling away from the intimate contact, deeply relieved that he couldn't know how much he had affected her. Having unlocked her hands from the nape of his neck and got them as far as his shoulders, she found her attempt to extract herself from her boss thwarted by the tightening clamp of his arms.

'The band will start another number soon,' was his excuse.

Lucy took a deep breath, needing a full blast of

mind-clearing oxygen. She was *not* going to get carried away on a fantasy again. It was too shaming when she knew perfectly well it was Buffy Tanner he'd be going to bed with tonight.

'This dance is over,' she stated with frosty finality, pushing at his shoulders to make her intent clear.

He marginally loosened his embrace, enough for her to lean back and look him straight in the eyes. Which was a big mistake because the eyes that looked straight back into hers were smouldering with desire, confusing her sensible train of thought.

'Don't say you didn't enjoy it, Lucy,' he challenged.

She took another deep breath. 'You're a very good dancer, James,' she answered, wary of committing herself to anything more than that.

'We flowed together,' he insisted.

'Well, the music finally got to me,' she parried, proudly determined on not admitting anything else had got to her. Buffy was still in the wings. 'Now if you don't mind, the music has stopped and I would like my own space back.'

His eyes glittered. 'Because I'm your boss?'

Her chin tilted defiantly. 'That's one reason.'

'Are labels more important to you than people?'

'It was you who labelled me *your punctilious secretary,*' she flashed back at him.

'Which was very wrong of me and I apologise for it,' he said, sweeping that mat out from under her feet.

She struggled to keep it there, not knowing where

this was leading and feeling intensely vulnerable. 'I'm not your partner here tonight,' she blurted out.

'And if I said I wish you were…?'

Her mind went into another spin of doubt and desire. 'I think you must have drunk a lot of champagne.'

'Is it so impossible to think you could be the wine in my blood, Lucy?'

The eight months of non-interest blasted his contention. 'Since when, James?' she demanded sceptically. 'Since I turned up with Josh tonight? Did that titillate your fancy? Not so *boring* after all?'

'You have never bored me,' he declared vehemently.

'So you told me earlier. Me to entertain you, Buffy to satisfy your other needs,' she threw at him savagely. 'So let's just keep to the rules.'

Having hurled down that bitter gauntlet, she shoved herself out of his embrace, stepping back on trembling legs and swinging towards the stage where a man was announcing something over the microphone. She concentrated fiercely on grasping what was being said, determined on blocking James out until the violent turbulence he'd stirred could be brought under control.

'…and the winner is…Lucy Worthington…of Bellevue Hill, Sydney!'

Stunned at hearing her own name being blared out through the auditorium, Lucy couldn't apply any sense to it. Suddenly Josh burst through the crowd on the dance-floor, picked her up and whirled her

around, laughingly crowing, 'The Alpha Spider
sports car! It's yours, Lucy love! You've won it!'

The raffle!

The *wish* prize!

Miracles could happen to her, she thought dizzily.

And maybe—just maybe—if she threw the rules
away and acted like Buffy, another miracle could
happen!

CHAPTER FIVE

JAMES stood with his hands clenched, fighting the violent urge to rip Lucy away from Josh Rogan and smash his handsome face in. Never had he felt so aggressively possessive of a woman. The adrenaline pumping through him was priming every caveman instinct he had, adding to the problem of easing the hard-on that dancing with Lucy had aroused. He fiercely told himself he'd look an absolute fool if he tried any move at all.

Buffy slid out of the dance crowd and hugged his arm. 'How lucky can you get?' she exclaimed, heaving her lush breasts in a huge sigh of envy.

Having her rubbing against him should have been some consolation. It wasn't. The whole sum of Buffy's delectable femininity couldn't turn him on at this moment. In fact, it had the opposite effect. The discomfort Lucy had left him with was instantly lowered—from a rod to a turkey in no time flat.

'I'd love a car like that,' Buffy purred.

And a man like Josh Rogan, James thought viciously. Not that he cared about Buffy wanting Lucy's partner. She could have him. The sooner the better, detaching Josh from Lucy and freeing her of scruples about sticking to partners. Though James knew in his bones this wasn't going to happen. Josh was only too happy to be with Lucy, sweeping her up on stage to find out how to claim her prize.

The band started up again, a joyous jazzy number. There was no joy whatsoever in James as he resigned himself to dancing with Buffy. He wanted Lucy back in his arms. And she was totally wrong about him not fancying her before tonight. It was just that tonight the desires she'd been stirring had zoomed into flesh and blood reality...holding her, feeling her responding to him, the sheer sensual surrender she'd given him in their dance together.

Lucy unbuttoned...not yet in actuality, but he'd certainly got the sense of what she would be like when all her inhibitions—and clothes—were shed.

A series of highly erotic scenes occupied James' mind as he danced on with Buffy. He'd been left in little doubt that sticking to partners was the order tonight, but come Monday, when he had Lucy to himself in the office, the rules were going to change. She couldn't put Josh Rogan between them then. Nor Buffy. And if she arrived all buttoned up tight in her secretary role...well, he'd take great pleasure in probing for button-holes.

Lucy was riding high on a rainbow of delight. She'd won a pot of gold with the Alpha Spider sports car. Of course, she wouldn't get the full value of the flashy red convertible when she sold it back to the dealer, but she would still be able to pay a huge chunk off her mortgage on the apartment, as well as buy the furniture she wanted.

'I still can't believe my luck! You'd better pinch me, Josh,' she whispered as they left the official who'd explained how the prize could be collected.

He laughed. 'You're definitely on a winning streak.' Cocking a wicked eyebrow, he added, 'Seemed to me the course of true love was running hot as you danced with your boss.'

She grimaced. 'Hardly true love.'

'Lust unlimited?'

'There are limits on the dance-floor, but it was...'

'Stimulating?'

'Mmmh...'

'Never underestimate chemistry.'

The dance-floor had emptied. As they crossed it towards their table, Lucy looked nervously for James, secretly hoping Josh was right about chemistry, though she couldn't help doubting the factors that had stirred it tonight. Would she be making a fool of herself if she did give out some encouraging signals?

Maybe she shouldn't hand in her resignation. Maybe she should wait and see if something real developed between James and herself, not just a flash in the pan fancy, brought on by unusual circumstances. If she was still the wine in his blood in the cold light of day in the office...Lucy heaved a fluttery sigh. Hope certainly had a way of worming through a whole thicket of thorny doubts.

Her heart skittered all over the place when James turned in his chair and smiled warmly at her as Josh saw her seated. 'Congratulations!' he rolled out with every appearance of pleasure in her winning luck.

'I'm sick with envy,' Buffy declared, 'but it's fantastic for you, Lucy. You must be tripping on Cloud Nine.'

'I am,' Lucy happily admitted, flicking an appreciative look at James. 'Thank you.'

'Here comes the red terror on the highway,' one of the other men joked.

It spurred a string of light-hearted comments around the table.

'You'll have to be careful of police patrols. A sports convertible is like flashing up a speed sign to them.'

'Great fun driving one though.'

'And you'll be fighting guys off with a stick. You'll have to watch out, Josh.'

'The sun in your face, wind in your hair...heaven on wheels.'

James laughed and shook his head. 'I'll bet right now none of that will happen.'

'Why not?' Buffy demanded.

'Because Lucy will never drive that car.' He looked knowingly at her. 'She'll make a deal with the dealer and take the money.'

It was precisely what she had planned, but hearing James say it with such smug confidence had the perverse effect of making her want to deny it. 'Why do you think so?' she demanded, her hackles rising over the *boring* image again.

His eyes filled with amused mockery. 'Because it's the sensible thing to do.'

Sensible! She seethed over the word, despite how true it was of her.

'And you are always very sensible about money, Lucy,' he added, rubbing it in. 'You never do anything extravagant.'

That was even more true, she had to concede, but it was a truth she suddenly wanted to blow to bits, and to hell with being sensible! She wanted to wear outrageously sexy clothes like Buffy. She wanted to whiz around in a red sports convertible with the wind in her hair. She wanted to seize the pleasures of the day and forget about tomorrow. She wanted to rock James Hancock so far off his feet with her *unpredictability* he wouldn't know if he was coming or going with her.

'I'll be taking Monday off, James,' she stated recklessly.

He frowned, not liking this turn of events. 'What for?' he demanded.

'I can claim my car on Monday and that's exactly what I'm going to do,' she went on, hurling common sense to the winds.

'You're taking it?' His voice rose incredulously.

The tone of utter disbelief was music to Lucy's ears. James Hancock could just pull her right out of the pigeon-hole he'd put her in and think again!

'I hope it won't inconvenience you too much,' she said sweetly, 'but I do need the time off. Of course, I won't expect you to pay me for the day...'

His eyebrows beetled down. 'I'm not that mean, Lucy.'

She smiled. 'I can be quite extravagant when I choose to be, James. I don't mind...'

'Don't be absurd,' he cut in tersely. 'You've never even taken a sick day off.'

Her smile tilted into irony. 'It's my curse to be healthy.'

'And I'm very grateful for it. You're entitled to a free day on full pay. It's nonsense to suggest otherwise.'

'As you wish,' she conceded, feeling an exhilarating zing of triumph at having flouted his picture of her and extracted what she wanted from him.

'Can you drive?' he shot at her.

Lucy bristled. Did he think her so stodgy and narrow in the life she lived, that handling a car had never entered into it? She ungritted her teeth enough to say, 'Like most people, James, I got my driving licence in my teens.'

'Handling a sports car is a bit different to driving a sedate sedan.'

Sedate! Lucy's teeth ground together again. She'd show him, she thought wildly. His worthy Miss Worthington was going to be the most unsedate secretary he'd ever seen, come Tuesday morning.

'I think I'd better take Monday off, too, and come with you when you take possession of the car,' he went on, frowning over her possible incompetence. 'Run you through its paces so you can feel secure with it.'

Secure! He was hitting all the buttons that made her so unexciting! 'That's not necessary,' she grated.

'Lucy...' He looked earnestly at her. 'It's often inexperience that causes accidents. I care about you.'

Did he? Did he really? Or was he worried about having to do without his secretary if she smashed herself up?

'You could underestimate the power, the acceleration,' he explained. 'And because you're lower to the ground in a sports car, the road will feel different, look different.'

'James does know,' Buffy put in helpfully. 'He drives a Porsche.'

Such wonderful common sense, Lucy thought bitterly, and common sense had nothing to do with all the things she planned to do between now and Tuesday morning. While it was nice of James to offer help with the car—condescendingly nice—she didn't want to be in his company again until she was good and ready. There was one way to squash this whole idea and she took it.

'Josh drives an MG,' she told Buffy, then turned to James. 'It's very kind of you to offer your services, but I truly don't need them. I'll be fine, thank you.'

He looked put out, his mouth tightening, his jaw jutting, his eyes momentarily flashing a savage glitter as he said, 'Then I can confidently expect you in the office on Tuesday morning.'

'No problem,' she assured him, though she

fiercely hoped she'd be giving him a lot of problems when she arrived.

'James took me to the MG Restaurant where they have those cars on display,' Buffy told Josh. 'They looked fabulous.'

'Mine is a much older vintage,' he dryly informed her. 'A fifties model which I've restored to its former glory.'

This sparked interest around the table and Lucy relaxed, glad the spotlight was now off her. Having embraced madness, she started plotting her moves for the next three days. The car was a windfall anyway, she argued rebelliously to the thrifty voice inside her head, and it wouldn't break her to buy a few new clothes. The furniture could wait. The payments on her mortgage would simply stay the same.

But what about the cost of car registration?

Insurance?

Fuel?

Parking fees?

Stop it! she commanded. If James Hancock could be won with these tactics, she was going to do it, no matter what. A woman was entitled to one period of madness in her life. She might be dead next week. Seize the day. No shilly-shallying. Just go for it!

James sat in seething silence as the rest of the party carried on about vintage cars. Lucy's determination to hold him at arm's length was extremely frustrating. Even out of the office on her day off, it was no go. She had him pigeon-holed as her boss and there he was going to stay, despite the indications of what they could have together. And the deceptive image she had carried off all these months had clearly been designed to put him off, too.

Not that it had completely fooled him. His instincts had been aware there was more to Lucy Worthington than met the eye. Her *real* life was spilling out tonight.

He turned to her, suspicion wanting proof. 'You wore this standby little black dress tonight because I'm here,' he stated bluntly.

She looked startled. 'I beg your pardon.'

'It's a *work* dress, isn't it? And that's your *work* hair-do, too.'

She affected bewilderment. 'I'm sorry if you think I'm inappropriately dressed.'

'Not at all. I'm just working you out, Lucy Worthington. It's been quite an enlightening night,' he declared tauntingly.

Her face lit with a smile that seemed to say he hadn't even scratched the surface of her. She reached out, picked up her glass of champagne, and raised it in a toast. 'Well, here's to better days!'

And nights, James darkly vowed, as he echoed the toast with mocking grace and drank with her. If it was the last thing he did, he'd find out all there was to know of Lucy Worthington. Every intimate detail! Monday was now a write-off, but come Tuesday…if he had to shake her out of her buttons, he would.

CHAPTER SIX

NOT even the coolness of the night lowered the fever in Lucy's brain. The ball was over but her feet still felt like dancing as she and Josh walked from the convention centre to the parking station. She had hooked James Hancock's interest. No doubt about it now. The trick was to pull out all stops to hold it engaged.

'What are you going to tell your mother?' Josh asked, a curious lilt in his voice.

'Mum?'

A spear of guilt pierced Lucy's intoxicating dreams of conquest and triumph. Her mother wouldn't approve these wild and wanton plans at all. In fact, she'd have a pink fit if she even heard a whisper of them.

'I'm not going to tell her anything,' she said decisively, and cast Josh a stern look. 'And don't you dare gossip to your mother, either. You know they belong to the same Businesswomen's Association.'

He held up both hands in a gesture of innocence. 'Mum's the word. Your secrets are my secrets, Lucy love.'

'Good! Just keep them that way,' she insisted.

Josh and his mother were close, invariably telling each other everything. In fact, Lucy had often envied the very open loving relationship they shared. Sally Rogan was a warm, happy person. Widowed when Josh was only three, she had opened a fashion boutique which was a thriving business because she'd always taken the time to chat to her customers and get to know what appealed to them.

Her own mother tended to preach to her customers. She ran a health food shop and styled herself as an authority on what was good for everyone. In personality, Ruth Worthington and Sally Rogan were chalk and cheese. Being sensible came first with Ruth, while having fun came first with Sally.

The two women didn't mix in any social sense, though they'd both lived and worked in the same town for over thirty years. Being in business was the only thing they had in common, and when they went to those meetings they were usually polite to each other, prompted, no doubt, by the long-term friendship between Josh and Lucy, which also occasionally led to the swapping of family news. Tonight's news had to be kept off that agenda at all costs.

Lucy knew what she would be in for if it wasn't. Her mother didn't approve of extravagance and didn't know the meaning of fun. Or she'd lost all sense of it when her husband had left her for another woman. Lucy had no memory of a father. He'd gone before she was two years old, but she'd been drilled in lessons from that desertion for as long as she could remember.

You can't count on men to look after you.

Make your own security.

Never lose your head over a man. He'll take advantage of you.

And so on, and so on, and so on.

Now bent on breaking just about all of those rules, Lucy didn't want any accusing lectures from her mother. She'd suffer her own grief from this decision if she had to, but inviting a battering stream of 'I told you so's' would only add misery to misery if nothing worked out as she wanted it to.

'So how are you going to hide the car?' Josh quizzed.

She heaved a sigh, knowing full well what her mother would say about running a red sports convertible. 'I'll keep it in Sydney.'

'You're still going to catch the train to Gosford every time you visit your mother?'

'Easier than flaunting that extravagance in her face. It would be like waving a red rag at a bull. Besides, it's not as if it's a long train trip.'

In fact, it was only an hour and ten minutes on the fast northbound trains between Sydney and Gosford. She usually read a book, which she couldn't do driving a car—one of the reasons she preferred public transport. Lucy had never found it a hardship to do without her own vehicle.

'Waste of a great car, not using it on the expressway,' Josh remarked. 'You should let yourself enjoy it and to hell with what your mother thinks.'

'I will enjoy it. But I'll probably end up selling it so why cause a hassle?'

'Ah!'

The 'Ah!' was so full of understanding, Lucy blushed. 'You said I should be unpredictable,' she reminded him.

Josh laughed and started singing, *'This is the moment...'*

She laughed, too, her tingling feet performing a pirouette as she threw out her arms and exultantly sang *'This is the time...'*

Josh caught her waist and lifted her up to the stars—metaphorically speaking—and they laughed in a mad, joyous celebration of victory over the frustration that had originally driven Lucy this evening. Miracles were definitely in the air.

'Well, Lucy love, if you're really going to *show* him you'll have to let your hair down,' Josh merrily advised as he set her on her feet again.

'I intend to.'

'Some shopping is in order.'

'Will you help me, Josh? Do you have some spare time tomorrow? I want some really modern sexy stuff to go with the convertible but I don't want to look too tarty.'

'We'll trawl the streets tomorrow afternoon,' he promised.

'Great!' She hugged his arm as they proceeded into the parking station. 'You've got such a good fashion eye. I'm bound to choose the wrong things.'

'Flattery will get you everywhere.'

'You're the best friend!'

He patted her hand with indulgent affection. 'Lucy love, it will be a huge pleasure to see the butterfly emerge from your mother's narrow little cocoon.'

She frowned. 'Have I been so stodgy?'

'Not stodgy. Never stodgy,' he assured her. 'But to a large extent you have lived by the constraints your mother put on you. If you get too fixated on being *safe,* you miss out on much of the fun in life, and you never live life to the full.'

But you don't fall down a hole, Lucy argued to herself, then realised her thought was parroting what her mother said. She shook her head, disturbed by the idea she was living a brain-washed life instead of a life of her own.

'Take the suits you wear to work,' Josh went on seriously. 'They armour you against risk. They're safe, beyond criticism, properly professional, but they don't express the real Lucy. Not the Lucy I know. They're a reflection of your mother.'

'I guess they are,' she answered thoughtfully.

'Nothing exciting about wearing those clothes.'

'That's true. I just bung them on and go.'

'It shouldn't be like that, Lucy. You should love the clothes you wear.'

She gave him an arch look. 'This is *your* mother talking now.'

'Mum's right. Clothes should lift your spirits, make you feel good about yourself. The attitude of *this will do,* is an expression of compromise, accepting you're not worth more. It's a downer. You should never do that to yourself.'

'Well, I'll let you have your way with me tomorrow,' she declared, feeling she had let herself down in this area.

'Not *my* way. *Your* way.'

'But I might get it wrong.'

He shook his head. 'It will be in the smile on your face, the zing in your heart. The right clothes for the person you are do that for you. All you have to do is go with that flow. Trust it and don't let anyone else's opinion spoil it.'

Lucy took a deep breath and resolved to be boldly free, choosing whatever thrilled her and made her feel sexy. No more *work* clothes. No more *work* hair-do. She grinned at the thought of James trying to work out the new Lucy Worthington when she presented her on Tuesday morning.

Having arrived at the parking slot where they had left the MG, Josh steered her to the driver's side. 'Better get in some practice,' he pressed.

Lucy baulked. 'I can't drive your pride and joy.'

'To my knowledge, the only car you've driven is your mother's Ford with automatic gears. James Hancock had one thing right tonight. A sports car is different.' He opened the door. 'Get in. I'll give you a lesson.'

'But what if I dent it or something getting out of this parking station?' she fretted.

He gave her a devil-may-care grin. 'I'll take the risk.'

The dancing challenge in his eyes spurred her on. After all, it was what she'd determined to do...*take the risk*. She stepped into the MG and settled herself in the driver's seat. Her hands curled around the wheel.

This is it, she told herself.

I'm going for it.

Starting now.

By Tuesday morning she'd be on a roll and James Hancock wouldn't know what hit him. It was a delicious thought.

'Right. Give it some juice,' Josh instructed, having settled beside her.

She giggled and switched on the ignition.

Juicy Lucy...

Starting now.

CHAPTER SEVEN

With a spring in his step, a smile hovering on his lips, and a lively sense of anticipation tingling through the rest of him, James opened the door to his secretary's office, fully expecting to find Lucy at work preparing for his arrival. It was instantly deflating to see no sign of her.

He checked his watch—five minutes short of nine o'clock. She wasn't exactly late, yet she invariably came in earlier than this. He'd never known her not be here before him. Her failure to do so on *this* Tuesday morning was aggravating, particularly since he'd given her Monday off.

As it was, he'd hardly done any work yesterday, distracted by her absence from the office and the gnawing desire to move their relationship onto new ground. Despite telling himself over and over again it was stupid to mess with what had been an ideal working partnership, he couldn't block out the temptation that had been raging through him since Friday night.

He *wanted* Lucy Worthington.

He hadn't even stayed with Buffy after the ball. Nor had he felt the slightest spark of interest in any of the women at the party he'd attended on Saturday night. There was only one woman he wanted to be with and she was frustrating him again right now.

A hopeful thought struck. He strode across her office and opened the connecting door to his. She wasn't there, either. Feeling doubly vexed, James didn't even think of settling to work without Lucy. He walked over to her desk and propped himself against it, arms folded in displeasure, ready to confront her with her tardiness when she did arrive.

There was no excuse for it. Getting from Bellevue Hill to this office building in Woolloomooloo presented no real difficulty. She didn't have to drive through inner-city traffic and Lucy wasn't ignorant of how to get into the basement car-park. She'd been a passenger in his car many times. He was not going to be drawn into worrying about the possibility of an accident. A woman in as much control of her life as Lucy Worthington was, did not have accidents.

Everything seemed unnaturally quiet, now that the other offices on this floor had been vacated and the company of solicitors that had taken them over wouldn't be moving in until next week. He had no client appointments this morning so there was only Lucy to come—Lucy to break the loneliness that had so irked him yesterday.

The hurried clack of heels on the tiled corridor leading from the elevators, momentarily straightened him up. Aware that his body was suddenly buzzing with tension, James forced himself to relax against the desk again. He was not going to look eager for Lucy's arrival. He was the boss here, not a lap-dog panting for his mistress's attention. The situation could get completely out of hand if he didn't remain master of it.

A woman whirled into the office, closing the door he'd left open, arrogantly assuming the right to seal off privacy. Annoyed by the unwelcome intrusion, James snapped upright again. A few terse words were about to spill off his tongue when the woman swung around and froze, shocked at being directly faced with his unexpected presence.

'James!' His name hissed out on a long, shaky breath.

Lucy?

Stunned disbelief rendered him speechless. A wealth of shiny brown hair swirled around her shoulders, wisps of it flying out as though electric from being in the wind. Her face was vibrant with colour...glowing cheeks, glossy red lipstick and sparkling green eyes. Quite clearly green, and fringed by long dark lashes. She wasn't wearing spectacles!

And what she *was* wearing hit him like a punch in the gut, taking his breath away. The clingy lime-green singlet top was a *long* way from conservative. Not only did the bold colour leap out at him, but so did her breasts, the stretchy material outlining them perfectly. Small breasts compared to Buffy Tanner's but firmly rounded and delectably tip-tilted at him— no sag anywhere, sideways or downwards—and she certainly wasn't wearing a bra to aid their shape.

Much, much better without one. No aid needed at all.

Floating between the provocative peaks was an embroidered butterfly—its wings a neon glow of violet and red and green. And it wasn't the only butterfly. Her skirt was printed with them—a virtual kaleidoscope of brilliant butterflies on a white background, flying every which way. It was a short straight little skirt—shorter than anything Lucy had ever worn before—hugging her hips and ending mid-thigh, with a couple of rows of frivolous little frills around the hem, giving a swinging effect that was very cutely sexy.

Her legs were bare—more leg than he'd ever seen on his secretary—and proof positive that they were, indeed, very shapely. On her feet she wore what looked like ballet slippers, with straps crossed over around her ankles, but they weren't black. They were lime-green.

James had the mad thought that she had danced all the way to the office, twirling around in that provocative little skirt, and ruffling her long hair into loose havoc, swinging the silky-looking lime-green bag she was carrying. Not a proper, clipped up leather hand-bag, a more casual, open-topped, cloth one.

No buttons in sight anywhere!

His heart started hammering. This had to be the *real* Lucy Worthington. And was she *something!* To think she'd been right under his nose all along, hiding her true self from him, wasting time that could have been spent exploring the full potential of a relationship between them.

Resentment at her duplicity fired every aggressive male hormone in his body. No more pulling the wool over his eyes. He had her in his sights now and he wouldn't be content until she was his in every sense there was.

'I'm sorry if I've kept you waiting,' she rushed out.

The tantalising little witch had kept him waiting eight months for this!

'I got into the wrong traffic lane,' she babbled on, 'and ended up being forced to go through the harbour tunnel, then on to North Sydney before I could turn around and come back over the bridge.'

She heaved a sigh that fixed his gaze on her breasts again. Buttons there, underneath the stretchy fabric, pushing it out, two perky buttons that blatantly invited a tug of his teeth.

'I'm just not used to driving in city peak hour.'

James dragged his gaze up from her peaks—reluctantly past her crushed-strawberry red mouth—to the glistening appeal in her eyes. Fantastic green eyes. Those bland spectacles had blurred their impact. Deliberately, no doubt. So why was she showing them now? Good question!

His mind belatedly clicked onto the excuse she'd been offering for her lateness. 'Takes experience,' he agreed sympathetically, needing to slide into probing her motives.

'I won't make the same mistake again,' she assured him.

'No problem.' He made an airy gesture, forgiving her confusion on the road, his mind busily occupied with finding the best way through her formidable defences.

She frowned reflectively. 'You know, I think it's the red sports car. It seems to spur other drivers into being aggressive. Like they want to block it in or beat it.'

While getting as much as an eyeful of you as they can, James thought.

With a very sexy shrug, she added, 'Anyhow, it was really hair-raising out there this morning.'

'So I notice,' he said dryly, his gaze flicking to the long wild tresses.

'Oh!' She lifted an arm and attempted to pat down the wayward strands. 'Guess I'm a bit wind-blown. I'll tidy up shortly.'

'Don't on my account.' He smiled, feeling like a shark on the prowl all primed to bite into a tasty morsel...the lifted breast, the soft underarm... 'I like the new image,' he said, laying the obvious on the line for her to pick up and explain.

She blushed, then instantly took evasive action as though suddenly aware of having raised attention that might prove uncomfortable. 'Blame Orlando for that,' she tossed off as with quick purposeful steps she skirted him to get around behind her desk.

He swung to keep her in sight, grimly digesting this new unpalatable information. 'Orlando? You've thrown Josh over for some other guy?' he quizzed, his eyes mocking her fickleness as his stomach clenched at the thought of more competition to get rid of.

'No.' She dumped her bag on her chair and faced him with a look of defiant pride. 'Josh will always be...special. We understand each other.'

'I take it he understands Orlando,' he retorted sardonically, unable to believe that any man would like sharing Lucy with other lovers.

'Yes, he does.' A smile tugged at her mouth. 'I christened the car Orlando.'

James blinked. 'The car?'

'Calling it an Alpha Spider seemed all wrong to me. Spiders are creepy-crawly.' She shuddered expressively before breaking into a full-blown grin. 'The dealer said owning an Alpha was like having an Italian love affair and the name flashed straight into my mind...Orlando...' She drawled it seductively.

James laughed in sheer relief. This he could understand. She'd fallen in love with the car. He relaxed, hitching himself onto her desk, feeling more the master of the situation than he had before. Lucy was here with him, showing herself in her true colours, and he could proceed to pin the butterfly down.

'I take it you're now dressing for Orlando, the thrill of doing so having suddenly become more important to you than continuing your secretary role.'

She looked at him uncertainly. 'I'm still your secretary...aren't I? I mean...you don't actually *need* me to dress...'

'Like a prim spinster?'

She blushed again, no doubt inwardly squirming at his accurate description.

'No, I don't need that, Lucy,' he went on, enjoying the sense of being on top. 'I never did need it. I'm just wondering why you did it. After all, my business is *show* business.'

The green eyes flashed with some indecipherable but strong emotion. 'Considering the people you deal with, James, I thought you'd be more comfortable with a contrast.'

'Ah, thinking of my comfort, were you?'

Her chin tilted. 'I think you found it very comfortable, having the *worthy* Miss Worthington—' a scathing edge there '—be your ready handmaiden.'

The knives were out! A buzz of exhilaration zipped through James. Office hours had often been enlivened by verbal duels with Lucy, but this one was slicing open fascinating territory.

'All an act for my benefit, was it?' he challenged.

'No. It suited me, as well. I've simply shifted my priorities,' she declared.

'No longer caring about my comfort zone.'

'I didn't notice you caring about my comfort zone on Friday night,' she flashed back at him.

'Ah! The plot thickens. It's not entirely Orlando pressing your buttons.' He slid off her desk, impelled to prove what he was saying. The memory of how she'd melted in his arms brought an exciting wave of confidence. 'I got under your skin, didn't I? A little payback, Lucy?'

Her eyes simmered with a wealth of feeling. 'Why shouldn't I do what I want to do?' she hotly retorted.

'You should,' he agreed silkily. 'You very definitely should.'

As he rounded the desk, she gripped the back of her chair as though to stop herself retreating. The tension flowing from her was electric, pumping his excitement higher. She stood her ground, tossing her head like a cornered thoroughbred, her nostrils flaring rebellion, eyes daring him to cross her space.

'It's not a payback,' she proudly insisted. 'I simply decided to please myself.'

'Fine! You please me, too.'

She took a deep breath. Her breasts lifted, luring him on. James knew he was probably suffering a major rush of blood to the head, but the need to catch this butterfly woman in his net before she took flight was overpowering.

She wrenched her gaze off him and flicked an agitated glance at the filing cabinet. 'Is there something urgent you need for work?'

'You expect me to think of work with you dressed like this, Lucy?'

Her eyes flashed back to him, glittering with counter-challenge. 'You told me yourself it was time to stop putting my life into little pockets.'

'And I was right. It's a major crime to fold such glorious hair into a pinned up pocket. It should flow free.' He reached out, lifting the long fall of hair from her left shoulder and trailing it through his outspread fingers...sensual silk.

She didn't make the slightest move. No protest, either verbal or physical. It was as though she was holding her breath, she was so still. There was no shock/horror in her eyes, more a mesmerised wonder, and the wild urges thrumming through James received a huge kick of encouragement. She *had* melted in his arms. Was everything within her poised to feel the same sensations again?

He had to know.

His gaze dropped to her mouth. Her lips were slightly parted, soft and red and glossy, as though moistened with the juice of berries. His arms moved instinctively, winding around her, pulling her close, pinning her to him as he tasted what he was driven to taste, and she gave her mouth to him, willingly, passionately as he plundered the sweetness within. No holding back. Her hands were around his head, pressing him on, eager, demanding, expressing an urgency that was wild for satisfaction.

All the erotic thoughts he'd had about Lucy raged through his mind. He remembered the temptingly pert jut of her bottom and ran his hands over it, wanting to squeeze the fullness of her cheeks. But the fabric of her skirt was stiff, not soft and giving. He hauled it up. Naked flesh...*naked!* No panties? Yes, a G-string dipping down the cleft. Nothing to get in the way, though, and he revelled in the lovely bare curves, cupping them, lifting them to fit her more closely to the rampant hardness stirred by her readiness to come his way.

Her way, too. No doubt about that.

She wriggled against him. Seductively. And her mouth was in a stormy tangle with his, both of them simulating what they really wanted, the excitement intense. She was on heat, definitely melting for him, except for the hard nubs pressing against his chest, more intoxicating proof of her arousal.

Buttons, he thought, and the desire to undo them shot through him, moving his hands to the sexy stretchy top she wore, shoving it up, pushing it over the mounds of her breasts, sliding a palm over them, rubbing the marvellous protrusions, so tight, bigger than he'd anticipated, big aureoles, too, feeling the different skin texture of them.

He had to look, had to see.

He wrenched his mouth from the hot intimacy of hers, grabbed a great hank of her gorgeous long hair and bent her back from him. Perfect, perfect breasts, the aureoles gleaming like ripe plums, and in the centre of them, such long nipples drawing him towards them. Irresistible.

He scooped Lucy off her feet, sliding her body up his until he could take one of the provocative peaks in his mouth, tugging at it with a greed he'd never felt before. She gave a throaty animal cry and the sheer wanton need he heard in it drove him to her other breast, and the hands in his hair, kneading, clutching, pushing, were telling him yes, yes, more,

more…but his body was screaming for its own satisfaction.

The desk. He'd fantasised having her there. His legs instantly chose to move to the end of it and he laid her down along the top, her hair sprawling out in a picture of glorious abandonment, her breasts thrust up to him, still irresistible. He leaned over and gave them his avid attention as he unfastened his trousers and unleashed his own needy flesh.

Already positioned between her thighs, her supple legs wound around his hips, ready to pull him into her, James paused only long enough to push the flimsy G-string aside. He could feel her urgent desire, hot, moist, quivery, and he plunged himself forward, travelling fast to the innermost depths of her, exulting in the convulsive welcome she gave him, the arch of her back as she lifted herself to take all he could give…sheer ecstacy, her coming instant, wine in his blood.

A moan of almost agonised bliss erupted from her throat as it arched, as well, making her hair ripple and swirl.

He rocketed out of control, pumping in a frenzy of exultation as she came again and again and again, crying out for more—'Yes, yes, yes…' her head writhing, her body writhing, the hot voluptuous flow of her making him feel like a king amongst men, riding triumphant, and she lay in front of him, his prize, surrendering all she was to his power.

His climax burst from him like a fountain of exquisite pleasure, and she arched once more, feeling it, wanting it, loving it.

She was beautiful, incredible, magnificent. While still revelling in the honeyed heat of their intimacy, he leaned over and kissed her breasts, wanting to capture the throb of her heart, the whole inner life of her beating for him, with him.

The peaks were still aroused, wonderfully sensitive to his caressing, but her legs had fallen limp, sliding down the back of his thighs. Knowing their connection couldn't last, he gathered her up in his arms and joined his mouth to hers, savouring her response to their kissing and holding her close, soothing her tremors as separation inevitably came.

But it had been great—totally mind-blowing—and as he ended their kiss, a grin of sheer happiness spread across his face and his joy bubbled into words.

'Now that, my dear Lucy, is the way to start a day!'

CHAPTER EIGHT

THE WAY to start a day?

Lucy couldn't believe her ears. She'd just been through the most body-shattering, mind-ravaging, heart-drumming, out of this world experience, and James marked it down as *the way to start a day?*

Like any old day?

Nothing special at all?

A quick fix in the morning to get him happily through his work hours?

Somehow she mustered the strength to lift her eyelashes enough for her to see his face while still veiling any tell-tale expression he might seize on for making some other crass comment.

He was beaming with the kind of elated energy one associates with winning a million-dollar jackpot in a lottery. Macho male scooping the pool. Lucy's mind went clickety-click through a series of thoughts that raised her sense of vulnerability to an all-time high.

He'd had her.

She'd fallen to him.

Game over.

He'd won.

She was just another woman who'd provided him with a kick-start to the day.

Never mind that the desire had been every bit as mutual as she had craved, Lucy's heart was wounded and her pride unbearably stung. A vengeful rebellion surged across her mind, firing up a drive to puncture *his* pride. And his smugly male satisfaction in having done what he wanted with her also needed to be dealt with.

'Is that *it?*' she asked, the need to shame him clawing through her.

He looked startled, astonished. His beaming face tightened up. His eyes narrowed into piercing challenge. 'Don't tell me *you* didn't get off on it, Lucy.'

'Oh, I did. It was great!' she conceded dismissively, hating him for reminding her how *easy* she'd been. An absolute pushover. She picked her hands off his shoulders and rolled her stretchy top back over her breasts, settling it down to her waist in a clear demonstration she was not on offer any more.

Her mind furiously sought ways to take the edge off his triumph. She was sitting on the edge of the desk. He was still standing between her legs and her skirt was crumpled against him, hiding his vital parts, but the unzipped zipper sparked wicked inspiration—a reason for being so easy for him. Words tripped out before she could have second thoughts.

'Buffy told me...'

No, she couldn't say it. She hated anyone being reduced to a lump of meat. It was wrong. Even though he considered her his *starter* for the day, retaliating in kind was beneath her.

'What did Buffy tell you?'

'Oh, nothing. It was just woman stuff,' she quickly excused.

His expression relaxed into smug indulgence. Probably priding himself on what a great lover he was, serving Buffy on Friday night, her this morning—and no doubt Buffy had told him he was great, too! A violent jealousy erupted in Lucy.

'You and Buffy were talking woman stuff?' he commented, obviously amused by his two women connecting.

If he went back to Buffy tonight…she couldn't bear it. The come-hither model was just using him. The way she'd gone after Josh, she certainly wasn't in love with James. She just liked having what he could give her, especially in the sex department, while Lucy yearned for much more.

'Like what?' he prompted, curiosity dancing with amusement.

Could she say it? Would he see how shallow his relationship with Buffy was?

'Come on, Lucy. Out with it,' he pressed. 'I want to know what you two found in common.'

You…but not after this, she thought vehemently. She would not be the starter of the day and let Buffy be the finisher. She would do the finishing herself. Right now!

'Buffy told me you had a big…' She still couldn't say it.

'A big what?'

Why was she hesitating? It would re-arrange his

thinking, wouldn't it? Make him see how crass he'd been. Buffy, too, in labelling him like that.

'That you're really built...where it counted to her,' she blurted out.

'What?'

He looked utterly floored. Some protective instinct rose to the fore and he hastily achieved a respectable appearance, his face quite red as he tucked himself under cover—red from embarrassment or anger she couldn't tell until he raised savagely glittering eyes.

'She discussed me with you...in those terms?' he growled.

Definitely anger.

Goodbye, Buffy, Lucy thought, feeling no regret whatsoever at ruining the other woman's playground. Besides which, if James had only been using the swimsuit model for sex, he deserved to have that smacked in his face. He probably thought of Buffy in similar terms—big boobs. At least, he couldn't think about her like that.

'Some women do talk about their lovers,' she explained, furiously justifying what she'd done, though beginning to feel agitated about it. She smoothed her skirt over her thighs, nervously needing more respectability herself. 'Buffy considers *big* important,' she explained further.

His eyebrows beetled down. 'Do you?'

Desperately hoping he felt more than an impulsive lust for her, she earnestly declared, 'I consider lots of things important, James.'

'I'm glad to hear it,' he said grimly. 'Though apparently you didn't mind hearing intimate details about me.'

'I didn't ask for them,' she defended.

Seething disbelief glared back at her.

Her heart jiggled uncertainly. Somehow this was all rebounding on her, making everything tacky. She didn't know how to extract herself from it. The truth spilled off her tongue.

'Buffy offered them, wanting to dig out details about Josh, if you must know.'

His eyes glittered. 'Did she get *his* details?'

'No, she didn't. I really don't think of people like that,' she strongly asserted.

'But you have been thinking of me like that or it wouldn't be still in your mind right now,' he retorted fiercely. 'What else did she say about me?'

It was getting worse, not better. She desperately wished she hadn't started this. Jealousy was a terrible thing. She shook her head in shame. 'I'm sorry. Please…can we just let this go?'

She slid off the desk, onto her feet, intending to side-step away from him.

His hands clamped on her shoulders, halting her attempt at escape. 'Tell me!' he commanded.

'I must go and tidy up. Truly I must,' she begged, squirming to get out of the black hole she'd dug herself into.

'I'm sure you can spell it out in very brief terms,' he bit out relentlessly.

Apologetic appeal was her last resort. 'I don't

think you want to know, James. I seem to have said too much already. Sorry…' She wriggled out of his grasp and grabbed her bag from her chair, hoping to make a fast exit.

'Dammit, Lucy! If Buffy has been maligning me behind my back…' He looked about to explode.

'No, no no! Not maligning you, James,' she emphatically assured him. 'Really, I'd call it flattering.'

'Meaning I didn't live up to it in your view?' he thundered.

Lucy lost it.

The words just came tumbling out in a frantic effort to put this disaster behind her.

'Buffy said you could go on and on. But since this was just a starter for the day, I quite understand that's all you wanted. We are supposed to be working, so it's only right to stop and get on with what we're really here for,' she reasoned, frenziedly trying to save the pride she had so successfully wounded, ruining everything in the process.

'A starter for the day?' he bellowed at her.

She almost jumped out of her skin. 'That's what you said!' she hurled back at him—the wound to her own pride. Then to mitigate all the offence, she blabbed, 'I'm sure you're a great lover when you don't have to think about work.'

'But you thought…*that was it?*'

He was in a towering fury.

To Lucy's shattered mind, escape was the only answer. 'I'll go and get ready for work,' she mum-bled, heading for the door into the corridor, intending to bury herself in the washroom at the end of it.

'Hold it right there!' A blistering command.

She paused and cast him a look of desperate appeal. 'I do need to go.'

His eyes were flashing blue murder. 'All right!' he tersely conceded. 'But don't think we've finished this.'

Lucy trembled all the way down the corridor.

The realisation that she'd left James thinking she'd been merely trying out his equipment for size and stamina was deeply mortifying. She wasn't like that. She'd never been like that. In wanting Buffy out of his life, she'd done herself a damage that might very well be irretrievable.

And spoilt all the intense, amazing, ecstatic pleasure she had felt with James. An anguished moan ripped through her whole body as she closed and locked the washroom door. She rested her head against it, wishing she could die. No, wishing she had died before he had spoken *his* spoiling words. He'd given her a taste of heaven, and now she had completely blighted any chance of ever recapturing it.

Hell couldn't be worse than this, she thought in wretched despair. How was she going to face James again? How? She'd wanted so much to be special to him—uniquely special. She didn't want to live the rest of her life on her own and her heart said James Hancock was the one who could fill the lonely gaps better than anyone else ever would. But now…he probably wouldn't even want her as his secretary.

Unfortunately, she couldn't skulk in the washroom forever. *Don't think we've finished this,* he'd said. If she didn't reappear soon he might come and bang on the door. More shame!

Lucy forced herself to set about using the facilities. She felt like weeping buckets. Only the fear of losing her new contact lenses, which might swim out of her eyes on a flood of tears, held her inner misery contained. All the trouble she'd gone to in order to spark his interest and hold it…and she'd blown it all with her a self-defeating burst of pride, compounded by a bitter edge of black jealousy.

So what if he thought their intimacy had provided a great start to the day?

It was a start, wasn't it? A start she might have turned into more and more.

Why did she have to go and bring Buffy Tanner into it?

She stared at her kiss-swollen lips in the mirror above the sink, remembering the wild passion that had erupted between her and James. Mutual. Very, very mutual.

Don't think we've finished this!

Maybe there was still a chance, a feeble hope whispered. If she could straighten out the misunderstanding with James, confess her real feelings…her mind instantly shied from laying herself on such a vulnerable line. Best to assess his attitude first before diving headlong into more disaster. Which meant facing him.

Lucy took several deep, calming breaths. She brushed her hair until her hand was steady enough to re-apply lipstick without wobbling. Courage, she sternly told herself, deciding her appearance was as good as it was going to get, and there was no point in lingering in the washroom any longer. Waiting might not improve James' temper.

The walk back down the corridor felt like a walk to the guillotine. Her heart was in a nervous flutter. Her pulse was drumming in her ears. Remembering the flash of blue murder in James' eyes, she almost wished she had a black hood over her head. At least then she wouldn't see him working up to chopping her out of his life.

As it turned out, he was not waiting in her office. He had left the scene of the crime. Maybe he had decided to forget it and was setting up for work, all primed to put her firmly back in her secretarial place. Lucy was riven with uncertainty as to what to do now—wait for him to call her or take the initiative of telling him she was back?

The connecting door between their offices was open, beckoning her forward. She forced her somewhat tremulous legs to cross this last daunting distance, the need to see James—to gauge where she stood with him—driving her on.

He was not sitting at his desk. He was standing by the huge picture window, his back turned to her, his attention apparently fixed on the view of Sydney

Harbour. His back looked very stiff, his shoulders squared, and his arms were not hanging loose. Folded across his chest, Lucy surmised, which instantly formed a forbidding picture.

Panic seized her.

She had gone too far, tossing Buffy's words at him.

Her wayward tongue felt so thick she couldn't speak. She swallowed hard, desperately working some moisture into her mouth. No point in panicking. Best to confront whatever was going on in his mind. Then she'd know the worst. Open the conversation with business. That was relatively safe.

'Did anything happen yesterday that I should know about?' she asked, trying her utmost to project an efficient secretary voice.

He swung slowly around, a frosty glare in laser blue eyes.

Lucy's stomach was instantly reduced to jelly. He'd had second thoughts about what he'd done with her—second, third, fourth and fifth thoughts! In fact, he hated being faced with a reminder of it. His gaze sliced down and up her as though he wished he could disembowel her on the spot.

'We'll deal with this morning's e-mails first,' he stated icily.

'Oh! I thought since you arrived earlier than I did, you might have already dealt with them,' she gabbled, sick with relief that he was prepared to continue working with her.

'No, I haven't.' A positively arctic response.

'Fine. Okay. I'll get right onto them.'

She fled, her heart almost bursting with pain. It *was* finished...

James watched her swift exit, seething over her air of crisp efficiency. The saucy little skirt twitched provocatively as she turned her back on him, reminding him of how little she wore under it. How he was going to block that knowledge out of his mind for the rest of the day he didn't know, but be damned if he'd let her pull his strings any way she liked.

Whether Buffy had said those things or not, Lucy had definitely used them to gain the upper hand on him, reducing him to nothing more than an experience she'd fancied trying. He'd almost been goaded into whipping her off home with him for a day-long session in bed. But he didn't have to prove anything to her and he wasn't about to invite any further critical appraisal, either on his physique *or* his performance.

Lucy Worthington was not going to dominate him, not physically or mentally. She could play those manipulative games with her other lovers, but she'd find him a harder nut to crack. He'd satisfy her curiosity in his own good time, and on his terms. And one thing he was determined on with her— exclusive rights! If she thought she could juggle both him and Josh Rogan and anyone else she took a fancy to...

A bolt of shock hit him.

He strode to the connecting door, needing the question instantly settled. Lucy was seated at her desk, fingers tapping away at the keyboard with the firepower of a woodpecker—efficiency plus!

'Do you have a clean bill of health?' he shot at her.

Her head snapped towards him but her expression seemed totally blank, as though her mind hadn't connected to what he said.

'We just had unprotected sex, Lucy,' he bit out tersely. 'Is there a problem I should know about?'

'Oh!' Heat scorched her cheeks. 'Do you mean…could I get pregnant?'

'No.' He frowned over her interpretation. 'I mean you've been with Josh Rogan and God knows who else.'

Enlightenment dawned, along with a look of stricken horror. 'You've been with Buffy Tanner and God knows who else,' she shot back at him.

'I'm clean. I always use protection.'

'So do I. You have nothing to worry about.'

Clearly she was highly discomforted by the conversation. Her face was glowing with heat and her gaze jerked back to the monitor screen, her long loose hair swinging forward to block him out.

'Do I take it today was exceptional?' he drawled, pleased at getting under *her* skin and making her burn.

'You…umh…took me by surprise,' she excused in an embarrassed mumble.

'That doesn't usually happen to you?'

She visibly took a deep breath and looked him straight in the eye. 'No, it doesn't. What excuse do you have for not practising safe sex?'

'I was taken by surprise, too,' he answered, barely repressing a grin. 'Interesting, don't you think?'

'What do you mean?'

'Oh, just interesting,' he drawled and retreated to his office, his heart considerably lighter.

She hadn't gone along with him out of curiosity. There'd been no control at all, just hot wild passion all the way. Same as himself. Highly mutual desire running rampant.

It made James feel really good. He had the truth of it now. Measuring him and his performance had absolutely nothing to do with Lucy's response to him. Sheer wool over his eyes to put herself on top after the event. Well, it wasn't going to work. He'd have Lucy Worthington and he'd whittle down her defences until she confessed she wanted him every bit as much as he wanted her.

Let her simmer over what they had already shared. He was confident in his own mind she would want to try it again. It was only a matter of time. Meanwhile, he would revel in being master of the situation. Nothing to worry about.

James was in top humour for the rest of the day, getting through a prodigious amount of work with Lucy. He found it intensely gratifying that she was slightly on edge, watching him apprehensively as though on guard against being grabbed again and responding as she had this morning. It was further confirmation that this was new ground for Lucy Worthington. He'd stirred something in her that no other man had.

James exulted over this thought. He was also incredibly excited by it. In fact, he couldn't recall ever having been so excited by a woman. He could barely contain himself. He started watching the clock, determined on waiting out the full work-day, but impatient to set up another intimate encounter with his secretary.

He noticed Lucy checking her watch, too, as the afternoon drew closer to leaving time. Was she eager to get away? Finding the undeniable sexual tension between them tearing at her nerves? Control not so easy any more?

At ten to five she picked up a bunch of files from his desk to return them to the cabinet in her office. She walked so fast, the butterflies on her skirt flipped from side to side. Flight in progress, James thought, and was instantly compelled to lay down a trip-wire.

'Do you have any special plans for when we finish up here?' he tossed at her, keeping his tone casual.

She halted, her back going ram-rod straight. For several nerve-tingling seconds she stayed like that, not moving, not answering. James sensed an inner conflict raging, and with all his energy, willed her to give in to what *he* wanted. What he was convinced they both wanted.

'Nothing special,' she finally replied, half-turning

to look at him, her expression very guarded and wary. 'Why do you ask?'

He shrugged, leaned back in his chair, offered an encouraging smile. 'I wondered if you'd have dinner with me.'

'Dinner?' she repeated as though stunned by the idea.

'I'm not doing anything. If you're not doing anything…why not enjoy a meal together?' he reasoned affably.

She stared at him.

He could almost see the wheels going around in her head. He didn't really mean…just dinner. He meant bed and breakfast, too. And where would that lead? She had her job to consider. The sensible thing to do was…

'All right,' she said.

His heart leapt at the victory.

Temptation had won out.

'Good!' James approved, doing his utmost not to reveal his elation. He didn't want her to feel threatened in any way. He wanted her *with* him.

'Where were you thinking of going?' she asked.

'Where would you like?'

'I'm easy,' she said, and blushed a bright red.

'My place then,' he pressed decisively.

Her chin jerked up.

James suffered a searing stab of doubt. Had his eagerness pushed him too far too fast?

'Your place,' she repeated, her eyes glittering a

fierce challenge over the heat in her cheeks. 'In that case, I'll follow you there in my car.'

And leave whenever she wanted to.

James received the message loud and clear but he wasn't troubled by it. 'Fine,' he said, glancing at his watch. 'We'll take off in fifteen minutes or so. Okay?'

'Okay,' she agreed and made a fast exit from his office.

Done, James thought.

Although it wasn't a done deed yet, he reminded himself.

It was only the first step towards doing.

No…*undoing!*

And he grinned.

CHAPTER NINE

His place!

The intimacy of the invitation had Lucy's nerves in a riot. It felt as though the butterflies on her skirt had come alive and flocked into her stomach. If James had touched her as she accompanied him into the elevator which took them from their office floor to the basement car-park, she probably would have jerked away from him, frightened more of her own wild feelings than of him.

She stepped briskly to the rear of the compartment, leaving him to press the panel button and giving herself some space to get her mind clear and her skittish body under control. She'd wanted to step into his private life. This was her chance. Going to his place might not be very sensible, but what did she have to lose at this point?

Nothing.

Absolutely nothing.

And she had everything to gain.

Even if James had a sexual marathon in mind...so what? Hadn't she fantasised this kind of experience with him? She had to exude confidence, not apprehension. Seize the day. Seize the night. Seize anything he offered. There was no going back to the old worthy Miss Worthington image. Not after the raging heat of this morning's encounter on her office desk.

Besides, if for some reason, she decided this wasn't what she wanted, she had her own car to leave in whenever she chose. James surely understood that. The important factors were he was no longer angry with her and she had another chance with him.

'I don't know how to get to *your place*,' she said, doing her utmost to project a calm acceptance of this progression in their relationship. 'I know you live in Balmain, but...'

Balmain—one of the oldest suburbs of Sydney, like Woolloomooloo, where the dockyard workers had lived in earlier times. Now it was a very up-market trendy area, close to the inner city, the old terrace houses expensively renovated, trees cultivated along the narrow sidewalks, lots of fashionable eateries and the kind of shops that invariably catered to money.

'Just follow me in your car,' he advised. 'It's easier than explaining.'

'What if the traffic separates us?'

He smiled. 'I'll take very great care not to lose you, Lucy.'

It was like a warm caress all over her skin—that smile, that look in his eyes. He still wanted her. He was not going to lose her. And Lucy's fevered mind clutched his words, nursing them as though they were a promise of more than just sex between them—a promise of continuity, of value that went beyond a fleeting physical thing.

She definitely had to go with him. Her future was hanging on this journey. When the elevator stopped and the doors opened to the basement car-park, Lucy's legs moved automatically, compelled forward by a sense of commitment that had been seeded the moment she had decided to keep the red Alpha Spider convertible. Not the safe, sensible road. She was risking everything—*everything*—to have this man.

She took the car-keys out of her bag and pressed the unlocking device attached to them. James strode past her and opened the driver's door, a courtesy she hadn't expected. She paused, her heart drumming in her ears as her eyes searched his face for some sign of deeper feelings than desire.

'This isn't business, Lucy,' he stated pointedly, interpreting her pause as some feminist stance. 'You're my guest.'

He was treating her like a woman in his personal life, someone to be looked after, cared for. However facile the gesture was, it made Lucy feel like a winner already. 'Thank you,' she purred at him and slid into the driver's seat with as much feminine grace as she could manage.

He closed her into the car, his eyes gleaming satisfaction in her acquiescence. 'Sit on my tail,' he instructed, then grinned a devil-may-care challenge at her. 'Be aggressive if anyone tries to cut in.'

She watched him swing away to his black

Porsche—this man she had craved so long—and felt a fierce surge of possessive aggression. Let any woman try to cut in now that James had chosen to take up with her, and there'd be blood on the floor, including his if he proved fickle.

The drive to Balmain was something of a blur. With almost obsessive tunnel vision she saw only the black Porsche ahead of her, responding instinctively to its every move, slowing, stopping, accelerating, turning, feeling herself being irrevocably towed towards a place where her fate would be decided.

Was he taking her to a bachelor love-nest?

How many women had been there before her?

Would she become just one of a passing parade?

Stop it, she berated herself. What good was there in letting the past blight the present? James wanted *her* now. Nothing else mattered. She took a deep breath and muttered, 'Just take one step at a time. Live for the moment and meet the future as it comes, Lucy Worthington.'

She tried to focus more on where they were going since she would eventually have to find her way home. As they turned down a hill out of the main stream of traffic, she caught a glimpse of the harbour. The street was narrow with housing on both sides, most of the residences being terraces or semi-detached cottages, no obvious blocks of apartments. They travelled right to the end of the road before the black Porsche led her down a steep concrete driveway to a private parking area at the back of what had to be quite a large waterfront home.

Lucy was surprised. All the single career people she knew had minimum upkeep apartments, relatively free of maintenance problems which might take up their leisure time. A house such as this seemed too much to handle for a bachelor involved in a demanding business, as well as a high-flying social life. Nevertheless, it certainly reflected the kind of financial status that impressed people and undoubtedly made him even more attractive to those who counted such things.

Could she really compete with the likes of Buffy Tanner and all the socialites on the party circuit?

I'm here. They're not, Lucy firmly told herself, feasting her eyes on James as he skirted her car to open the driver's door. He wasn't as dashingly handsome as Josh, but he had a male animal magnetism that curled her toes. She wanted to see him stripped of clothes, wanted to feel the whole naked power of his masculinity. Everything had exploded on her this morning, all so sudden, so fast, but tonight...

The desire coursing through her was so strong, the touch of his hand was electric as he helped her out of the car, and her legs were definitely tremulous.

'Here we are, safely arrived,' James cheerfully remarked, guiding her to a flight of steps at the side of the house.

Probably the only *safe* thing done today, Lucy thought. 'You were right,' she acknowledged with a smile. 'I doubt I would have found this place by myself. Better to be led.'

'So now you can relax.'

Easier said than done. Lucy was wound up so tight, it was difficult to pluck out any line of normal conversation. 'Nice position you have here, right on the water,' she commented, sounding like a real estate person, buying or selling property.

'Yes. It's always good to come home to,' he replied, warm pleasure in his voice.

Was it especially good, having her with him, Lucy wondered—hoped—and would being in his home reveal more of the heart of the man?

There were three flights of steps down to the waterfront with landings marking the split levels of the house. The door James unlocked for her was off the first landing. Lucy preceded him into a hallway, her shoes clacking noisily on polished wooden floorboards, giving the house an empty sound. It made her very conscious of being really alone with him, and the door closing behind her punctuated the risk she was taking.

Every nerve in her body tensed but there was no sudden pouncing. James simply ushered her around a corner into a spacious foyer at the rear of a huge living area. As they stepped past the staircase which led upstairs, the whole ground floor, with all its dramatic interest, captivated her attention.

The foyer led into a kind of mezzanine level which virtually staged a magnificent black grand piano, and beyond it three exotically patterned sofas were grouped around a fire-place situated on the far wall which stretched up both storeys of the house to a domed ceiling of glass which flooded the area with light.

On the right of this level, a few steps led down to a dining-room, at the end of which were glass doors which gave a superb view of Sydney Harbour. On the left, matching steps led to an open-plan kitchen, its glass doors leading out to a large covered verandah which held more casual furniture for lounging or eating outside. Upstairs, a balcony ran around what had to be bedroom wings on either side of the mezzanine level with the high spectacular ceiling.

So struck was Lucy by all these fascinating features, she was barely aware of James moving past her to the kitchen, discarding his suitcoat and tie on a coat-rack along the way. This architectural wonder of a house, not to mention its prime location on the waterfront, had to be high in the millionaire class, and she felt swamped by what she had stepped into.

Would James ever see her as *belonging* in such a place as this? The office seemed like a world away. Yet he had chosen to bring her here, Lucy reminded herself.

'What would you like to drink?' he asked, jolting her back to the highly questionable issue of *why* he had invited her into the privacy of his home.

He had undone the top buttons of his shirt and was rolling up his sleeves. His virile energy hit Lucy anew, sending quivers through her stomach.

'Gin and tonic if you have it,' she answered, smiling ironically as she remembered having started all this recklessness last Friday night with a gin cocktail. *Mother's Ruin,* Josh had called it, and it would probably be her ruin, too, but she'd gone too far now to reconsider the wisdom of an intimate involvement with James Hancock.

'No problem,' he responded with an ironic smile of his own. 'You can hang up your bag on the coat-rack.'

Getting rid of extraneous items.

Lucy took a deep breath to calm her nerves and did as he said. 'This must be a great place for entertaining guests,' she remarked, trying to sound natural.

'Yes. Most people find it friendly.'

He was busy making their drinks...ice-blocks and tonic water from a big, double-sided refrigerator, a lemon from a well-stocked bowl of fresh fruit, a bottle of Tanqueray gin from a liquor cupboard. Lucy stepped down to the kitchen level, ready to take her glass when it was ready. There was an island work-bench with stools around it and she was about to draw out a stool and sit on it when a voice rang out, freezing all activity.

'Darling! So glad you're home early...'

A female voice, rich with seductive delight, and coming from the balcony above them, the balcony that clearly led to bedrooms!

Lucy's stunned heart burst into a killer drum-beat. She shot a sizzling glare at James. 'Overlooked something?' she hissed, venomous words spilling forth. 'Like not telling *darling* up there that you play musical beds and her time was up?'

'She shouldn't be here,' he muttered, frowning up at the apparition on the balcony.

Lucy spun around to get an eyeful of the competition. The woman was striding along the balcony towards the staircase, a gorgeous silk gown patterned with fiery dragons billowing around her, tousled red hair being finger-raked back from a face which was still obscured from Lucy's view.

'I've been resting but it's definitely time for drinkies,' the woman declared, obviously expecting her wishes to be served.

Lucy burned. Let James sort this out in front of her. If he didn't send the woman packing, she would flay him alive with her tongue, not to mention telling his erstwhile lover what he'd been up to today. It was totally outrageous that he'd left this redhead in his bed, then within minutes of Lucy entering his office, slaking his sexual needs all over again with her. Buffy was certainly right about one thing. He was a pistol with women. And as far as Lucy was concerned, this was the showdown at the OK Corral.

'Why aren't you in Melbourne?' James suddenly thundered up at the scantily clad woman who was ruining his set scene.

So the bird was supposed to have flown, Lucy thought caustically.

'The black plague hit,' came the insouciant reply.

'I decided to escape any possibility of infection by getting right away from everyone.'

'There's been no news of a black plague,' James argued, vexation pouring from him.

'Chicken pox,' came the airy correction, an arm waving away any protest from him as she went on. 'What could be worse, darling? Apart from getting deathly ill, I'd run the risk of having my face scarred. I told Wilbur he'd just have to write me out of the show until the danger was over. It was all his fault anyway for bringing the poxy child into the cast.'

An actress. Probably as voluptuously endowed as Buffy Tanner, and just as fixated on the physical. Models, actresses… Lucy seethed over James' choice of women.

'You could have called me,' he shouted.

'What for? Wilbur understood. I'm not breaking the contract, just having a break. I haven't made any trouble for you.'

James muttered something violent under his breath and shot an anguished look at Lucy. She gave him back a merciless stare. Trouble was certainly coming if he didn't get rid of this woman. In fact, his ammunition would be highly endangered by a sharp knee to the groin if he didn't extract himself from the redhead in Lucy's favour.

'It's not what you think,' he grated.

'What is it then?' she asked sweetly.

'Pour me a gin and tonic, darling,' the order came from the top of the stairs.

'No wonder you've got the ingredients handy,' Lucy mocked.

'Make it a double gin,' the voice trilled. 'It's so good to be home.'

'Home? This is *her* home?' Lucy was so shocked her voice came out half-strangled.

'It's my mother,' James bit out, his face a study of intense frustration. 'And yes, this happens to be home to both of us.'

'Your mother…' Incredulity gripped Lucy, her mind automatically rejecting a situation that didn't seem at all real to her. 'You still live with your mother?'

'Something wrong with that?' he snapped.

It had to be real. The fierce blaze in his eyes clearly resented any implication that living with his mother was in any way odd at his age. So the woman coming down the stairs had to be Zoe Hancock, star of both stage and television, and currently a key-player in the high-rating hospital soap opera, *St Jude*.

Lucy had never met her in the flesh. She had seen her on screen and would definitely recognise her when they finally came face-to-face. She was also aware that this family background in show business gave James an edge in managing his clients, but she had no idea the mother-son relationship extended to sharing the same home.

'Well, it will be very interesting to meet her,' Lucy said decisively, and her eyes challenged him to make the introduction with good grace.

No way in the world was Lucy about to be treated as a piece of skirt he'd like to sweep under the mat. She might have been invited here for sex, but enjoying a family evening with James and Zoe Hancock suddenly loomed as an extremely attractive alternative…a fast-track insight into the very heart of their private lives.

CHAPTER TEN

JAMES gritted his teeth. Not only was the evening he'd planned ruined, but Lucy now had the impression he was living under his mother's thumb. Which meant she'd have to see for herself that he wasn't. Otherwise, any respect she held for him would be shot to pieces, and that was one outcome he wouldn't tolerate.

Whipping her away to dinner in a restaurant would not get him what he wanted. That was glaringly obvious. She was unsettled by the situation. There were questions to be answered, and if she wasn't satisfied, Lucy was perfectly capable of making unshakable judgements—mind over matter, regardless of how tempting the *matter* was.

'Oh, you have a guest! What an unexpected pleasure!' his mother trilled, sighting Lucy as she swanned down the stairs. A second thought clearly struck and she shot an arch look at James. 'Is this why you sounded a bit cross? Am I *de trop,* darling?'

'Not at all,' he dryly assured her, resigning himself to the inevitable. 'Lucy was just saying she'd be interested to meet you.'

'Lucy...' A warm, welcoming smile was beamed at her. 'Do please forgive the deshabille—' a graceful gesture excused the exotic dressing-gown '—but

I am at home, you understand.' She looked expectantly at James. 'Lucy who, darling? Don't leave me in the dark.'

'Lucy Worthington…Zoe Hancock.'

'Worthington… Worthington… I'm simply terrible with names. Should I know it?'

'Lucy is my secretary,' James stated to cut the agony short.

'*The* secretary?' His mother looked at Lucy in astonishment—looked her up and down—then raised her eyebrows at him as though he'd lied through his teeth.

'A double gin coming up,' he said, refusing to get into explanations about Lucy's change of image.

'Have you been my son's secretary very long, Lucy?' his mother pressed on with totally unabashed curiosity.

'About eight months,' came the matter-of-fact reply.

'Well, I must say James made you sound quite different to what you are.'

'On the contrary,' he cut in. 'I said my secretary was the most sensible woman I've ever met and she is still the most sensible woman I've ever met.'

He added a twist of lemon to the drinks and carried them to the two women, seizing the opportunity to clear up the situation since Lucy might well decide any further intimacy with him was unwise and she was better off out of it.

'What I didn't tell you and what I've come to realise,' he said to his mother, then turned his gaze to Lucy, deliberately locking eyes with her, 'is that she is also the sexiest woman I've ever met.'

He could feel the power drill of Lucy's brain boring into his. *'Ever?'*

She was smart, utterly delectable, and infinitely exciting in her ability to challenge. 'Ever,' he confirmed emphatically.

Electricity crackled from her. 'Surpassing the beautiful Buffy?'

'Buffy is no longer even desirable.' It was the absolute truth.

'You seem rather fickle in your desires.'

'Superficial distractions. I've had one constant desire burning in me for some time now. Only on Friday night did I discover it was mutual.' She couldn't deny that and James topped it with more undeniable truth. 'As with everything you do, Lucy, you hid your light under a bushel with superb efficiency.'

She blushed. Something she couldn't control, James noticed, which excited him even further, wondering if her whole body blushed. At the very least, it was a sign of vulnerability to him, and nothing was going to stop him from exploiting that vulnerability.

His mother coughed. 'This conversation…'

'Is necessary.' He flicked her a derisive look. 'When you floated out on the balcony, Lucy thought I was playing musical beds.'

'Me?' She laughed, reached out and patted Lucy's

arm indulgently. 'My dear! What a compliment, taking me for one of James' women.'

'He does tend to run through them rather quickly,' came the acerbic comment.

'Perhaps because they fawn on him,' his mother remarked with knowing amusement. 'I can see you don't. Very sensible.'

'Well, I guess you have the best standpoint to judge these things, Mrs Hancock,' She shot him a look that was loaded with dubious thoughts as she added, 'having lived with James so long.'

He tensed, realising he hadn't won anything yet. Lucy's guard remained up and this moving straight into the question of his sharing a home with his mother was a clear signal her mind was still assessing the situation. Her hand-bag was in easy stepping distance, hanging on the coat-rack, and although he'd put a glass in her hand, that could be quickly disposed of.

'Shall we take our drinks out to the verandah?' he swiftly suggested, wanting to put distance between her and her car-keys.

'Good idea! Fresh air to blow thoughts of the plague away,' his mother approved, collecting Lucy as she moved forward. 'And please call me Zoe, dear. Hancock is actually my maiden name. I didn't marry James' father, you know.'

James winced at his mother's garrulous habit of letting everyone know he was a bastard. Supposedly it reflected well on her for shouldering the task of bringing him up alone—the brave single mother—

but it always made him feel belittled, having been fathered by a man who hadn't cared enough to stick around.

'I'm sorry. I didn't know,' Lucy muttered, sounding embarrassed by the revelation.

'It simply wouldn't have worked,' his mother burbled on. 'A brief fire in our lives, not a lasting passion. I didn't marry at all until I met my wonderful Hugh, and James was fifteen by then.'

She was off and running and, James knew from experience, impossible to stop with a new audience to lap up the more colourful details of their lives.

'Should I know your Hugh?' Lucy asked, being drawn in by the excessive story-telling.

'Really, James,' his mother huffed. 'Haven't you told Lucy anything about your life?'

'I'm sure you'll make up the deficit,' he replied, ushering them out to the verandah. At least his mother was adept at carrying guests with her, which was something to be grateful for. He was acutely aware of how elusive Lucy could be.

'Hugh…Hugh Greenaway…was a marvellous father to James,' his mother rattled on. 'Just what he needed after years of being dragged around with a bunch of actors, living in temporary digs and having to fit in with the mad hours we worked. It's amazing he wasn't taken away by social workers, now that I think about it.'

'I had lots of aunties and uncles, remember?' James put in dryly, trying to correct any impression of being an object of pity.

He wouldn't swap his childhood for any other. As an education in life and people, it had covered a very broad spectrum. Yet there had been many times he'd envied other boys their fathers and the activities they shared with them. If he'd had a father like Hugh, right from the beginning…

'But it was a rackety existence, darling,' his mother insisted. 'Always changing schools.'

That wasn't good, James silently agreed, but he'd learnt to go with the flow.

'Sit here, Lucy.'

She waved to the cane armchair adjacent to the fan-backed one she always favoured herself—the queen taking her throne, usually surrounded by courtiers. There was only Lucy to entertain this evening, and James watched them sit down together, confident his mother would hold her audience captive for a while.

'I'll get some nibbles,' he said and back-tracked to the kitchen, relieved to have Lucy settled and within easy reaching distance.

She could make what she liked of what his mother told her. It was irrelevant to him…as long as she stayed.

Lucy's mind was in a whirl, knocked for a loop by the idea that James had fancied her for some time, even *before* the charity ball! Was it true? And was Buffy—every other woman—completely out of the picture now? Did he really think she was the sexiest female he'd ever met? It felt…too much to believe.

On top of that she was now sitting here with his mother, which was as unexpected as everything else, and she was being fed information so fast she could barely take it in. With James having taken himself back to the kitchen, relieving her of the distraction of his overpowering presence, she tried to recollect herself enough to focus on Zoe Hancock.

The older woman had glorious hair, thick with curls and waves, its rich colour undoubtedly provided by a hairdresser since she had to be in her fifties, but her pale skin suggested she had once been a natural redhead. Her face was relatively unlined, perhaps due to cosmetic surgery, yet it radiated a vivid personality through the fascinating mobility of her mouth and expressive blue eyes. James had the same eyes but Lucy could see no other similarity to his mother.

His father—the brief fire in Zoe Hancock's life— must have been in the tall, dark and handsome mould. Lucy wondered if he knew he'd fathered a son. How brief was *brief*? From what she'd been told so far, he'd played no part in James' upbringing. She wondered if James felt as deprived as she had by her father's desertion.

'This was Hugh's place. I think I fell in love with it before I fell in love with him,' Zoe remarked, gazing at the view down the harbour to the great coat-hanger bridge that spanned it. She heaved a sigh and flashed a wry smile at Lucy. 'He left it to us when he died, but I'm away more than I'm home these days. It's lucky James is always here to look after everything.'

'I imagine he feels lucky to have the pleasure of it.'

She nodded. 'It's the only real home he's ever known. God knows where he might have ended up without Hugh settling him into a proper education and guiding him through law.'

'Guiding him?' Lucy queried, thinking James was not the kind of person to be guided anywhere he didn't want to be led.

'My incredibly clever husband was a top-flight barrister,' Zoe proudly declared. 'He taught James all the tricky things about contracts, putting him wise on what to look out for in the entertainment business. That's a good part of why he's so successful at managing his clients.'

'Meticulous attention to detail,' Lucy agreed, privately reasoning that James had probably taken every opportunity to pick Hugh Greenaway's brains, already knowing where he wanted to go. He wasn't a follower. Having worked so closely with him, Lucy was fairly sure James always had and always would forge his own path.

'There is the personality angle, too,' she pointed out to his mother. 'He's very good with people.'

Zoe laughed. 'Well, something of me had to rub off on him.'

That could be so, but coping with all the honorary aunts and uncles and constant changes of school had more likely made getting along with people a sur-

vival art, Lucy thought. She wondered what, if anything, had ever touched him deeply. Maybe superficial relationships had become a habit—here today,
gone tomorrow, enjoying whatever pleasure they
gave him.

'Have you been a widow long?' she asked, really
wanting to know more of James' relationship with
his stepfather.

'Longer than I was a wife,' she answered ruefully.
'I only had nine years with Hugh. He loved sailing
and always crewed for a friend in the Sydney to
Hobart yacht race. Ten years ago a dreadful storm
blew up during one of those races and Hugh was
swept overboard, drowning before he could be res-
cued. It was a wicked, wicked waste of a life.'

'He died as he lived, doing what he wanted,'
James sliced in, carrying out a cheeseboard with a
plate of crackers and olives. 'And if he hadn't been
a risk-taker, you wouldn't have married him. One
thing he didn't do was waste his life, playing everything safe.'

His gaze swung to Lucy and the challenge in his
eyes thumped into her heart. It was what she had
resolved herself—not to play safe—and he wasn't
playing safe, either. They were both risking their
work relationship, compelled to explore a desire that
was by no means fulfilled...yet! Where it would
lead—where it would end—neither of them knew.
A brief fire or a lasting passion?

'You've told me that a thousand times, darling,

but it doesn't stop me missing him when I come home,' Zoe said plaintively.

James set the food down on a coffee-table within easy reach of the armchairs and shot his mother a sharply inquiring look. 'Have you broken up with Wilbur?'

'No, no. Wilbur's a dear sweet man and he understands me. We do share a lot, but...'

'There will never be another Hugh,' came the quiet admonition.

Zoe rolled her eyes at him. 'Do you have to be so sensible, James?'

'It's my job,' he returned dryly. 'Excuse me while I get my drink.'

'Honestly!' Zoe huffed at Lucy. 'He's been like that since he was a boy, making me face up to things instead of letting me float along in my usual haphazard fashion. Is he a terribly bossy boss?'

'I've always found him very reasonable,' Lucy replied, which was true, for the most part.

'Ah, yes, but you're sensible, too. Like minds, no doubt.'

Lucy had to smile. Being sensible was certainly not part of the current equation. But it was interesting to learn Zoe Hancock's view of her son. It seemed that she looked to him to keep her life in order and there was no such dependency the other way. No mother domination at all. James was, without a doubt, what he had made of himself, and Lucy found that strength of mind and purpose immensely attractive.

He re-emerged from the kitchen, jiggling his drink as he took command of the conversation. 'So, am I to understand there's no problem in Melbourne apart from the threat of chicken pox?' he demanded of his mother. 'You haven't come flying home for any other reason?'

'Truly, darling, everything's fine,' she assured him. 'Wilbur doesn't want me to risk my health, either. It's just a precaution, nothing more.'

'I'm glad to hear it.'

He settled onto the cane armchair directly across the table from where Lucy sat, leaned forward, cut off a slice of brie from the selection of cheeses, spread it on a cracker and offered it to her, his vivid blue eyes appealing for her to take it.

'Thank you,' she murmured, her pulse beginning to gallop as he watched her lift it to her mouth and bite into it.

A sensual smile played on his lips as he proceeded to serve both his mother and himself. Lucy remembered how sensational his mouth was…kissing her…and as enlightening as Zoe Hancock's presence had been, she wished his mother elsewhere.

'It's such a lovely, balmy evening,' Zoe remarked. 'Who would have thought it would still be this warm in March?'

'A late summer,' James said and gave Lucy a look that simmered with hot invitation. 'Would you like to have a swim in the pool before dinner?'

Pool? She quickly recalled the flight of steps going down beyond the landing that must lead onto this verandah and realised there was a ground level she hadn't yet seen. 'I'd love to, but...' Surely he didn't expect her to go skinny-dipping with his mother here, though she squirmed sensually at the wicked thought of swimming naked with him. She'd never swum nude in her life, but with James...

'But what?' he pressed, offering her the dish of olives.

She shook the wild fantasy out of her head. 'I don't have a swimming costume with me,' she answered ruefully, choosing a black olive.

'We keep a selection for guests in the cabana. I'm sure there'll be something to fit you.'

'Oh!' She almost choked on the olive as his eyes burned into hers, feeding images of them being in the water together, none of them remotely connected to actually swimming. The *something to fit her*...did he mean him? She could barely catch enough breath to answer, 'Okay. Sounds great!'

She could feel the strength of mind and purpose she so admired encompassing her, tugging on her like an irresistible magnet, and every nerve in her body was dancing in response.

'What were you thinking of doing for dinner?' Zoe asked.

'Whatever appeals when we feel like it,' James answered, his eyes still locked on Lucy's, promising to please her in every way. 'There's plenty to choose from in the refrigerator.'

Could his mother feel the sexual energy being

emitted? Was he always so open about it in front of her? Even being conscious of his mother being a spectator, Lucy couldn't tear her eyes from his.

'Then why don't I prepare something while you two have your swim?' Zoe brightly suggested.

'Fine!' James agreed. 'Is there anything you particularly don't like—' He paused, raising goose-bumps on Lucy's skin as he let the question linger suggestively before adding '—in the way of food, Lucy?'

She sucked in a deep breath, trying to focus on the practical question being asked. 'I don't really enjoy burn-your-mouth food like chillies and hot Indian curries.'

He smiled. 'No de-sensitising your taste-buds.'

For kissing, Lucy instantly thought, though she had never connected such things before this. It was James, messing with her mind, the desire emanating from him exciting her own madly wanton urges.

'Then that's settled,' Zoe said with satisfaction, apparently happy to accommodate her son's program for the evening. 'I'll just potter around the kitchen and see what inspires me.' She aimed a warmly encouraging smile at Lucy. 'It occurs to me that I've been rattling on about our life and I know nothing about yours, apart from being James' secretary. Do tell me more.'

This distraction was deeply unwelcome, yet courtesy demanded she answer something. Lucy took a quick sip of her gin and tonic to cool herself down. It was difficult to pluck anything sensible out of her fevered brain with James still watching her, listening intently, alert to her every response, both verbally and physically. Her whole consciousness was vibrating on a more immediate level—what was going to happen next, not what had made up her life before this.

'I really have nothing out of the ordinary to relate,' she said with a dismissive shrug. The last thing she wanted was to sound boring when James was finding her exciting...*the sexiest woman he'd ever met!* Somehow she had to live up to that, keep his interest running.

'Where do your family live?' Zoe persisted.

'At Gosford. But I don't really have a family. Only a mother.' Like him, she quickly reasoned. Common ground. It was okay to say that much. She wanted a bond between them that went beyond work and sexual excitement, and she exulted at the gleam of interest she saw in his eyes. 'I was an only child,' she added, eager to re-inforce the bond, let him know she'd been fatherless, too. 'My parents were divorced when I was very young and my father went off travelling. I have no idea where he is.'

'Your mother didn't re-marry?' Zoe asked, seeking more background.

'No. I guess you could say she became a career person, preferring to be on her own,' Lucy answered reluctantly.

'Ah!' James murmured, as though she'd just said something enlightening.

Lucy's skin prickled. What did he think she had just revealed?

'What does your mother do?' Zoe asked curiously.

'She runs a health food business,' Lucy answered, still wondering why the career tag was meaningful to James.

'With all the nutritional fads and diets these days, it must be a thriving business,' Zoe pressed.

'It suits my mother,' Lucy replied, not wanting to comment further. She couldn't guess what either James or his mother were reading into this information and she felt discomforted by Zoe's persistent probing for more background. Wasn't it enough that she was a person in her own right?

'Well, healthy food is fine, but all dietitions say it should be accompanied by exercise,' James drawled, pushing up from his chair and giving his mother a look that warned her off any further cross-examination. 'If you'll excuse us...'

'Of course, darlings.' She eloquently gestured her generosity of spirit over the move. 'Do go and enjoy the pool. Work up an appetite for dinner. I wouldn't want my culinary efforts wasted.'

Relieved to be off the hook where his mother was concerned, Lucy quickly put her glass down and eagerly took the hand James offered to pull her up from her chair. Just the feel of his fingers closing around hers set her body abuzz with appetites that had nothing to do with food.

'Take your time,' James advised his mother. 'We're not in any hurry for dinner, are we, Lucy?'

'No,' she agreed.

But there was a sense of urgency pulsing between them, and as James led her off the verandah to the steps that presumably took them to the pool and cabana, the hand holding hers tightened to a hotly possessive grip and her heart started drumming in her ears.

Her mind shut down on where this was leading.

James was orchestrating the moves.

Let him lead.

CHAPTER ELEVEN

'THE pool is solar-heated. The water is like warm silk this time of the evening,' James told her as they descended the flight of steps.

His voice was like warm silk, Lucy thought, a sensual encouragement to feel all there was to feel. She shivered in anticipation. 'Do you swim every day?' she asked, tinglingly aware of his strong, muscle-toned physique.

'Depends on the weather, but most days, yes.' He flashed her a wicked grin. 'I enjoy swimming and it's supposedly the best physical exercise. It makes keeping fit a pleasure.'

Lucy's mind instantly skipped to the other physical pleasures that undoubtedly gave his body a good work-out. If Buffy had spoken the truth...but she wasn't going to think about Buffy, or any of his other women. This was here and now with her.

They reached ground level and there was the pool stretching out in front of them, clear blue water rippling in the balmy breeze. Most of the area surrounding it was paved with slabs of blue-green slate, but along the high side fences of the property, ensuring privacy, was a profusion of fern-trees, palms and tropical shrubs with shiny, colourful leaves, creating an environment that was visually exotic as well as inviting total relaxation.

Underneath the shade of the verandah were sun-loungers and occasional tables. Behind them was a third level to the house, presumably what they called the cabana, a large glass-fronted room, its layout curtained from view. James released Lucy's hand, removed a key from under a pot-plant, unlocked a sliding glass door, opened it, lifted the curtain aside and waved Lucy into what appeared to be more a guest suite than a casual entertaining area.

Her gaze was instantly drawn to the queen-size bed, her imagination running riot with the sexual fantasies she'd woven around James in the long months of her employment as his secretary. Only vaguely did she hear the click of the door closing, the rustle of the curtain dropping back into place, but all her senses leapt into vibrant life as James' arms wound around her waist, scooping her back against him, and the warmth of his breath caressed her ear as he lowered his head to hers to murmur seductively intimate words.

'I've been anticipating this moment all day and I can't wait any longer. Say it's what you came for...that you can't bear not to feel again what exploded between us this morning.'

His hands moved up under her top, taking possession of her breasts, kneading them, revelling in their soft giving to his touch. Her bottom was nestled against his groin and there was no doubting the urgency of his desire, his arousal only too evident in its hard, erotic pressure. Lucy was dazed, thrilled that he could want her so much, that this morning's passion had not abated and was just as strong— stronger—now.

'Say it, Lucy. Take the risk. Break your rules. Don't hide from me any more. You can't anyway. I know.'

His voice throbbed with confident knowledge.

She didn't care that he knew what she felt.

She didn't care about anything but having him.

'Yes…' The admission poured from her heart. 'I do want more of you.'

More than he was thinking of, but it would come, Lucy told herself. It had to, or this flood of feeling for him was a terrible misdirection of nature.

'Yes,' he echoed, a hiss of triumphant satisfaction. 'So let it *be* more. No clothes this time.'

His hands moved swiftly, whipping off her top. Momentarily freed of his embrace, Lucy whirled around to face him, her eyes blazing with her own need to have him stripped, as well. 'You, too, James. This is a two-way deal,' she insisted feverishly, her fingers attacking the buttons of his shirt, uncaring if he thought her brazen. It wasn't right, James taking without giving her all of himself. The word, *mutual,* was pounding through her mind.

He laughed, seemingly elated by her positive counter-action, pulling off his shirt as she opened it. His tanned skin was gleamingly taut over his chest and arm muscles, somehow glorifying his beautiful masculinity which was so sleek and strong, everything female in Lucy started fluttering in a purely pagan response to the man he was. Even the nest of black hair across his chest suggested an animal virility that touched something deeply primitive in her.

Impossible to stop her fingers speading through that hair, luxuriating in the feel of it. Under her palm the thump of his heart transmitted a charge to her own heart, an exultant pulse of joy and need that she knew, beyond any possible doubt, was intensely mutual—such exhilarating, intoxicating knowledge, like swimming in dreams that had taken on flesh and blood reality.

'Stopping there, Lucy?' James teased, his voice husky now, affected by her absorption in him.

She looked up into eyes that had darkened to deep blue. 'You had the advantage of me this morning,' she reminded him. 'I didn't get to touch you.'

'Satisfy yourself then. As I will.'

He reached around her waist, unclipping and unzipping her skirt. Driven to match him, she slid her own hands down over his stomach to unfasten his trousers, wanting him stripped at the same time, both of them equally naked. Clothes were discarded in a rush of eagerness, shoes, too, everything tossed aside with a wild sense of abandoning all inhibitions because this reality was a thousand times more exciting than anything she could dream.

At last she was free to know all of him and he crushed her to him as though the need to imprint her flesh and blood reality on his was of the utmost

urgency, as though he, too, had wanted it for months
and the waiting and fantasising were finally over.

'No pins—' he growled, grabbing a fistful of hair,
winding it around his fingers '—and all buttons undone.'

'I didn't have buttons,' she said distractedly, revelling in the lean line of his hips, the powerful hardness of his thighs, the taut curve of his buttocks,
filling her hands with every tactile sensation within
her reach, even as she soaked in the sheer bliss of
feeling her breasts squashed against the heat of his
bare chest and his erection furrowing her stomach.
He was perfect—incredibly, wonderfully perfect.

'You've been primly pinned and buttoned up
from the day I employed you, Lucy Worthington,'
he gruffly accused. 'But I've got you now—the
woman I always sensed was underneath it all.'

Always?

He started walking her backwards, dominantly
purposeful. Lucy found the movement so exciting,
her mind barely grasped the idea that James had
been thinking of her as a woman, not just as his
worthy secretary.

'Why did you never say anything?' she cried, remembering the anguish of her own secret wanting
which he'd given no hint of returning.

He tumbled her onto the bed, kneeling over her,
hauling her into a more comfortable position, smiling into her eyes. 'I liked the tantalising mystery…the way you fenced with me.' He lifted her
arms up over her head, holding her wrists to keep

them there. 'But more and more I've wanted you like this, Lucy, open to me, wanting me, responding with the passion I sensed in you.'

Was it true? Had the attraction been there all along, building towards this on both sides?

He bent and ran his tongue between her lips, making them tingle. She lifted a leg and caressed the back of his knee with her foot, instinctively denying him complete mastery over her. His head jerked up. Then with a rumbling growl he released her wrists, burrowing an arm under her hips as he plundered her mouth with a swift challenging drive to arouse and excite the passion he wanted to feast on.

Lucy gave it to him, as greedy as he was for the same ravishing intimacy, the same heady explosion of sensation, the same sense of an ecstatic inner sharing that broke all normal boundaries, that zoomed them into a world owned only by them.

She felt the hot hardness of his penis being moved against the soft moistness at the apex of her thighs, caressing, inciting an almost unbearable excitement, back and forth, back and forth until she wrenched her mouth from his and cried for its insertion. 'Enough! I need you now...now....'

And he plunged into her, so deliciously full and fast, dispelling the terrible yearning for him, answering the throbbing need with a force that arched her body in exquisite satisfaction, and she could feel her inner muscles convulsing with the intense pleasure of it, squeezing him, relaxing to let him pump the sheer splendour of this fantastic togetherness higher and higher, climbing to peak after peak of quivering ecstasy, her legs wrapped around him, driving him on, her hands blindly urging, her eyes closed, her whole being inwardly focused on this wildly compelling mating with James…James…her man…and she his woman…bonding…melding…

Climax!

Shattering in its power, tempestuous in its rolling rush through every cell in her body, blissful in its aftermath.

Then a long, sweet, sensual kiss, gentling hands, contented sighs, a slow, reluctant parting.

They looked at each other, in their eyes a wordless acceptance of having experienced something special. How special it was to him, Lucy had no idea. In her need to draw some heart-warming admission from him, she remembered a claim he had made earlier today.

'You said you always used protection,' she blurted out, secretly—anxiously—watching for some sign that it was different with her for a host of reasons that were emotional, as well as physical.

His mouth curved with some private pleasure. 'I didn't want anything to come between us.'

'But to break a personal rule…'

He smiled into her eyes. 'Isn't that what we're both doing, Lucy? Breaking all the rules we set ourselves? Messing with our work relationship because we wanted this?'

The realisation that it wasn't sensible for him, either, gave her hopes a boost. But giving in to temptation after eight months...was that really a sign that she was special to him or merely an admission that desire had finally overridden good business sense?

'Besides, you said I didn't need protection and you wouldn't lie about that, Lucy,' he went on. 'Not about control. It's too important to you.' He trailed his fingers down over her stomach making her flesh leap at his touch. 'Even just now you called the shots.'

'Hardly,' she protested, amazed that he thought she had any control at all over what she felt.

His eyes teased. 'Didn't I move to your command?'

Her mind jolted with the memory of Josh inadvertently suggesting he was a slave to her whims and James then thinking she had dominatrix tendencies. But surely he didn't really believe that.

'I don't remember standing over you with a whip. More like you did what *you* wanted, as well,' she replied, mocking his assertion.

He laughed, a happy gloating in his eyes. 'No complaint. But I shall contest your timing in the next round.'

'Round? Is that what you call it?' Again her heart fluttered apprehensively. Did he see this as some kind of contest he had to win? Was that what had *really* excited him?

'There's always a battle of the sexes,' he answered sardonically, stroking her hair away from her face. 'And I see no surrender in your eyes. In all probability you're plotting the next move.'

She didn't want a battle with him. Never had. Just two people finding love and holding onto it. Why did it have to be so complicated between them? Couldn't he simply feel they were right for each other?

She shouldn't have deceived him with Josh. Yet hadn't that deception triggered the change in his attitude towards her, heightening his interest and sharpening the desire he'd repressed for the sake of not messing with his business set-up?

Desperately needing time to think, she said, 'If we don't soon move to the swimming pool your mother will start to wonder.'

'Ah! To the shower!'

He swung off the bed, scooped her up and carried her to an ensuite bathroom. Caveman style he hoisted her over his shoulder as he opened the door to the shower stall and turned on the taps. Lucy didn't get any time to think. He no sooner set her on her feet under a streaming spray of water than he grabbed a bar of soap and started sliding it over her.

Her hair was getting wet and it would be a mess— was the last rational thought she had. He soaped her breasts with a slow sensuality that trapped her into a fascinated thrall. It was as though he was rapt in the structure of them, and as fascinated as she was by their response to his caressing. Then the glide of the soap over her abdomen and down between her legs. Never had she been washed so intimately, and she felt his fingers circling, drawing more intense excitement.

Mindlessly, she lifted her hands to his shoulders, instinctively seeking a steadying support. The hair on his chest was plastered into tight curls. His naked body somehow seemed magnified this close— big...big all over, overwhelmingly male, intensely physical, powerfully sexual.

Suddenly he lifted her, lifted her against the shower wall and his mouth was lashing her breasts, licking, sucking, wildly tugging on her tightly extended nipples, and she was embracing his head with a fierce desire to hold him there, her legs encircling him just as possessively, and when he pushed inside her again, her only thought was a sweetly savage... Oh yes! Yes...yes...her whole being exulting in the compulsive madness of it, the incredible arc of pleasure from her breasts to her womb, the pumping of it to another intense climax. She was totally consumed by the tumultous power of it, even when it was over.

James gently eased her down to stand on her own two feet. 'This could get addictive,' he murmured, his eyes simmering with a lust for more. 'But I guess we'd better go and swim.'

'Yes,' she managed to reply, struggling to appear as composed as he seemed about what they'd just shared.

He turned off the taps, stepped out of the stall, grabbed a towel and wrapped it around her, touching her cheek in an oddly tender salute as he said, 'I'll find you something to wear.'

Had he given up the idea of *battle,* she wondered, watching him leave the ensuite bathroom, aware of every nerve-ending in her body buzzing with pleasure and wantonly anticipating being served with more and more of it. No control at all, she dazedly thought, and decided it didn't matter. She could only hope that whatever was driving James would last beyond tonight because she was beyond controlling anything.

He came back with a silvery maillot. 'This should fit. Stretchy fabric.'

There was no bra structure in it and the leg-line was cut high to her hips. The thin nylon provided little more than a second skin over what it covered. Didn't matter, she reasoned again. Only he was going to see her. Possibly his mother, too, she belatedly remembered, but that would only be in the pool if Zoe Hancock happened to look over the verandah railing.

The brief black costume James had put on was just as revealing. Her gaze strayed to the heavy bulge at the apex of his thighs. Three times today already, Lucy thought, wishfully—lustfully—wondering if he was planning on more. It was a terrible thing about lust. Having it so brilliantly satisfied seemed to generate more.

'Let's go,' he said, taking her hand.

Even that contact felt intensely sexual.

He released it when they reached the edge of the pool, letting her dive in alone.

The water *was* warm and silky, a lovely sensual liquid flow around her body, doing nothing at all to cool her mind, inciting an even deeper seduction towards simply luxuriating in feeling. Her hair which had been heavily wet from the shower, floated around her, weightless, as she turned on her back and floated.

'You look like a mermaid,' James said, treading water beside her.

She smiled, enjoying her own wicked thoughts as she replied, 'Having a tail might be inconvenient.'

He laughed, and his pleasure in her was a further intoxication. She started swimming, spurted on by a glorious burst of energy and wanting to share all his pleasures with him. He didn't attempt to make a competition of it, matching her leisurely stroke, apparently content with the companionship, which warmed Lucy's heart. When she tired and rested at one end of the pool, he stopped with her, reaching out to draw her into an embrace. She went willingly, loving the slow entanglement of his legs with hers.

His eyes were midnight-blue in the gathering twilight of the evening. They searched hers, as though wanting the response of her mind as well as her body. 'I'm beginning to think we're natural partners…at work and play,' he said quietly, seriously.

Yes, her heart sang. She smiled. 'We seem to fit together very well.'

His answering smile was loaded with sensual appreciation. 'In every sense. So I think we should explore how far it goes, don't you?'

'James… Lucy?' Zoe Hancock called from above. 'Are you coming up soon? I've got everything ready to start cooking when you give the word.'

His mother! And soon to come—facing her across a dinner table! Lucy's lifetime habit of looking respectable—according to her own mother—came crashing into prominence. 'I'll need at least twenty minutes to do something with my hair,' she warned James in an anxious whisper.

He frowned quizzically at her, as though the state of her hair was totally irrelevant to him, then called back, 'Give it half an hour and we'll be ready to eat.'

'Half an hour,' Zoe repeated. 'That's fine…' Her voice trailed away.

James frowned again at Lucy. 'Don't be worried by my mother. She has nothing to do with us.'

'She's here…' *Summing me up, assessing me, and she'll discuss me with you when I'm gone…* but Lucy choked up on admitting she wanted his mother's approval. It assumed too much of their relationship. 'We can't keep ignoring that, James,' she pleaded.

'Agreed,' he conceded. 'Just don't let her interfere with this.'

He kissed her with ravishing intensity, wiping out the rest of the world. He peeled the flimsy maillot from her body, baring it to his again, and the water lapping them made the flesh to flesh contact even more erotic. When he hauled her up to sit her on the edge of the pool, Lucy was still rocking from the explosion of sensation spiralling through her. The maillot was drawn off and tossed onto the paving behind her. He moved between her legs, opening them wide.

'Lean back, Lucy, and think of me wanting to do this, and more, as you sit at the dinner-table with my mother.' He grinned wickedly. 'And know I'll be thinking of it, too.'

He parted the intimate folds of her sex and kissed her there, with even more ravishing intensity than he had kissed her mouth. Lucy automatically arched back, her arms supporting her as waves of pleasure issued from the exquisite caressing. He hooked her legs over his shoulders and she felt his tongue delve inside her, swirling, inciting an incredible excitement, driving her into another shuddering release which he soothed with gentle stroking until the quivering ceased.

'Hold onto what you feel now,' he murmured, his eyes burning with hot purpose. 'Don't let it go no matter what my mother says or does.'

Impossible to let it go. The acute sexual awareness he had stirred was pulsing chaotically through her bloodstream, throbbing through her mind.

He left her alone while she showered and washed her hair, going to fetch her bag from upstairs so she could apply fresh make-up and use her own hairbrush as she wielded the hair-dryer in the bathroom. But she didn't feel parted from him. Not for a moment. It was as though he had infiltrated her entire being.

Every sense was heightened with this feeling when he came back. While she attended to her hair and face, he was in the bathroom with her, showering and towelling himself dry, and she could barely stop herself from staring at him, so entranced was she by the naked physique of the man.

Even when he dressed she kept seeing him as he was without clothes. He watched her, too, waiting for her to be ready to confront his mother again, and all the time she felt his sizzling desire for every possible intimacy with her.

To Lucy, dinner with his mother seemed to take place on two levels. One appeared to be relatively normal. Conversation was carried on and she took some part in it because she heard herself speaking from time to time. The meal Zoe Hancock had cooked—a beef and vegetable stir-fry with noodles—was eaten, although Lucy couldn't recall tasting any of it.

On a secret and far more dominant level was the unrelenting and explicit message in every look James gave her—a simmering promise of more and more of what she had already experienced with him. It made her breasts tingle. It shot little shivers down her thighs. Her inner muscles clenched with the memory of all he'd made her feel—was still making her feel.

She grew so self-conscious of her response to him that she felt his mother couldn't fail to sense what

was going on under her nose. Zoe Hancock couldn't
know what had transpired in the cabana and by the
pool, but she would have to be as thick as a brick
not to pick up on what was humming between James
and his secretary. She had to know that the moment
she left them alone together...

Lucy couldn't bear the thought of his mother
knowing. Being here under the same roof and knowing. It wouldn't be private. Not emotionally private.
And that felt horribly wrong to her.

James had said—*Don't let her interfere with this.*

But what was *this?*

If she was more than a lay for the night...if he
really thought they were natural partners...that
would still be true tomorrow.

She couldn't stay.

Not with his mother here.

It wouldn't feel right to her.

Dinner was over. Coffee had been served. Best
she leave now while Zoe was still indulging herself
with the chocolate mints she'd brought with the coffee. She stood up, determined on taking her leave,
regardless of how deeply she was still aroused by
the promise of *more* with James.

'It was a lovely dinner, Zoe. And a most enjoyable swim, James. But I really must be going now,'
she rattled out, giving them both what felt like a
glassy smile.

Surprise stamped on both their faces.

'If you'll excuse me...'

'Of course, dear, if you must,' Zoe graciously supplied.

'There's work tomorrow,' Lucy babbled and headed straight for the coat-stand where her handbag had been hung again on her return upstairs.

There was a scrape of chairs behind her, making her nerves leap in wild agitation.

'I'll see you out to your car,' James stated, and his firm tone brooked no opposition.

He said nothing more, not inside the house, nor on the climb up the flight of steps outside, but Lucy felt his dark brooding presence encompassing her, tugging on the sexual promise that was still wreaking its inner havoc, and her heart pounded with fearful uncertainties. Was she breaking something she should have stayed with?

She fumbled in her bag for the car-keys. It was too late to change her mind about going. Besides, she didn't want to. It *didn't* feel right with his mother there. And she wanted more than sex with James.

'Why are you running away?' came the harsh demand behind her.

'I'm not. I'll be at the office tomorrow,' she argued, reaching the driver's side of her car and almost flinging herself into the seat, anxious not to be stopped, not to be drawn into an embrace that could change her mind.

He closed the door for her and stood there, still gripping it. 'Then don't be late for work, Lucy,' he warned, an underlying threat of retribution in his tone.

She inserted the ignition key and looked up at him. His eyes were narrowed slits but she felt the force of the will behind them, fiercely probing and determined on a resolution that went *his* way.

'I'll be there…on time,' Lucy promised, then gunned the engine.

James nodded and stepped away.

She backed out of the parking slot and drove off, tremulously aware of her conflicting needs and James at the centre of them.

Tomorrow, she kept repeating to herself. Tomorrow she would have more answers to where she was heading with James Hancock. Nothing was predictable. Nothing was safe or sensible, either. Which probably meant she'd completely lost her mind.

Everything depended on *him*.

CHAPTER TWELVE

FOUR weeks…the four most wonderful, exhilarating, sensational, worth living for weeks she'd ever lived, Lucy reflected, even if there was a lifetime price to pay for it. Though she shouldn't think like that. Not yet. There was no sign at this point that James was getting the least bit bored with her, which left a possibility that their relationship might wear what she had to tell him.

The sex between them was still red-hot, invariably igniting an urgency that drove them to take wild chances, and even when they were concentrating on work, their desire for each other simmered around the edge of it, waiting to be satisfied again…and again…and again. In fact, Lucy didn't feel she belonged to herself any more. Everything she did, thought and felt was linked to James.

Which made today's decision not to fly to Melbourne with him a wrenching one, but she couldn't think about the future when they were together, and they were together so constantly, it was all too easy just to let herself be immersed in the excitement and pleasure of being with him, and put off dealing with what really did have to be faced.

A massive pile of washing and ironing to do, she'd pleaded to James. Which was true enough,

Lucy thought ironically, as she trudged up the stairs to her apartment. But it was the shocking and frightening knowledge of her pregnancy that she couldn't keep pushing aside. How it had happened, given she had not once missed taking her contraceptive pill, she had no idea, but a missed period and a pregnancy test had wiped out any doubt about it.

Maybe James was just so potent, he'd worn out her protection. She wished now that he'd kept on his practice of always using condoms. Though there was no point in thinking about *how* or *if only*. It was a done deed.

Her first impulse—after the shock of finding out—was to hide the fact from James and hang onto what she had with him for as long as she could. It felt as though she'd waited all her life for this one man, and still wanting him so much, she kept shying away from presenting him with the knowledge they'd made a baby.

It would change everything—whether for better or worse she didn't know and was too scared to lay it on the line.

Nevertheless, as much as she longed to hide her pregnancy and pretend nothing was different, a deeply rooted core of common sense insisted she couldn't keep holding such a huge secret from James, not when their relationship was so very intimate. Besides, the deception would inevitably play on her mind, spoiling things anyway. Somehow she had to decide what to do.

Sighing heavily, Lucy pushed open the door that

led from the stairwell to her floor. As usual it banged shut behind her. Ahead of her she noticed the door to Josh's apartment standing half-open, and wondered if it was an invitation to drop in. Being in no mood to talk to anyone, she went no further than her own apartment, feeling slightly guilty at the little contact they'd had since Josh had helped re-vamp her image.

'Ah! Caught you!' his voice rang out, halting her as she was about to insert her key in the lock. 'The intrepid sleuth strikes again!' he declared triumphantly.

It teased a smile from her as she turned to return a greeting. 'Hi to you, too.'

He leaned against his door-jamb and surveyed her, his eyebrows waggling above wickedly dancing eyes. 'A little tired from constant romping with James?'

'A house-keeping night,' she dryly replied, letting him know it was not for socialising.

'But it *is* going well with him?'

'You could say that.' She was not about to dump her current problem on Josh before thinking it through herself.

'Your mother called,' he announced with more waggling of eyebrows. 'You've neglected her dreadfully. In fact, you're in the dog-house. She has called and called and you are never home. She had to ring me to find out if you were still alive.'

'Oh, hell!' Lucy muttered, sagging against the wall.

'Bad, bad girl!' Josh mockingly chided. 'Nor have you been up to visit her for six weeks. Any minute now you're going to wear the label of the prodigal daughter.'

She grimaced, mentally hearing her mother rolling out these complaints to Josh. 'It's true,' she confessed. 'I've been totally selfish the past few weeks. And I didn't want to lie to her about what I've been doing so I just plain avoided it.'

He gave her a sympathetic look. 'Being in love is not a crime, Lucy love.'

'Oh, no? Risking my job by getting involved with my employer? My mother will have a field day on that one, let alone keeping the convertible and...' She bit down on the worst sin of all—getting pregnant outside of marriage.

'And?' Josh instantly prompted.

'Never mind.' She gave him a glum look. 'My crimes against common sense are legion at the moment.'

He adopted a stern headmaster pose, shaking his finger at her. 'Well, may I advise you...don't forget her birthday, which she let me know was this weekend, and if you don't call and grovel, and subsequently turn up with the fatted calf...'

'Mum's birthday!' Lucy smacked her forehead with the heel of her hand. 'Oh, Josh! I am awful!'

'Not at all. Intensely pre-occupied might cover it.'

'I'll go and call her right now.' She pushed herself off the wall, tossing him an apologetic wince. 'Thanks for catching me.'

He grinned. 'Just don't kill the messenger boy.'

It won an ironic laugh. 'You're safe, Josh.'

The safest person she knew, Lucy thought as she let herself into her own apartment. He never judged. He was there for her when she needed a friend. He listened and tried to help. But her current biggest problem was painfully private and not up for discussion...yet.

First things first, she told herself, heading for the telephone on the kitchen bench.

She had to talk to her mother.

Her mother...who had married the man who'd made her pregnant, a mistake in judgement that had scarred the rest of her life, all because of her need to be *respectable*. Though she would have hated the social blight of being an unmarried mother, which might have been just as scarring for her.

It had been different for Zoe Hancock. Respectability hadn't meant so much to her, not enough to marry a man who had only been a brief spark, not a lasting passion. She seemed to have taken being an unmarried mother in her stride...with a lot of help from the people James called honorary aunts and uncles.

Neither woman had considered an abortion and Lucy knew she wouldn't, either. She was twenty-eight years old and had no doubt in her heart there would never be another James. Whatever his response to her pregnancy, she would have the baby and keep it. But she desperately wanted to be the lasting passion in James' life.

Four weeks…it really wasn't enough time to be sure this was a rock-solid relationship to James. He had never talked about *love*. What if his passion for her reached burn-out before she was even visibly pregnant?

Should she wait, holding her secret from him until she was as sure as she could be that she was the only woman he would ever want, not just the sexiest woman he'd ever met up until now?

Yet if he truly felt they were natural partners…

Lucy shook her head.

It was all so terribly risky, whichever way she looked at it.

And she had to call her mother.

Four weeks, James reflected, claiming his Porsche from the airport car-park and happily eager to drive to the office and get back to Lucy. Best four weeks of his life, he decided. Not one falling out with Lucy over work or play, and she suited him brilliantly in both areas.

In fact, the trip to Melbourne had been a drag without her. He'd missed her company—missed her comments on the client and situation he'd had to deal with, missed her smiles and the sparkle of shared understanding in her eyes. And the hotel bed would definitely have provided more comfort and satisfaction—not to mention pleasure—with her in it.

What they had together was great. No doubt about it. Even the sluggish pace of the traffic into the city could not fray his good mood this morning. It gave him more time to plan what he'd do with Lucy over the coming weekend. For once, he was entirely free of work and social commitments. They could do anything they fancied. James entertained himself with various highly desirable fancies all the way to the office.

And there she was, waiting for him, saucily sexy in a little scarlet shift with a gold chain belt dangling provocatively around her hips. Her green eyes had that look of eating him up which always excited him, and even as a grin of sheer pleasure broke across his face, he could feel himself stirring, wanting the more intense pleasure of connecting physically with her.

'How did it go in Melbourne?' she asked.

His office, he decided.

'Everything settled,' he assured her, not the least bit interested in going into details.

With his briefcase occupying one hand—something he had to get rid of—he hooked his free arm around Lucy, drawing her with him as he headed for the connecting door and his larger, more comfortable, more private office. It felt so good, having her at his side again.

'All washed and ironed?' he teased.

'Enough to go on with,' she answered wryly.

'Good. Because I have big plans for us this weekend.'

He felt her body tensing. It alerted him to a problem even before she stopped, momentarily halting the purpose burning in his mind. Her face turned up to his, her eyes filled with an eloquent appeal for understanding.

'I can't be with you this weekend, James,' she said, the decision clearly paining her.

'Why not?' he asked, trying to sound reasonable against a rush of frustration.

'I have to go home. To Gosford, I mean.'

'Visiting your mother?'

'Yes. It's been six weeks and...'

'It's okay.' Not what he'd fancied, but he could ride with it. 'I'll go with you. I don't mind meeting your mother. You've met mine.'

'No!' she cried, showing clear signs of agitation. 'I mean...it's just not appropriate this weekend, James. It's her birthday.'

'So?'

He frowned over her obvious reluctance to introduce him to her mother. What was the problem? Why was she acting so oddly, floundering in the face of his perfectly logical question.

'It's a mother/daughter thing. We always celebrate her birthday together,' she babbled, actually wringing her hands.

His gut told him it was more than this. 'Which day is your mother's birthday?' he asked, needing to get to the bottom of what was really going on.

'Tomorrow. But I've got my bag packed and in the car, and I'll be leaving straight after work. My mother has already made plans, James, expecting me to fall in with them, so I'll have to spend the whole weekend with her.'

There was an anxious appeal in her eyes that begged him not to interfere, not to make any claims on her. It clicked through his mind that she'd cried off going to Melbourne and now she wanted another two days without him. After four weeks of very mutual intimacy, why this? Then it hit him. Four weeks...

He heaved a relieved sigh as understanding cleared his concerns. Lucy was funny about some things...like being embarrassed about his mother knowing they were having sex together. Never mind that his mother was completely blasé about her own affairs! *And* she so clearly approved of Lucy as a partner for him, taking her out to lunches and showing her all her favourite shopping places in Balmain.

Good thing the chicken pox scare was over and she'd flown back to Melbourne. He preferred to have Lucy to himself. But since Lucy had been so good about *his* mother's foibles, it was only fair for him to give consideration to *her* mother.

He dropped his briefcase and turned to draw her into a reassuring embrace. She came stiffly, confirming his conclusion that sex was out for a few days. He gave her a soothing smile.

'It's okay. You don't have to be embarrassed about saying you've got your period. I am aware of a woman's cycle.'

A flood of heat swept into her cheeks. She dipped her head, her long lashes veiling her eyes. Clearly

she was *acutely* embarrassed. Did she think he
would have wanted sex anyway, not respecting her
feelings?

'I'd prefer it if you're open with me, Lucy, not
hiding anything,' he gently chided.

She bit her lips. Sensing a strong inner turmoil he
didn't understand at all, James decided to let the
issue drop for the moment, not wanting her to be
upset. 'Hey...' He tenderly tilted her chin. 'It's no
big deal. Just having your company is great to me.'

Her lashes lifted and the anguished uncertainty
that poured out at him gave James a severe jolt. She
couldn't think all he wanted her for was sex...could
she? Admittedly he could barely keep his hands off
her, but she'd been just as hot and hungry. Definitely
mutual desire! So what was going on here? Did she
only want *him* for sex?

Perplexed, disturbed, James retreated to familiar
ground. 'Let's get on with work. Okay?' He released
her, picked up his briefcase and proceeded to dump
it on his desk. 'Any e-mails that need urgent answering this morning?' he tossed at her.

'I'll get the print-outs,' she answered and fled like
a cat on a hot tin roof.

James sat in his chair, feeling like a pricked bal-
loon, all his earlier good humour totally evaporated.
He'd dealt successfully with people for too many
years not to know something was very wrong here.
Lucy's behaviour did not add up to what he felt
could be reasonably expected of their relationship.

She enjoyed his company. He knew she did.

No-one could fake the instinctively positive response he saw in her eyes, the easy rapport in their conversations, the body language that openly expressed pleasure in being with him. There had to be some other factor at play here, something more than being funny about her period.

Her mother?

Was Lucy holding some secret she didn't want to reveal about her mother?

Further thought reminded him of Lucy's discomfort when his own mother had started boring in about family background. Of course, no-one liked being so obviously cross-examined. All the same, Lucy had never brought up the subject of her mother herself—no reference at all to her life in Gosford—until now. And that was an unusual omission, given that most women did mention family, if only in passing.

His mind was revolving around this intriguing little mystery when Lucy re-entered his office, carrying the e-mail print-outs. He hadn't even opened his briefcase, but getting to work was not his priority here. Seeing that Lucy still looked tense, he leaned back in his chair, promoting a relaxed mood, and offered a friendly smile.

'I was just thinking…I don't even know your mother's name. I presume it's *something* Worthington,' he prompted.

'Ruth. It's Ruth Worthington,' she replied stiffly.

'And where in Gosford does she live?'

Lucy frowned, not welcoming this line of questioning. 'Green Point,' she bit out.

Not giving an actual address, James noted. 'Well, I wondered—' he pressed on '—would Ruth *mind* having me as a guest this weekend? I mean...does she disapprove of our relationship?'

Her feet instantly faltered. Her cheeks bloomed with hot colour again. 'It's a small house. It doesn't have a guest room.'

And there'd be no sleeping with her under her mother's roof, James instantly deduced.

'Besides,' she went on with a telling grimace, 'I haven't even told her I won the car yet. And I haven't told her about—' she took a deep breath '—about us.'

James had the strong impression that 'us' was a huge hurdle to be negotiated, and why anyone would hold back the news of winning such a car was a puzzle in itself. The mystery deepened.

'Might be easier just to present her with the lot in one shot,' he suggested, undeterred by the image of a dragon lady.

'No...' She shook her head, dropping her gaze from his, nervously fingering the pages in her hands. 'That wouldn't work at all well. Believe me—' another deep breath and her gaze lifted reluctantly, appealing for his forebearance '—I have to go and it's best I go alone. I'm sorry to...to disappoint you, but that's how it is.'

'Okay. It was just a thought,' he said dismissively, irony tilting his smile. 'I didn't know I was a deep, dark secret.'

Her chin lifted. 'You won't be after this weekend,' she promised with an odd intonation—like a mixture of pride and pain.

Was there some old private conflict with her mother she didn't want to share?

'Good!' he said, approving her decision to be open with her mother, if not with him. Though he didn't intend for that situation to continue much longer, either. 'Then I'll look forward to meeting your mother another time.'

'I hope so,' she muttered, resuming her walk to his desk, holding out the e-mails for his attention. 'These came in.'

Still he sensed turmoil in her mind. He thought about pursuing the subject, but decided it would not win him anything. Lucy's mind was made up and he sensed there'd be no changing it. But she wasn't happy about this trip back to the maternal home. She was expecting conflict.

James pondered the situation throughout the day, remembering how he'd accused Lucy of putting her life into neat little pockets. She'd broken that rule with him, but clearly there were other pockets which were still buttoned up. Why, was the question. What drove a young woman to divide up her life as Lucy did? What was the mystery about her mother?

She begged off lunch with him, saying she had to buy a birthday gift. The mission neatly avoided an opportunity for personal chat. It grew more and more obvious as the afternoon wore on that she was in a fraught, distracted state. Concern for her safety on the road drove him to suggest she leave early to beat the peak-hour traffic.

'You don't mind?' she asked anxiously, gesturing at the papers on his desk. 'We're not finished.'

'Leave it to me. Go on,' he urged.

She hesitated, eyeing him uncertainly. 'I am sorry about this weekend.'

'Can't be helped.' He shrugged and moved to give her shoulders a light, reassuring squeeze. 'Take care driving. I want you back here safe and sound on Monday. Okay?'

'Yes,' she whispered shakily.

He bent and planted a gentle kiss on her mouth.

She barely responded, breaking away quickly. 'Thanks, James,' she breathed on a ragged sigh, and was off.

One way or another, he was going to find out what was in this pocket which was being kept so tightly buttoned. Lucy might not consider her family situation *his* business, but he was going to make it his business. Something was wrong and it needed to be put right.

Apart from which, secrets were bad. They showed a lack of trust. They formed barriers to the intimacy he'd thought he had with Lucy. Those barriers had to be broken down. Right from the beginning he'd wanted to know Lucy Worthington inside out, and having come this far, he wasn't about to be stopped.

Not by anything!

CHAPTER THIRTEEN

LUCY managed to concentrate enough to get the car and herself over the harbour bridge and into the right lane that would take her north to the central coast. All she had to do then was virtually follow the car in front of her, which was just as well, because she was in a tangle of torment over letting James believe she had her period.

Her period! What a black joke that was! It had been on the tip of her tongue to tell him the truth. All day she had wavered over revealing her pregnancy or keeping it hidden. In the end, the lure of having him as her lover for another month overrode her conscience. She just couldn't risk a negative reaction. Not yet.

And he wouldn't guess the truth, not believing her monthly cycle was running as it normally would. By Monday she might get over feeling sick about the deceit. James would think her period was over and hopefully they would go on as before…if she could keep pushing her condition to the back of her mind. In her present mental state, that was a big *if*.

At least he hadn't pressed her too much about this weekend with her mother. He'd really been kind about letting her go early, too. Kind and considerate. Like he truly did care about her. Combining that with his assurance this morning that he enjoyed her company, with or without sex...maybe she could tell him the truth without everything blowing up in her face.

The torment of uncertainty continued while the car took her away from Sydney. She wasn't aware of having crossed the Hawkesbury Bridge and the big dipper of the Mooney Mooney Bridge—landmarks along the expressway. It was a jolt when she saw the exit sign to Gosford. It forcefully reminded her she would soon be facing her mother and she'd better get herself ready to fend off the criticisms that were bound to be aimed at her.

'What train will you be on?' she'd been asked last night.

'You won't have to meet a train. I'll be coming by car, Mum,' she'd answered, steeling herself to argue her way past her mother's concept of a sensible car.

'Well, if Josh is giving you a lift, you just tell him he'd better get you here safely in that dreadful old sports car of his. And he's not to roar into my driveway like a larrikin.'

The steel wilted. 'Josh is not a larrikin, Mum. And he's always been safe.'

Safe, safe, safe... Lucy mocked savagely to herself as she took the Gosford exit. Having flouted all the *safe* rules, she was now looking right down the barrel of the consequences. Which, of course, her mother had warned her about. Compared to falling pregnant to her boss with no marriage in view, showing up in a red Alpha Spider convertible and shocking her mother with it was the least of her worries.

Though the brief sense of cavalier bravado took an abrupt dive when she spotted her mother watering the garden and caught the astonished look on her face as the Alpha turned into the driveway with *her daughter* in the driver's seat. Lucy switched off the ignition and sat for several moments, trying to raise her sinking heart.

'What on earth are you doing in that car and why are you driving it?' came her mother's shrill demands.

Taking a deep breath, Lucy hauled herself out of the red sports convertible, shut the door, and stood beside it, her hand gripping it in a show of proud possession. 'I'm driving it because it's mine. I won it in a raffle.' She beamed a smile full of teeth at her mother. 'Big surprise!'

Ruth Worthington gaped—first at Lucy, then at the car, and back at Lucy, who'd forgotten she'd changed her style of dress in the turmoil of everything else. 'A raffle,' she said weakly, clearly not knowing what to make of anything yet.

'Isn't it great? It's an Alpha Spider, an Italian sports car, and I've christened it Orlando,' Lucy burbled on, projecting unquenchable enthusiasm. 'You know, Mum, I've never won anything in my entire life, and to win this...' She released the door to make an expansive gesture. 'It was so unbelievable I'm still getting used to it.'

And her mother would take even longer to get used to it. If ever. Oddly enough, Lucy found herself not caring. Josh was right. It was *her life.*

Ruth Worthington would only be forty-seven tomorrow but somehow she'd made herself sexless, wearing no-nonsense clothes and having her greying, salt and pepper hair cut in a short layered style that required no more than a quick comb through it. She was even wearing grey—flat-heeled grey shoes, grey skirt, grey and white tailored blouse—and if she chose to live a *grey* life, well that was her choice, but it wasn't going to be Lucy's, no matter how things worked out with James.

A wave of belligerent self-assertion lifted her chin at her mother's continued silence. Judgements were undoubtedly being made and any second now they would start raining down on Lucy's head. She could only hope some kind of truce could be drawn so the birthday weekend wasn't a complete disaster.

'You know, you've worn glasses since you were in primary school,' her mother mused with a little shake of her head. 'You look quite lovely without them, Lucy.'

The soft comment was so unexpected—and nice—Lucy ended up grinning. 'I finally decided to get contact lenses.'

'It makes a real difference to your face. And your red dress... I didn't realise... I would never have dressed you in red...but red suits you. Especially with your hair down and fluffed out.'

Lucy's heart suddenly soared. To get compliments, not criticism…it was almost as unbelievable as winning the car. 'How about putting down that garden hose so I can give you a birthday hug?'

Her mother actually laughed. 'Well, you certainly have given me a big surprise.'

The hose, of course, couldn't just be dropped. The garden tap had to be turned off. Long-time habits weren't discarded in one fell swoop, but her mother did move briskly and her arms were open, ready to hug her daughter back when Lucy met her halfway between the car and the tap.

'It's lovely to see you, dear,' she murmured, then pulled slightly away to offer a wry little smile. 'I'm sorry I was so put out on the phone last night, but I've missed your calls and when I couldn't reach you, I had a silly, panicky sense I was losing you.'

'You'll always be my Mum,' Lucy reassured her on a rush of guilt. 'I've just been caught up in lots of things lately.'

'So I see.' A few wise nods. 'Well, let's have a look at this prize you've won. Does driving…Orlando…?' She looked totally bemused at a car having been personalised with a name. 'Make you feel like a million dollars?'

'Yes, it does,' Lucy answered, surprised into impulsively suggesting, 'Hop in, Mum, and I'll take you for a spin around the block. Best way of showing you what it's like.'

She hesitated. 'The house is unlocked.'

'We'll only be a few minutes.'

'But…'

'Take a risk,' Lucy recklessly advised.

And to her further surprise, always-play-safe Ruth Worthington actually did, proceeding to settle herself somewhat gingerly in the low passenger seat.

It was only a short ride but her mother seemed to enjoy it, smiling at Lucy as the wind ruffled her hair. When they returned to the house, she got out and said thoughtfully, 'It gives you a sense of freedom, doesn't it?'

Lucy laughed, amazed and delighted she was getting such an open-minded response. 'And a bit of zip in my life.'

'Not too much zip, I hope. Speeding is not sensible.'

'I've been watching that I don't. The car has a cruise control button to save me from going over the speed limit on the expressway, even accidentally.'

'Good!' She waited until Lucy had collected her bag and they were walking to the house, then archly asked, 'So who is the man?'

'What man?'

It earned a dry look. 'I might be one year older tomorrow, but I'm not senile, Lucy. Everything adds up to a new man in your life. And I'm happy for you. After all, you are twenty-eight.'

'Mmmh…' A safe, non-committal reply.

'You can tell me all about him after you put your things in your room,' her mother invited with an indulgent smile.

Not *all* about him, Lucy darkly decided. Her mother didn't deserve to have her birthday ruined.

And she'd been so nice about the car, even seeming to understand why Lucy had kept it instead of trading it in. Although she didn't have the whole picture—the motivating force being the need to impress James with a new exciting image. Lucy wasn't sure how much of the picture—featuring James—could be given before disapproval kicked in.

She was trying to calculate this as she unpacked her bag and put away her clothes. The wretched weight of the deceit she had allowed to stay in place with James today crept up on her and it was suddenly very clear that she couldn't go through with deceiving her mother about anything. She would hold back about her pregnancy for a while, but not about James being her boss, nor how much the relationship meant to her.

She wanted her mother to understand, needed her to be supportive. That was probably expecting too much, but…what was their relationship worth if she couldn't confide her love for a man and hope for a sympathetic ear? Maybe it was weak of her but she was tired of being independent, working everything out for herself. Josh was a good friend—the best of friends—and being able to lean on his shoulder was a big help…but she really wanted her mother.

Tears pricked her eyes and she hurriedly blinked them away. Silly to get all wet about it. Nevertheless, if there was ever a time to confide, this was it, and Lucy headed out to the kitchen, determined to lay out the truth…except for the pregnancy bit.

However, in the hours of chat that followed, Lucy did do a bit of judicious editing—the very private stuff—although she could see her mother mentally filling in the blanks. To her deep relief, while a few worried frowns occurred here and there, no criticism came at all.

'You're very much in love with him, aren't you?' It was more a statement than a question, accompanied by a look that seemed to understand everything.

Lucy had to blink hard. 'Yes, I am,' she answered huskily. 'I was strongly attracted to him all along. I really lived to go to work, Mum. It's more so now.'

She nodded. 'And James…does he love you, Lucy?'

'He hasn't said so…but it *feels* like that.'

'Well, I hope it will turn out right for you.' She paused, reservations creeping into her eyes. 'I don't want to be a wet blanket, Lucy. It's lovely to see you all bright and beautiful and glowing with love. But…have you considered…'

'What if it turns out wrong?' Lucy said the dread words for her—the same words that resided in her heart, causing it to ache with uncertainty.

Her mother sighed ruefully. 'Sometimes these office affairs don't last. It's easy to fall into them…proximity. But you have such a close working relationship with James, I think your position would become untenable if he…decided he'd had enough and wanted to take up with someone else.'

Pain sliced through her. He couldn't go from her to another Buffy. It would kill her.

'What would you do, Lucy? Where would you go?' her mother pressed worriedly.

'I don't want to think about that. Not until I have to,' Lucy rushed out vehemently. 'I don't want to be negative, Mum,' she appealed.

'Of course not,' came the quick, soothing reply. 'It was only with James being your boss...'

'I know. And he considered that, too, holding back for a long time.' *Until she looked sexy.* Lucy shook off the disturbing doubt and clutched at a positive point, rushing it out. 'He wanted to come and meet you this weekend...'

'Well, that's a good sign.'

'Yes. Yes, it is,' Lucy fiercely told herself, more than answering her mother.

'Is he coming?'

'No. I put him off. It's your birthday and...'

'You hadn't told me about him.'

'I couldn't just land him on you, Mum.'

She nodded. 'You were worried about my response.'

'It wouldn't have been fair...to either of you. And we always spend your birthday together. I told him another time would be better.'

She smiled. 'I'll look forward to meeting him.'

Would there be another time?

Her mother was being so...*accepting*...somehow it made the deception about her pregnancy more wrong than ever!

Her desperate need for James might carry her through fooling him for a while longer, but...it was her mother who would still be here for her if things went wrong with him. That was the bottom-line truth she didn't want to look at. Nevertheless, it was a truth she couldn't ignore.

It played on her mind all through the rest of Friday night and Saturday, despite every effort to put a happy face on everything for her mother's birthday. She knew, on Sunday morning, she couldn't carry this burden any longer. They had shared a late breakfast and were sitting over coffee when Lucy finally took the plunge.

'Mum…' She lifted eyes filled with anguished appeal. 'I didn't want to tell you…but I can't *not* tell you…'

A frown of puzzled concern. 'What is it, Lucy?'

She hunted desperately for some not so shocking way to say it, but there was no escape to be found in words. Her stomach was a churning mess. Her heart felt as though it was in a vise. There was an almost impassable lump in her throat. Just spill out the truth, her mind screamed. Get it over with.

'I'm pregnant.'

Right before her eyes she saw her mother's face sag, age, her whole expression emptying of any pleasure in life. It was worse than anything she had anticipated. And Lucy was helpless to make it better. There was nothing she could say, nothing she could do.

The sin—the very same sin that had led to bad consequences in her mother's life—filled the silence stretching between them, making it heavier, loading it with guilt and shame and an escalating mountain of regrets for not taking heed, for choosing a wild, reckless path that tossed risks aside. There was no point in saying she had used contraception. Pregnant was pregnant, and excuses were useless.

The doorbell rang, making them both jerk out of the pall of memories. Her mother shook her head, frowned, then scraped her chair back.

'Are you expecting someone?' Lucy blurted out.

'Probably Jean from next door.' Her eyes were sick, her voice dull. 'She wanted some geranium cuttings. I'll tell her to take them.'

She pushed herself up and moved slowly towards the door into the hallway, like a sleep walker in the middle of a nightmare.

Lucy closed her eyes, buried her head in her hands, and waited.

CHAPTER FOURTEEN

THEY had to be at home, James assured himself, waiting for the doorbell to be answered. Lucy's car was in the driveway. It had made it easy for him to pick out the right house, although he'd also checked that the address matched the one he'd found in the telephone book. He looked with satisfaction at his Porsche, now parked behind the red convertible. The Alpha was blocked in, which gave him a negotiating position with this visit.

All the same, if Lucy and her mother were inside, they were slow to open the door. He thought about giving the button another press, then decided the bell must have been heard the first time. It *was* a small house. Very neat and tidy and scrupulously maintained. So was the garden and lawn. Ruth Worthington undoubtedly had a tidy mind, everything having to be just right and in its place.

Lucy was like that in her work. She used to dress like that, too, all neatly pinned and buttoned. James was pondering her mother's influence—and wondering what else he would discover today—when he heard the metallic click of the door being opened. He hastily composed a bright happy expression, smile hovering, persuasive patter ready to roll off his tongue.

He'd hoped it would be Lucy, but it wasn't, and the woman he was suddenly facing looked ill and defeated by the illness. Something life-threatening? James thought, and instantly regretted the urge that had driven him here, intruding on what could be a seriously private time between mother and daughter. Lucy's stress was easily answered if what he guessed was the case and she'd just found out about it—something badly wrong.

The woman looked blankly at him—washed out grey-green eyes. Despite her obvious suffering, her short greying hair was neatly combed and she was quite smartly dressed in navy slacks and a white and navy striped top. Appearances meant a lot to her, James thought, and savagely wished he'd waited until Lucy was ready to introduce him to her mother.

Too late now. He couldn't cry off with some lame excuse of coming to the wrong house. Sooner or later a meeting would be arranged and she might remember him. He had to go through with his plan, adapting it to the circumstances.

'Mrs Worthington?' he asked, making identification certain.

'Yes. Who are you? What do you want?' Her voice was flat, slow, disinterested, and he could see it was difficult for her to focus on a stranger's needs.

'My name is James Hancock. Your daughter...'

'James Hancock?' It was as though his name had snapped her back to life, her eyes suddenly sharp and piercing.

'Yes. I was...'

'The man Lucy works for?'

'Yes.'

'Did Lucy invite you here today?'

'No. But we are *more* than business associates, Mrs Worthington, and I thought…'

'Yes. Much more,' she retorted, with a ferocity of feeling that knocked James back on his heels. 'And I think you'd better come in because my daughter has something to tell you, and I want to see for myself what kind of man you are, James Hancock.'

It was a facade-stripping challenge that couldn't be refused by any man worth his salt and it spun James' mind right around. Gone were any thoughts of illness. Ruth Worthington had just been transformed into a fire-eating dragon lady and James was already sharpening his own weapons to fight for Lucy as he stepped forward.

'Thank you. I'd like to come in and hear what Lucy has to tell me,' he said, all his aggressive and protective instincts flooding to the fore.

Ruth Worthington stood back and let him in, her shoulders squared now, very upright and unyielding in her stance. James paused in the hall, giving her time to shut the door and precede him to wherever Lucy was. She marched down the hall ahead of him, obviously prepared to seize the fighting ground and make it hers.

James followed, determined not to be outplayed by what he now perceived as very definitely *the enemy*. Something *was* very wrong here and he was intent on rescuing Lucy from it. No mother had the right to dominate or screw up her daughter's life. Lucy felt free with him. She had every right to freedom of choice.

They entered a kitchen. Lucy sat slumped over a table, head in her hands, a picture of despairing dejection. Whatever had been going here, it was going to stop right now!

'Lucy?' he called, demanding her attention.

Her hands flew away from her face as she jerked it towards him, shock widening her eyes and parting her lips. 'James?' It was an incredulous whisper.

'I figured you needed some support and I'm here to give it,' he declared.

'Support?' she echoed, seemingly unable to take in his offer or what it meant.

'Well, we'll soon see about that,' Ruth Worthington said in a harsh, judgemental tone, raising James' hackles even further. 'Tell him, Lucy. Either you tell him or I will.'

It was an uncompromising threat, and Lucy turned to her mother, clearly appalled by it and desperately seeking some other course. 'Mum, it's…it's my decision,' she pleaded, her hands turning palm upwards in painful eloquence.

James seethed at the torment her mother was putting her through. 'You don't have to take her orders, Lucy,' he insisted vehemently.

Ruth Worthington ignored him, still holding Lucy's attention despite his strong assertion. 'I won't have you living in a fool's paradise as I did,' she said, surprising him with a complete change of tone. Determination was tempered by a note of anguished sympathy, and her hands made their own agitated appeal. 'You *must* tell him, Lucy. Then you'll know.'

Feeling somewhat confused by this new twist, James decided he agreed with her. 'I think that's a good idea. Then I'll know, too. The sooner, the better.'

A *fool's paradise…*

The words sliced into Lucy's heart and cut out any lingering temptation to carry on some deceit with James. They sliced into her mind, clearing it of the fog of desire that four weeks of unbridled lust had built up. Four weeks—only a month—but there'd been eight months of working together before that. James had more than long enough to know what he felt about her and how important she was to his life.

She gathered herself together and stood up. The flash of proud approval in her mother's eyes strengthened her will to face James with the truth. She straightened her shoulders, knowing she was not alone, whatever happened. Her mother would stand by her.

James stood proud and tall, too, at the other end of the table. His vivid blue eyes were blazing at her, projecting a fierce command to explain what was going on. He wore casual clothes—red sports shirt, cream slacks—and his male animal sex appeal seemed to be heightened by the tension in the room.

A warrior come to do battle, Lucy thought—big, indomitable and determined to win.

It made her feel very small, very vulnerable, very frightened of losing. Her frantic mind clutched at what he'd said a few moments ago—*he'd come to give her support.* Please let it be true, she prayed, though she didn't really know what he meant by it or what had brought him here. All she knew was she had to say it, so she forced out the fateful words.

'I'm pregnant.'

'Pregnant?' he echoed dazedly, disbelief and confusion chasing across his face. He shook his head. 'But you said...'

'No, I didn't, James. You assumed I had my period and I...' Shame burned her cheeks. She swallowed hard, working some moisture into her dry mouth. 'I let you because...'

'How can you be pregnant?' he cut in, looking bewildered. 'You said...you were safe.'

Safe, safe, safe... was that word going to mock her forever?

A tide of violent emotion swept through Lucy, spilling out a torrent of her own torment. 'I swear to you I didn't mess up the contraception. I never missed a pill. Every morning without fail I took it, so it's not my fault. You...I...we...' She faltered, losing the plot.

'You're blaming me?' he asked with a wry twist of his mouth.

Out of the whirl of her mind shot the one and only cause for failure she'd thought of. 'You're just too sexy, James Hancock. And obviously very potent. *Too* potent.'

'What?'

His stunned expression churned Lucy into a further wild indiscretion. 'You know perfectly well what I mean and don't you deny it!'

'Oh, I won't.' He shook his head. 'No way would I deny my part in getting you pregnant. Seems to me you're the one who's been in denial.' He frowned at her. 'Is this what you were so uptight about on Friday?'

Denial…deceit…in wretched shame Lucy offered the only excuse she had. 'I didn't know how you'd take it.'

'Lucy…' His tone was gently chiding. The frown disappeared and a smile started spreading across his face. 'So you're mostly upset because it wasn't planned.'

'No. Yes. I just didn't know if…well, I *didn't* know how you'd take it, James,' she finished helplessly.

'A baby…' He started grinning. 'This is bound to be one really special kid, being conceived against the odds.' Then he was coming around the table towards her, still grinning. 'We're going to have a baby.'

It was Lucy's turn to be stunned. Could she believe the pleasure he was emanating? 'Yes. Yes, we are,' she affirmed somewhat breathlessly.

'I know you like to feel in control of things, Lucy, but I guess nature decided on working a little mir-

acle for us, and now that it's happened…it doesn't
really matter, does it?'

Her turn to be bewildered. 'Doesn't it?'

'Not a bit,' he answered, his eyes glowing warm
assurance at her. 'Just means we've got to get our
heads around being parents now instead of in the
future.'

'Future?' she echoed.

He reached out and curled his hands around her
shoulders, his thumbs fanning her collar-bones as his
gaze locked onto hers with commanding intensity,
searing away any doubts she might be nursing.

'You surely didn't imagine I was going to let you
move out of my life.' His voice purred into her mind
and stroked her heart. 'A partner like you?' He
smiled, projecting all the confidence in the world.
'We were made for each other, Lucy.'

Still she couldn't quite take in what was happening. 'You don't mind…about the baby?'

'You and I…we make the best kind of magic,
Lucy. Why shouldn't we expect miraculous things
to occur when we're together?' His eyes sparkled,
seeming to dance with happy thoughts. 'However
we did it, we've made a baby and I think it's great.'

'You do?'

'I sure do,' he replied with resounding certainty.
'And since we're here with your mother—' he shot
the judge of this situation a hard, challenging look,
then softened his expression for Lucy '—we can
start planning the wedding right now.'

'Wedding?' Lucy was beginning to feel like a fish out of water, gaping and gasping.

'We are definitely getting married before our baby is born,' he declared with determined intent.

'I don't think that's a good idea,' Lucy instantly protested, casting an agonised look at her mother. 'It...it didn't work for Mum, getting married because she fell pregnant with me.'

'Ah!' James said as though suddenly enlightened with a wealth of understanding. He shot a venomous look at her mother, then increased the pressure of his hands as his eyes bored into Lucy's. 'It didn't work for me, not having a father I could call my own,' he said forcefully. 'I will not be shunted off, Lucy. And I won't let you take *my* mother's path.'

'I don't want to,' she cried, suddenly seeing where he was coming from. Concern for his child was the focus here, not her. 'But there's more to marriage than getting tied together because of a baby, James.'

'We're tied together now,' he argued. 'As intimately as two people could be.'

'It's only been a month. What if...'

'A month? What do you call all the time you were with me before that—almost a year—fitting together like hand and glove in our work...'

'While you went to bed with other women,' she accused hotly.

'I didn't want to lose you. If I'd laid a hand on you at work...or even made suggestive remarks...how was I supposed to know you wouldn't have accused me of sexual harassment and walked out in high dudgeon?'

'You went with those women because of *me?* Is that what you're saying?'

'Distraction. I *told* you that.'

'How can I believe you? How can I know I'm not just the latest on the scoreboard? What if I risked marrying you, only to find you seeking *distraction* afterwards?'

'Dammit, Lucy! You're the total count. The perfect number for me. Why would I even *look* anywhere else?'

'You've never said that before.'

'Well, I'm saying it now.'

'Because of the baby…'

'No! I'm saying it because it's true.' He heaved an exasperated sigh. 'Why are you going on like this? You know we're perfect together. Nothing could be better. Don't you *feel* that?'

He looked as if he wanted to shake her until she admitted it. Lucy bit her lips. He was talking about sex and work, but there'd been no mention made of love.

'There's no risk, Lucy,' he declared emphatically.

She made a decision. 'If you still want to marry me *after* I have the baby…'

'Oh, no you don't!' He glowered at her through narrowed eyes. 'You're not stringing me along like you did Josh Rogan—now I want you, now I don't.'

'What?' her mother squawked. 'Josh?' her voice climbed incredulously.

'That's past history!' James shot at her. 'And not to be nagged over.'

'But...' she looked at Lucy.

There was no time for explanations. James was focused back on her, compelling her undivided attention, pouring out vehement passion.

'I'm here to stay, Lucy, and you'd better get used to it. You're *my* woman, and this is *my* child, and we're going to stick together because nothing else makes sense, and you ought to know that!'

It sounded good, weakening her doubts and bolstering her hopes. She heaved a rueful sigh as she confessed, 'Josh has never been more than a friend to me. He's *gay*. He was just doing me a favour, going to the ball with me because you thought I'd bring someone boring.'

James frowned disbelief. 'That guy... *gay?*'

'Yes.'

He let out his breath in a whoosh and relaxed into a wry smile. 'Lucy, *boring* I might have been able to deal with, but that guy tipped me over the edge. Be damned if I was going to let any other man have you!'

He released her shoulders and cupped her face, searching her eyes for the response he wanted. 'I love you, Lucy Worthington.' His voice was soft and tender. 'I love you through and through. There's not one bit about you I don't love. I drove up here today because I was worried about you. You seemed so stressed on Friday and I thought you must have some problem with your mother. I wanted to fix it for you. I want to make everything right for you. Don't you see? I *love* you.'

She was utterly transfixed by the words he spoke, words that seemed to be pulled from his heart and reflected in the deep blue pools of his eyes. Before she could form any reply there was a loud throat-clearing by her mother. James reacted instantly, an arm shooting around Lucy's shoulders to hug her to his side as he turned them both to face the woman he saw as his opponent.

'Mrs Worthington, this is *our* life…mine and Lucy's. And our child's,' he declared with ringing conviction. 'Whatever your own experience was, this is different and I'd be obliged if you keep right out of it.'

Different…Lucy almost wept at the stand James was making for her—it touched her so deeply. Could she dare to believe it would truly be different? Blissfully different? She let herself luxuriate in the warm security of his hug…the warm *loving* security. It felt so good. So right. Surely it had to be right. She looked at her mother, silently pleading for verification, for support.

This isn't a fool's paradise, is it?

But her mother wasn't looking at her. Her gaze was fixed on James, still assessing him, weighing his words, his actions. A smile started to tug at her mouth. 'Make it Ruth,' she invited.

'Fine!' James said, seizing the advantage it seemed to give. 'I hope you like what you see, but if you don't, I'm going to have Lucy as my wife anyway. As soon as I can persuade her to marry me.'

Her mother's expression softened further as she looked at Lucy, then back to him. 'I don't think you're going to have to do much persuasion. My daughter was afraid of losing you, and that's not a good basis for marriage, James.'

'She'd have to run a long, long way to lose me, Ruth, and even then I'd chase her,' he retorted vehemently.

She nodded and gave Lucy a smile that seemed to brim with inner joy for her. 'I don't think it's a risk, darling. He *does* love you.'

'You're...you're okay with this, Mum?' Lucy barely got out over the lump in her throat.

'You weren't a fool...anywhere along the line,' came the soft acknowledgement. 'Your instincts were right, and you were right to follow them. Sometimes...not to risk...defeats what you really want. And true love is worth any risk.'

Lucy couldn't speak. Never before had her mother shown such intimate understanding. Tears misted her eyes as she realised that maybe she'd never given her mother the chance to...until now.

'I think I'm going to like you, Ruth,' James declared with a decisive infusion of warmth.

She raised an eyebrow at him but her eyes were actually twinkling. 'I've got some work to do in the garden. It may take an hour or so. Let me know when you've made Lucy feel confident of a happy future with you, and we *will* plan a wedding.'

James grinned back at her. 'Now I know where Lucy got that cut-you-off-at-the-knees sensible streak from. Thanks, Ruth.'

'I'll look forward to seeing you work some more miracles, James,' she retorted good-humouredly, sailing off to leave them alone together.

Lucy took a deep breath to relieve the tightness in her chest, turned to James, flung her arms around his neck and buried her face in the comforting flesh-warmth at the base of his throat. 'I'm sorry I couldn't tell you,' she whispered.

He gathered her body closer, his hands caressing her in possessive yearning as he tenderly rubbed his cheek against her hair. 'You can share everything with me, Lucy. Don't ever be afraid to say what's on your mind...in your heart.''

Released from all inhibitions, she gratefully gave him her heart. 'I love you, too, James. I just didn't know...how deep it went with you.'

'How about soulmate? Will that do?' he softly teased.

'Yes.'

His chest rose and fell, emitting a long sigh. 'It's going to be good...having a baby...the two of us becoming three of us. You're okay about that now, aren't you, Lucy?'

'Yes. Now that you're here with me.'

'I'll always be with you.'

She believed it. She could feel it in her mind, in her heart, in her soul...James, her mate in all things. Lifting back her head, seeing the love in his eyes, the joy of it was so intense, the desire for him so overwhelming, she went up on tip-toes and his mouth met hers...both of them so hungry for each other, there was no stopping the passionate need that seized them.

Ruth Worthington couldn't stop smiling as she moved around her garden with her secateurs and a basket, choosing and snipping off the geranium cuttings her next door neighbour wanted. She felt happier for her daughter than she had ever felt for herself.

Lucy had fallen in love with the right kind of man.

There was no risk to *this* marriage.

No risk at all.

She wondered what kind of wedding Lucy would want. She remembered her own shame, having to select a wedding dress that would cover up her pregnancy. It was different these days. Young women were now proud of showing off their pregnancy, married or unmarried. Lucy could wear any kind of dress she liked. Maybe she would ask Sally Rogan to find something lovely and romantic through her boutique contacts. That would be nice.

A baby...Ruth's smile grew broader...a grandchild. It had been a worry that Lucy would never find someone, never have children. Twenty-eight...good thing she *was* pregnant, starting a family straight away. It just wasn't sensible leaving it too late, especially if Lucy and James ended up de-

ciding to have a bigger family…two or three children. That would be *so* nice.

But…first things first. Whatever Lucy chose for
the wedding, it was going to be absolutely perfect
with the bride and groom loving each other so much.
Which was the most important thing of all. It was
what she'd dearly wished for her daughter—what
she'd never found herself.

True love.

And that was far, far more than *nice*.

It was wonderful.

The Hot-Blooded Groom

EMMA DARCY

CHAPTER ONE

'I WANT you married.'

Bryce Templar gritted his teeth. It wasn't the first time his father had made this demand. Undoubtedly it wouldn't be the last, either. But he hadn't come out of his way to visit the old man, still convalescing from his recent heart operation, to have another argument about his bachelor state.

He kept his gaze trained on the view, ignoring the contentious issue. The sun was setting, adding even more brilliant shades of colour to the stunning red rocks of Sedona. His father's winter residence was certainly sited to capture one of the most striking panoramas nature had to offer, here in the Arizona desert. And of course, communing with nature was another thing Will Templar preached—spiritual peace, clean air, clean living...

'Are you hearing me, boy?'

Bryce unclenched his jaw and slid his father a derisive look. 'I'm not a boy, Dad.'

'Still acting like one,' came the aggressive grumble. 'Here you are with your hair going grey and you're not settled with a woman yet.'

'I'm only thirty-four. Hardly over the hill. And you went grey in your thirties. It's genetic.'

It wasn't the only physical aspect of his father he'd inherited. They were both well over six feet tall, big men, though his father had lost quite a bit of weight over the past year and was looking somewhat gaunt in the face. They had the same strong nose, the same determined mouth, closely set ears, and while his father's hair was now white, it was still as thick as his own.

The only feature he'd inherited from his mother was her eyes—heavier lidded than his father's and green instead of grey. Will Templar's eyes had been described in print as steely and incisive, but right now they were smoking at Bryce with irritable impatience.

'I was married to your mother in my twenties.'

'People married earlier in those days, Dad.'

'You're not even looking for a wife.' He shook an admonishing finger. 'You think I don't hear about your bed-hopping with starlets in L.A.? Getting laid indiscriminately doesn't sit well with me, son.'

Bryce barely stifled a sigh as he thought, *Here comes the clean living lecture.* 'I don't bed-hop and I'm not indiscriminate in my choice of playmate,' he bit out. Hoping to avoid a diatribe on morals, he added, 'You know how busy I am. I just don't have the time to put into a relationship what women want out of it.'

It brought his father up from his lounger in a burst of angry energy. 'Don't tell me women don't want marriage. They all want marriage. It's not difficult to get a woman to say *yes* to that. And I'm living proof of it with five wives behind me.'

All of them walking away with a bundle, Bryce thought cynically. Except his mother who died before she'd got around to divorce. The billion dollar empire of Templar Resources could absorb the cost of hundreds of wives. It just so happened Bryce didn't like the idea of being taken for the pot of gold at the end of the rainbow ride.

If a woman wanted him…fine. Especially if he wanted her. But the occasional pleasure in bed did not warrant a gold ring and a gold passport to a hefty divorce settlement. Apart from which, he certainly didn't need the aggravation of a demanding wife. He much preferred a walkaway situation.

'You get married, Bryce, or I'll put Damian in control of business, right over your head. Make him CEO until you do get a wife. That will free up your time,' his father threatened.

'And give you another heart attack when he messes up,' Bryce mocked, knowing his half-brother's limited vision only too well.

'I mean it, boy! Time's slipping by and I'm feeling my mortality these days. I want to see you married, and married soon. With a grandchild on the way, too. Within a year. Just get out there and choose a wife. You hear me?'

He was going red in the face. Concerned about his father's blood pressure, Bryce instantly set aside the argument. 'I hear you, Dad.'

'Good! Then do it! And find a woman like your mother. She had a brain, as well as being beautiful.' He sank back onto the cushions of the lounger, taking quick shallow breaths. The high colour gradually receded. 'Worst day of my life when your mother died.'

Bryce couldn't remember it. He'd only been three years old. What he remembered was the succession of stepmothers who had waltzed into and out of his childhood and adolescence.

'Got to think of the children,' his father muttered. 'Damian's mother was a featherhead. Charming, sexy, but without a thought worth listening to.' His eyes closed and his voice dropped to a mumble. 'Damian's a good boy. Not his fault he hasn't got your brain. At least he's guidable.'

Watching fatigue lines deepen on his face, making him look older than his sixty years, Bryce was troubled by the thought there was more to his father's remark on *feeling his mortality* than he was letting on. Just how bad was his heart condition?

While they'd had this argument over marriage before, there'd never been a time-frame stipulated.

Within a year.

And the threat about Damian—empty though it was—added more weight to the demand, carrying a measure of desperation.

The sun had slipped below the horizon as they'd talked. The massive red rocks were darkening with shadows. Nothing stayed the same for long, Bryce reflected, and if time was running out for his father...well, why not please him by getting married?

It shouldn't be too much of a problem.

He wouldn't let it be.

CHAPTER TWO

SUNNY YORK's heart did not leap with joy when she spotted her fiancé shoving through the crowd of delegates waiting to enter the conference room. His appearance sent a shudder of distaste down her spine and she found herself gritting her teeth as a host of blistering criticisms clamoured to be expressed.

It was the last day of the conference, the last day to try and smooth over the bad impressions he'd made on others, and the most important day for her, which Derek knew perfectly well. And he turned up like this?

She shook her head in disgust, thinking of how early she had risen this morning, determined on presenting a perfect, go-getting image. It had taken an hour to get her unruly mane of rippling curls under reasonable control, carefully blow-drying out any tendency to frizz and ensuring the whole tawny mass of it looked decently groomed. Her make-up was positive without being overdone, and her sharp yellow suit was a statement of vibrant confidence.

There was absolutely nothing sharp about Derek. His suit looked rumpled, as though he'd dropped it on the floor and dragged it on again. His eyes were bloodshot, he'd nicked his chin shaving, and he was obviously in no state to get anything out of the morning session. She actually bristled with rejection as he hooked his arm around hers.

'Made it,' he said, as though it were an achievement she should be grateful for.

Never mind that he'd broken every arrangement for them to spend private time together. Turning up for her sales presentation did not make up for treating her like nothing all week. And turning up like this was the last straw to Sunny.

Her sherry-brown eyes held no welcoming warmth as she tersely replied, 'I expected to see you at breakfast.'

He leaned over confidentially. 'Had it at the roulette table. Free drinks, free food all night. They sure look after you at these casinos and I was running hot.'

Sunny's heart felt very cold. 'I'm amazed you tore yourself away.'

He grimaced as though *she* was acting like a pain to him. 'Don't nag. I'm here, aren't I?'

Four days they'd been in Las Vegas and he'd been gambling every spare minute, even skipping conference sessions when he thought he could get away with it. 'I take it the hot run ended,' she bit out, barely controlling a fiery flash of temper at *his* criticism of *her* attitude.

'Nope. I won a packet,' he slurred smugly. 'But I happened to see the big man come in last night and if he's showing this morning…'

'What big man?' she snapped, losing all patience with him.

'The head of the whole shebang. Bryce Templar

himself. He dropped into the L.A. conference last year to give us a pep talk, remember?'

Sunny remembered. The CEO of Templar Resources was the most gorgeous hunk she'd ever seen, almost a head taller than she was and with a big muscular frame that telegraphed *all man* to her, eminently lust-worthy, but so far beyond her reach, he was strictly dream material.

She hadn't heard a word he'd said at L.A. She'd sat in the audience, imagining how it might be in bed with all that strong maleness being driven by the charismatic energy he was putting out in his address to them.

His father had founded Templar Resources, back in 1984, and it was now the largest networking company in the world, producing and servicing software in most languages. Obviously the son was building on that, not just inheriting his position, which added even more power to his sex appeal. On any male evolution scale he was definitely the top rung.

'Guess he'll do the same today,' Derek babbled on. 'Thought I'd better turn up for it.'

Sunny cast a severely jaundiced look at the man she'd cast in the future role of her husband and father to the family she wanted. Having seen her two younger sisters married and producing adorable babies, she'd become hopelessly clucky, and when Derek had walked into her life, he'd seemed the answer to her dreams.

Those dreams had received an awful lot of tarnishing this week, and right at this moment, the reminder of a man as powerfully impressive as Bryce Templar did nothing to shine them up again.

Derek was the same height as herself—if she wore flat heels—and quite handsome on better days when his blue eyes were clear and his face more alive. His dark blond hair was still damp from a very recent shower so the sun-bleached streaks weren't showing so much this morning. He usually kept his rather lean physique toned up with sessions in the gym but he hadn't been anywhere near the hotel's health club this week.

All in all, he was much less a man in Sunny's eyes than he'd been four days ago. Whether this gambling fever was a temporary madness or not, he'd completely lost her respect, and she'd hand him back his diamond ring right now, except it might cause a scene that she could do without in front of the other delegates whose respect *she* wanted when she gave her presentation in just another hour's time.

Deeply disillusioned and angry with the assumption she would overlook everything, she unhooked her arm from Derek's as they moved into the conference room and gave him a stony warning. 'Don't think you can lean on me if you fall asleep.'

'Oooh, we are uptight, aren't we?' he mocked, looking uglier by the second. 'Nervous about performing in front of the CEO?'

'No. I just don't want to prop you up,' she grated.

'Fine! Then I'll sit at the back and you won't have to worry about it,' he sniped, sheering away from her side in a blatant huff.

Sunny walked on, rigidly ignoring him. No doubt

a back-row seat suited Derek very well. If Bryce Templar didn't show, he could easily slip outside and get on with his gambling. Though if he thought other people besides herself hadn't noticed what was going on, he was a fool.

The managing director of the Sydney branch had already commented on his absence from conference sessions, as well as his failure to attend any of the social functions at night. Derek might be considered a top consultant but playing the corporate game was important, too. He was earning a big black mark here in Las Vegas, not only on a personal level, but a professional one, as well.

Still inwardly fuming over his behaviour, Sunny made her way to the very front row of tables in the auditorium, where she was entitled to sit as one of the presenters this morning. Having settled herself and greeted the other delegates in the team she'd been attached to all week, she did her best to push Derek's disturbing behaviour out of her mind, concentrating on listening to the buzz about Bryce Templar's arrival on the scene.

Had he come to announce some new technologies being developed by the company? Was he here to reward someone for outstanding performance? Speculation was running rife.

It ended abruptly as the man himself made his entrance, accompanied by the conference organisers. A hush fell over the room, attention galvanised on the CEO of Templar Resources. He took the podium without any introduction but whatever he said floated right over Sunny's head.

From a purely physical viewpoint, she couldn't help thinking that Bryce Templar had to have the best gene pool in the whole world, and if she could choose any one man to be the father of the baby she'd love to have, he would top the stud-list.

The woman in yellow kept attracting Bryce's eye. She was the only spot of colour amongst a sea of grey and black business clothing. Since she was seated right at the front, he couldn't miss seeing her, and as women went, she was definitely worth a second look.

Great hair. Lush wide mouth. Big dreamy eyes. A strong impression of warmth, which stayed with him as he left the podium, niggling at the bitterness his lawyer had stirred with the call about yet another change Kristen was demanding in the prenuptial agreement. His fiancée was fast dissipating any warmth he'd felt for her.

As he sat down at the official table with the conference organisers, he reflected on the black irony of having thought he'd picked the ideal wife. Kristen Parrish had enough beauty and brains to meet his father's criteria, plus a very stylish career as an interior decorator, which meant she wouldn't be hanging on having a husband dance attendance all the time. She had a business of her own to run. Which suited Bryce just fine.

The problem was, her sharp brain was proving to be one hell of a calculating machine, and Bryce fiercely resented the way she was manipulating the situation. Just one mention that he wanted a child, preferably within the first year of marriage, and she'd started using it as a bargaining chip to ensure she would always have funds to raise their child should the marriage fail. She was literally bleeding him for all she could get, and if it wasn't for his father, he'd tell her to get lost.

Then she'd probably sue him for breach of promise.

And would he find anyone better?

His gaze flicked to the woman in yellow and caught her looking at him. Her head instantly jerked away, thick dark lashes swept down, and her cheeks bloomed with heat. Quite an amazing blush. She had to be in her late twenties or early thirties, and very committed to a career to be here at this conference. Hardly the shy type. She wouldn't be wearing yellow if she was shy.

Her cheeks were still burning, lending even more vivid colour and warmth to her face. It was a very appealing, feminine face, finely boned, though not quite perfect with the slightly tip-tilted nose. Her hair drew his attention again, copper and corn colours tangled through a tousled riot of waves and curls, the thick mass of it falling from a centre parting and tumbling down over her shoulders. It looked…very touchable, unlike Kristen's ice-blond sculptured bob.

He wondered what the woman in yellow would be like in bed, then put a firm clamp on those thoughts.

He'd made his bed.

Besides, would the woman in yellow prove any different to Kristen when it came to the money angle?

With a cynical shake of his head, Bryce reached

for a glass of iced water. No point in getting heated about anyone he didn't know…or Kristen's greed.

His forthcoming marriage was a done deal. Almost a done deal. He didn't have the time to settle with someone else. The doctors had told him it was a miracle his father was still alive and they were using experimental drugs to treat his condition. Such risky medication held out no guarantees, and Bryce didn't want to delay giving what peace of mind this marriage might bring, at least in the short term.

No point in brooding over the outcome for himself, either. He'd flown to Vegas to hand out awards and get a feel of how the rank and file were dealing with the company products. His mission this morning was to listen and observe. Which he proceeded to do.

First up was a panel who role-played selling the concepts of particular products to customers who have no idea how they would work in business, or that they even existed to be used. Bryce was favourably impressed by their understanding and the concise way they focused on customer needs to adopt and apply more profitable business practices.

Next came a sample presentation to a company board level, delivered by a Business Development Manager from Sydney, Australia. The program noted that Sunny York had the enviable record of always achieving her quota of sales. *Her*…a woman? His interest piqued, Bryce waited curiously to assess why she was so successful.

The conference organiser finished his patter on her, raised his arm in a welcoming gesture, and in a typically hyped-up voice, announced, 'Miss Sunny York.'

Up stood the woman in yellow!

She had a smile on her face that would captivate and dazzle even the hardest-headed financial directors. And she was tall—six feet tall, Bryce estimated—and more than half of that height was taken up by the longest legs he'd ever seen on a woman. He couldn't help watching them as she stepped up to the podium. Her skirt ended above her knees but it wasn't a mini. It simply looked like a mini on those legs, and she wasn't even wearing high-heels, just comfortable court shoes with enough of a heel to look elegant.

His gaze travelled slowly upwards from her feet...what would it be like to have those long, shapely legs wrapped around him...the curvy cradle of her hips underneath him...plenty of cushion in those nicely rounded breasts, too...that mouth, so full-lipped and wide, made for sensual pleasure...and her hair tumbling everywhere.

'Hi!' She spread her smile and twinkling eyes around the audience, drawing everyone to her with a flow of warmth that sparked responding smiles. 'I'm here to help you make money...and save money.'

She had them in her hand from that very first delivery and didn't let them go for one second in the whole forty minutes of her presentation. It didn't feel like a hard-sell. She came over as concerned to serve the customer's very best interests, her voice carrying a very natural charm, allied to a mobility of expression which was almost mesmerising. The line of logic she injected into selling sounded so simple and convincing, she left no doubt this was a winning move, and her own positive energy literally generated positive energy through the whole auditorium.

Bryce found himself totally entranced.

Even her Australian accent was endearing.

Sunny...

He could certainly do with a bit of that sun in his life. A lot of it. All of it. His stomach clenched as his mind skidded to Kristen. He didn't want a cool-headed calculator. Taking her as his wife went against every grain in his entire body...and that very same body was craving what Sunny York might give him.

His eyes feasted on her as she stepped down from the podium. He'd invite her to join him for lunch...test possibilities. Seize the day. Seize the night. A night with Sunny York would at least satisfy the compelling fantasies she'd been stirring, and if she was all she promised to be...

The flash of a diamond on her left hand pulled the hot run of thoughts up with a jolt. Bryce stared at the ring that declared Sunny York was engaged to be married, committed to another man, whom she probably loved. Her whole performance demonstrated she put her heart into everything she did. Heart and soul.

Bryce wasn't used to feeling like a loser. It hit him hard, the sick hollowness following on the wild surge of excitement she had evoked in him. He sat back in his chair and grimly reviewed his options.

He might be able to seduce her away from her fiancé. Inducements marched through his mind...

powerful attractions for most women. But if he did win her like that…would he still want her?

Give it up, man, he told himself savagely.

Kristen was ready and willing…so long as he paid the price she demanded. Which he could well afford. Settle with her and be done with it.

CHAPTER THREE

SUNNY headed for the ground-floor casino, determined on having a showdown with Derek. He hadn't come to the lunch—not even waiting outside the conference room to give her a courtesy comment on her presentation before skipping off—and he hadn't shown for the last session, regardless of the fact that Bryce Templar had been giving out awards. His respect for *the big man* obviously hadn't extended that far.

She didn't like the casino floor. The assault on her ears from countless bell-ringing slot machines was horrific. It was bad enough walking through it. Actually spending hours here was beyond her understanding. Having finally located the roulette tables, she scanned them for Derek and was frustrated at not finding him. Could he have gone to bed—the need for sleep catching up with him?

Frowning, Sunny moved from foot to foot, too worked up to walk away with so much angst playing through her mind. She shot her gaze in every direction, not really expecting to resolve anything, simply at a loss to know what to do next. It came as a shock when she actually spotted Derek, seated at a *blackjack* table, watching the cards being played by the dealer with an intensity that cramped her heart.

He was caught in a thrall that nothing was going to break.

It seemed that nothing else mattered.

Sickened by the realisation of how destructively addictive gambling could be, Sunny hesitated over confronting Derek, yet the relationship they had shared up until this week demanded that he at least recognise how he was treating it. The need to get through to him drove her over to the blackjack table. She waited until he threw down his cards in disgust, apparently having lost his bet, then tapped him on the shoulder.

'Derek…'

He sliced an impatient frown at her.

'…could I speak to you, please?'

'Can't you see I'm playing?'

'It's important.'

Grimacing at the interruption, he heaved himself off his chair and tipped the back of it onto the edge of the table to hold his place. 'What's so damned important?' he demanded, his bleary eyes snapping with frustration.

'It's the last night…'

'I've just lost the roll I won at roulette. My luck's got to turn…'

'Derek, we've got seats for the *Jubilee* show. And dinner beforehand.'

'The action is here. I'm not leaving it.'

'Don't I mean anything to you anymore?' she cried, trying to get through the obsessive glaze to some grain of perspective on what he was doing.

The personal tack clearly irritated him. 'I sat

through your presentation. You slayed 'em as you always do. Is that what you want to hear?' he said ungraciously, then waved a sharp dismissal as he added, 'If you're hot to go and watch some showgirl extravaganza, fine. But as you just pointed out, this is our last night here and I want to win my money back.'

'And what if you don't? What if you lose more?'

He looked shifty.

'Derek, just how much have you lost already?'

Feverish need flashed at her. 'I'll win it back. It's only a matter of time.'

An icy fear struck her. 'Have you been gambling on credit?'

'That's my business. We're not married yet.'

No sharing. No desire to share. Complete shut-out. Hurt and disappointment held her silent for a moment as she realised beyond any doubt that there could be no happy future for them. A bitter urge to show him what he'd done, how low he had fallen, had her wrenching the diamond ring off her finger.

'Here!' She held it out to him. 'You can pawn it. Get some more money to throw down the drain.'

It rocked him. 'Now look here, Sunny...'

'No. Try looking at yourself, Derek. It's over for me.'

'Well, if you feel that way...' His eyes glittered as he took the ring. 'You'll change your mind when I win a bundle.'

He was unreachable on any level. 'I won't change my mind. We're through, Derek,' she said with absolute finality.

His gaze had dropped to the diamond in his hand,

and Sunny had the gut-wrenching impression he was assessing what he could get for it. Her eyes blurred— all the inner torment of hopes and dreams being just swept away suddenly catching her by the throat. For their eight-month-long relationship to come to this…

She swung away, swallowing hard to stop herself from bursting into tears and making a spectacle of herself. Her legs moved automatically, driven by the need to get out of the casino, out of this dreadful playground which trapped people and drained them of any soul she could relate to.

The slot machines jangled around her, a cacophony of sound that seemed to mock her misery. She completely lost her bearings, not knowing what direction led to an exit. A moment's enforced reasoning told her to head for the hotel's reception desk from where the lobby was definitely in view.

It was such a relief to break free of the vast gambling area, tears swam into her eyes again. This time she simply put her head down and followed the walkway to the lobby, hoping not to run into anyone who knew her.

The limousine was waiting. His plane was waiting to fly him back to L.A. Kristen was waiting for him to return to her, no doubt ready to sweeten her prenuptial demands with how well she would accommodate his needs. Bryce Templar told himself that what he'd just witnessed didn't change anything, but still he lingered in the lobby, watching Sunny York.

She'd taken off the diamond ring.

The man she'd handed it to wasn't following her.

Her haphazard flight from what was clearly a distressing scene had finally been checked and she was heading towards him. Not consciously. She hadn't seen him. She wasn't seeing anything except the floor stretching ahead of her.

'Your bag is in the car, sir,' the bellhop informed him.

He nodded, unable to tear his eyes away from the long beautiful legs of Sunny York, walking her towards him. The memory of her warm vibrancy played havoc with his usual cool decision-making processes. Here was opportunity. The guy at the blackjack table was one hell of a big loser and that loss was right in front of Bryce to be capitilised upon. The urge to do so was more compelling than any urge he'd had for a long time.

She was free.

He wasn't, Bryce sternly reminded himself. Kristen was wearing *his* ring. But not a wedding ring yet. And before he could have any further second thoughts, a fierce surge of highly male instincts moved him to intercept Sunny York's path to the exit doors.

'Miss York…'

Legs were planted in front of her—the legs of a big man—and that voice…her heart quivered as a weird certainty crashed through the daze of misery in her mind. Bryce Templar was addressing her. Bryce Templar!

Her feet faltered, hesitating over making a wild sidestep to escape him. Even blinking furiously, she couldn't hide the moisture in her eyes. Impossible to face him…yet impossible not to. A man like Bryce Templar would not be snubbed. Not by an employee of his company.

'I was looking for you after the awards presentation,' he said purposefully.

It surprised her into raising her gaze to his. 'Looking for me?' His eyes were green, pouring out interest in her, and despite her embarrassment, Sunny found she couldn't look away.

He smiled. 'You impressed me very much this morning.'

At the vivid memory of how he had impressed her, heat whooshed up her neck and scorched her cheeks. It reduced her to total speechlessness.

'You have a remarkable gift for selling,' he went on.

Somehow she managed to get her mouth around, 'Thank you.'

'I wondered if I could interest you in a proposition.'

Like having a baby with me?

Sunny blushed even more furiously at that terribly wayward thought. Her mind was hopelessly out of control. Bryce Templar had to be talking about a business proposition, which was stunning in itself…the big man thinking she had a special talent for sales.

'Were you on your way somewhere?' he asked.

Realising her gauche manner was probably putting him off—*putting Bryce Templar off!*—Sunny tried desperately to adjust to this totally unexpected situation.

'I...I was just going for a walk. Out of the hotel. We've been closeted inside all day...'

'Yes, of course,' he said understandingly. 'I'll walk with you. If you'll just excuse me a few moments while I rearrange my schedule...' He smiled again, showering her with warm approval. '...I would like to talk to you.'

She nodded, completely dumbstruck at the prospect of strolling down the street, accompanied by Bryce Templar. Her whole body started tingling as she watched him stride over to the concierge's desk. He was rearranging his schedule to be with *her!* It was incredible, world-shaking.

Green eyes...she hadn't been close enough to see their colour before. They gave his face an even more striking character. Or so it seemed to her.

She watched him command the concierge's attention. He would naturally command attention anywhere, Sunny thought, even without the weight of his name and position. His height, the breadth of his shoulders, the sheer physical authority of the man, drew the gaze of everyone around him.

For once in her life, Sunny had the uplifting feeling of her own tallness ceasing to be a burden that had to be bypassed in her reaching out to others. She was short enough to hold her head high next to Bryce Templar without diminishing his sense of stature in any shape or form. Not that her height would be of any concern to him—a man of his power—but it was a relief to her not to feel conscious of it.

He made some quick calls on a cell phone, then spoke again to the concierge. Sunny was grateful for the time to pull herself together. A business proposition, he'd said, which was what she should be focusing on instead of letting foolish personal responses to him turn her into a blithering idiot. She had a future to consider…a future without Derek.

Yet when Bryce Templar turned back to her, his green eyes targeted her with an intensity that didn't feel business-like at all. Sunny was instantly swamped with an acute awareness of being a woman, every feminine instinct she had positively zinging with the electric possibility that *he* found her worthy of mating with.

It blew her mind off any consideration of business. Her pulse was a wild drumbeat in her temples. Her stomach clenched at his approach. He stretched one arm out in a gathering-in gesture and some madness in her brain saw him naked and intent on claiming her. Then his other arm pointed to the exit doors and the crazy anticipation rocketing through her was countered by a blast of sanity.

A walk…

That was the sum of his invitation.

Somehow she pushed her shaky legs into walking.

Bryce Templar did not, in fact, touch her. A bell-hop rushed to open the door. When they emerged from the hotel, the big man fell into step beside her and Sunny instinctively chose to turn right because he was on her left and bumping into him was unthinkable in her dreadfully hyped-up state with fantasies running riot.

'Have you enjoyed being in Las Vegas?'

It was a perfectly natural question but his voice

seemed to purr in her ear, heightening her awareness of him. Sunny kept her gaze trained straight ahead, not trusting herself to look at him and keep sensible. *Business, business, business,* she recited frantically.

'I haven't really had much time to explore the city,' she answered carefully. 'The conference has been pretty much full-on. Which is what we're here for,' she quickly added in case it sounded like a criticism. 'And I have learnt a lot.'

'You apply what you know extremely well,' he remarked admiringly.

She shrugged. 'I like giving our customers the best deal I can.'

'Well, you've certainly done an excellent job of serving Templar Resources.'

'I'm glad you think so.'

'Oh, I think you'd be an asset to anyone, Miss York. Or may I call you Sunny?'

'If you like,' she gabbled, trying not to read too much into his charming manner.

'It suits you. You project a warmth that makes everyone want to bask in it.'

He was projecting a warmth that was sending her dizzy. She was tempted to glance at him, to check the expression on his face, but didn't quite dare. It was difficult enough to remain reasonably sensible when she was so affected by his close presence. If he caught her looking at him and held her gaze, she might melt into a mindless heap.

'What do you wish to see on our walk?' he asked pleasantly.

She had no plan. Her only thought had been to get

out of the casino. 'I...I just wanted...more of a feel
for the city...before I leave.'

'I suppose, in a way, you could call it a very romantic city...full of dreams.'

Shattered dreams if you're a loser.

The flash of Derek was unwelcome, bringing with
it the empty feeling of no marriage and no babies to
look forward to. But she could never accept Derek as
a husband or the father of her children now. It was
definitely for the best that she'd found out what she
would have been getting in him.

'The re-creation of romantic cities in the newer ho-
tels—Venice, Paris, New York. They're quite fantastic facsimiles of the real thing,' Bryce Templar remarked, continuing his *romance* comment. 'Have you
had a look at them?'

Sunny struggled to get her mind back on track with
his. 'The Venetian and Paris, yes. They're amazing.'

'Well, we're walking in the right direction to see
New York, New York. The Excalibur and the Luxor
are further on beyond it. Very striking with their
Medieval and Egyptian architectural themes.'

Suddenly struck by his indulgence towards what he
perceived as her wishes, Sunny began seriously wondering what he wanted with her. Here he was, strolling along the Boulevard, playing guide to her tourist...what was it leading to? They reached an
intersection and had to stop for the traffic lights to
change. Taking a deep breath, and steeling herself to
cope with the nerve-shaking magnetism of the man,
Sunny turned to face him.

'Your time must be valuable,' she stated, her eyes quickly searching his for a true response.

'Isn't everyone's?' he replied.

'Yes. But…' She floundered as he smiled, showing obvious pleasure in her company.

'You need to relax. So do I. Is there any reason we shouldn't relax together?'

'No,' she answered breathlessly, her pulse going haywire at the realisation he *was* attracted to her, man to woman attraction. No mistake. No flight of fancy. The spark of sexual connection was in his eyes—the keen interest, the desire to know more, the hunter's gleam that said she was worth pursuing and he meant to pursue.

'Good!' There was a wealth of satisfaction in that one simple word. He reached out and gently cupped her elbow. 'The lights have changed. Let's go with the flow.'

The flow Sunny felt had nothing to do with the stream of people crossing the street with them. She was barely aware of them. The hand lightly holding her arm had the mental force of a physical brand…like Bryce Templar was claiming possession of her, burning his ownership through the sleeve of her suit-coat and making her sizzle with possibilities she would not have believed in a few moments ago.

Bryce Templar…wanting *her*. She hadn't been completely crazy back in the hotel lobby. But what did it mean to him? Was it his habit to pluck a woman out of a crowd—someone he fancied—and just go after her? It probably was that easy for a man like him. What woman would refuse the chance to…?

Shock stopped that thought from reaching its natural conclusion. Fanciful lusting was one thing. Real flesh-and-blood lusting was something else. Did she want to be a one-night stand for Bryce Templar, finishing off his trip to Las Vegas—a bit of relaxation, satisfying a sexual urge? Surely that was all it could be. She was an Australian, on her way back to Sydney tomorrow. An easy goodbye.

'How would you feel about transferring to the U.S., Sunny?'

It startled her into a fast re-think. 'You mean...leave Sydney...for here?'

'Not here. Your base would be Los Angeles. Or New York. They hold our biggest operations.'

Business!

Was she hopelessly out of kilter, imagining the sexual stuff?

Totally confused, Sunny tried to come to grips with this new question. A career move...an upward career move...out of her own country.

'Would you find that too much of a wrench?' he asked quietly. 'I realise it's a big ask, particularly if you're close to your family.'

Her family...Sunny almost groaned as she envisaged telling her mother and sisters she'd broken her engagement to Derek. No wedding. No marriage. No babies. She'd been a failure as a woman in their eyes for years and there she'd be, proving it again. Almost thirty and couldn't find Mr. Right. Sympathy would be directed to her face, pity behind her back, and she'd hate every minute of it.

'I have my own life to lead,' she said on a surge of proud independence.

'No family?' he queried.

'I have two married sisters and my mother is very involved with her grandchildren. My father died some years ago. I'd be missed…and I'd miss them…' She flashed him a look of self-determination. '…but I would certainly consider an offer.'

Triumph glinted in his eyes. 'Then I'll make it as attractive as I can.'

Her heart jumped into another gallop. It wasn't her imagination. This was highly personal. And he wanted her on hand *for more than one night!*

'The package would include a generous travel allowance,' he assured her. 'Which will enable you to visit your family on a reasonably frequent basis.'

Behind her, music suddenly boomed out over loudspeakers. So dazed was Sunny by the revelation that Bryce Templar was very intent on getting her where he wanted her, she almost leapt out of her skin at the fanfare of trumpets, her head jerking around, half expecting to see a triumphal parade for the victory being planned in the green eyes.

'It's heralding the dance of the fountains at the Bellagio,' Bryce informed her. 'Come…it's worth seeing.'

His arm went around her waist, sweeping her with him and holding her protectively as he steered her through the crowd gathering along the sidewalk to enjoy the promised spectacle. He didn't push or shove. People simply gave way to him, standing back to let him and his companion through to a prime watching position against the Italian-style balustrade that edged the man-made lake in front of the Bellagio Hotel.

He stood half behind her, dropping his hand onto the balustrade on her far side to keep her encircled in the shelter of his arm, though no longer touching her. It was an extraordinary feeling—being protected and cared for by this big man. Sunny couldn't help revelling in it. She was so used to fending for herself, it was wonderful to wallow in the sense of being a woman whose man was looking after everything for her, ensuring her pleasure.

Except he wasn't actually *her man*. But could he be? In a very real sense? The very male solidity of the body so close to hers was real enough. So was her response to it. If she leaned back...made deliberate contact...what would happen?

Recognising the wanton recklessness in that temptation, Sunny held still, telling herself to wait for his moves. It ill behove her to instigate anything, especially when she wasn't in his social league. She'd made a fool of herself, believing she could share her life with Derek. How big a fool might she be, reading far too much between the lines of Bryce Templar's proposition?

A row of high water spouts started running right across the lake. Circles of fountains shot into the air. The music moved into the tune of 'Big Spender' and the high lines of water looped and swayed and bopped to the rhythm like a human chorus line, dancing to a choreography that required perfect timing.

It was an entrancing sight, yet the song being used

struck a raw place in Sunny, reminding her this city
revolved around gambling and all the lavish glamour,
luxury and service were designed to draw people into
big spending. Derek could very well be ruining himself here. Though the responsibility for that lay
squarely with him, no one else.

Would she be ruining her life, impulsively linking
it to whatever Bryce Templar wanted?

A gamble, she thought. A big gamble on a big man.
An absolutely magnificent man who made her
feel...exceedingly primitive.

The fountains whooshed high in a fabulous finale,
then seemed to bow before gracefully dropping back
under the surface of the lake, their dance over.

'That was lovely,' Sunny breathed, and with her
eyes still sparkling appreciatively, turned to look directly at the man who was fast infiltrating every aspect of her life. She realised instantly that his gaze
had been fixed on her hair. It slid from the soft mass
of waves to meet hers, transmitting a sensual simmering that caught what breath she had left in her
throat. The rest of her words emerged as a husky
whisper. 'Thank you for showing it to me.'

For one electrifying moment he looked at her
mouth. The blast of raw desire she felt emanating
from him scrambled her mind. Her lips remained
slightly parted, quivering in wanton anticipation.

Then he dragged his gaze back to hers, locking
onto it with searing force as he murmured, 'Your
pleasure is my pleasure.'

Her breasts prickled. Her stomach clenched. A
tremor of excitement ran down her thighs. Her only

conscious thought, rising out of the raging desire he
stirred was…

It *was* real…his wanting her…as real as her wanting him right back…and if she didn't take this gamble
she might be missing the experience of a lifetime.

CHAPTER FOUR

BRYCE only just managed to stop himself from kissing Sunny York right then and there. The desire to ravish the mouth she seemed to be offering him was totally rampant. Only a belated sense of where they were—on a public street with a crowd of tourists around them—gave him pause, and his brain seized the pause to flash a neon-bright danger signal.

He was out of control.

Even so the physical rebellion against the warning was sharp and intense. But being in control had ruled his life so long, his mind automatically equated that factor with success, and losing this woman with rash action at this point was unacceptable. She had been skittish up until now. Moving too fast might frighten her off. It wasn't smart to assume too much too soon, not when so much was hanging on the outcome of one night with her.

Dumping Kristen.

Marrying Sunny York.

Persuading her into a pregnancy she might not want.

It was a huge leap for him to take. How much bigger for her, without his cogent reasons firing the impulse to take this alternative road?

He stepped back, gesturing a continuation of their

stroll. 'A little slice of New York awaits you up ahead.'

Her beautiful amber eyes reflected inner confusion. Her vulnerability to what he was doing smote his conscience for a moment. She was afloat from her broken engagement, undoubtedly wanting an escape from the hurt to both heart and pride, and he was ruthlessly intent on drawing her into his net.

But he would look after her and give her a life full of riches if she came his way.

With that soothing justification riding on the advantage he knew he was taking, Bryce slid into charm mode, offering a whimsical little smile as he sought to ease her personal turmoil with outside interests.

'The Statue of Liberty, the Brooklyn Bridge, and the Empire State Building are somewhat scaled down since they're merely dressing up a hotel, but very recognisable,' he said encouragingly.

She gave her head a little shake, alerting Bryce even more forcefully to the danger of moving too fast. She'd have to be totally insensitive to miss the sexual signals he'd been giving out and he suspected she was all too aware of them, given the way she'd been evading looking at him and the tension emanating from her. Although part of that could have been the need to hide her distress over the guy she'd just broken with.

'Have you had any first-hand experience of New York?' he quickly asked, talking to re-establish a more comfortable connection for her.

'Yes, but only a few days' sightseeing.' She hesitated, her eyes scanning his uncertainly. 'Not…not business.'

'What was your impression of it?' he pressed, relieved when she stepped forward, indicating her willingness to go on with him.

'It had an exciting energy…the sense of a lot happening.' Her mouth curved into a musing smile. 'Extra-wide sidewalks. Hot dogs, with an amazing range of choices for spicing them up. Delicatessens with exotic food. Caramel apples…'

He laughed. 'You must really enjoy food.'

'Yes, I do.' Her smile turned lopsided. 'My sisters accuse me of having hollow legs.'

'That has to be envy.' Her incredibly sexy legs were an instant source of erotic fantasies.

'Oh, I doubt they envy me much…except not having to diet.'

'Then I hope you'll have dinner with me. I shall enjoy eating with a woman who likes food and doesn't see it as the enemy to be kept at bay.' He slanted her a teasing glance. 'You will eat more than lettuce leaves?'

She laughed. It was a delightful gurgle, spontaneous, warmly responsive. 'We can skip salad altogether if you like.'

'I take it that's a yes to dinner?'

She scooped in a big breath. 'Yes.'

Elation zoomed through him. He didn't care if this was some kind of emotional payback to the guy back in the casino, who clearly hadn't valued her enough. She was coming *his* way…plunging ahead with reckless disregard for caution.

After all, he triumphantly reasoned, what did she have to lose? His cynical side told him if it was pride driving her, he represented a top replacement in the lover stakes. What he was offering had to be all gain from her point of view—better prospects for her career, a transfer away from her erstwhile fiancé, and an enviable reason to remove herself from any criticism by her family with the CEO of Templar Resources taking a personal interest in her.

But falling into bed with him might not be on her agenda.

She might not see that as wise—in her position as his employee—or, indeed, desirable in a personal sense, given her very recent disillusionment with her fiancé. On the other hand, there was always *impulse*.

Bryce started planning a seduction scene as he continued chatting to her, building a rapport to bridge what *he* had in mind.

Sunny couldn't believe her luck. Dinner with Bryce Templar. Dinner for two. Beautiful man, beautiful food, beautiful wine—probably the finest champagne to celebrate her taking up his proposition. Except she didn't quite know what his proposition was, apart from its involving her transfer to the U.S. *And the personal element.*

A convulsive little shiver ran down her spine. Was sex on the side the pay-off for a big career promotion? She quickly shut her mind to that creepy-crawly thought. Bryce Templar *liked* her. She could tell from the way he was talking to her. He wasn't just making conversation. He was enjoying the to-and-fro, smiling, laughing, connecting on *all* levels.

He was clearly interested in her as a person—what level of education she'd had, the various positions she'd held, leading to her current one, everything she'd done with her life so far, her likes, dislikes. In fact, Sunny was so intoxicated by his charm, it took her a while to realise he was actually conducting an in-depth interview while they wandered along the boulevard.

This was a somewhat sobering thought. Though reassuring, as well. It had to mean he was seriously considering where she could best be used in the company business, and more importantly, he didn't seem at all put off by anything she'd said.

He wasn't touching her, either. From the moment he'd stepped back from that highly charged moment in front of the Bellagio Hotel, he'd made no physical contact with her. Plenty of exhilarating eye contact, but nothing physical. Perhaps he had stepped right back from sexual temptation, deciding an intimate liaison with her was inappropriate.

Which, of course it was, Sunny told herself. If she held his high esteem, well…that was something very positive. Yet she couldn't stop her gaze from surreptitiously wandering over him whenever he paused in his role of tourist guide, pointing things out to her.

The muscular breadth of his chest caught her eye as they lingered under the Statue of Liberty at New York, New York, watching the roller-coaster that looped around the hotel, its riders screaming their excitement. A woman would surely feel safe, held to all that strength, and as a father, he would easily be able to carry two or three children, clutched in his arms or perched on those shoulders.

Then his hand captivated her attention, directing her to look at the figure of the magician, Merlin, in the windows of one of the turrets forming the Medieval castle which was the Excalibur Hotel...a large strong hand, deeply tanned, long fingers, neatly buffed nails. To have such a hand holding her breast, stroking her...did it know how to be gentle? Was he a caring lover?

When they stood between the giant Sphinxes that flanked the great pyramid of the Luxor Hotel...he didn't look at all dwarfed by them...more like a powerful pharaoh of his time...a man astride the world he was born to...and what would spring from the loins of this king of kings?

Sunny had to take a stern grip on herself. Secretly lusting over Bryce Templar was bad enough. She had to stop thinking about babies, especially connected with him. Whatever the deal he had in mind for her, babies would most certainly not be part of it.

They took the pedestrian overpasses to cross the street to the other side of the boulevard. The second one led them into the vast MGM complex, and an Elvis Presley impersonator strutting ahead of them and revelling in the notice he drew, evoked a bubble of shared amusement.

'I've never understood that,' Sunny murmured.

'What?'

'Why people want to be someone else.'

'You never entertain a dream world?'

She blushed, guiltily conscious of her x-rated dreams about him. 'Not to the extent of actually copying another person.'

'You're content to be you.'

'I guess I think…this is *my* life, however imperfect it is.'

The twinkling green eyes intensified to a sharp probe. 'What would make it perfect?'

Sunny couldn't reveal that, not when her idea of perfection revolved around the man he was. She could feel her blush deepening and frantically sought some kind of all-purpose answer.

'I don't think we can expect perfection. Making the most of who we are is probably the best aim.'

'So a good career in your chosen field would satisfy you?'

Was he testing how long she might stay in his employ? She couldn't bring herself to lie. A career that interested her was great but it wasn't *everything*. 'Well…not completely,' she admitted, hoping he didn't need total dedication to her work. 'I think most of us would like to have a…a partner…to share things with.'

Surely he would, too. Being alone was…lonely. Though he probably never had to be alone if he didn't want to be. Here she was…providing him with company, simply because he chose to have it, and he hadn't even met her before today. Maybe he was self-sufficient enough not to need any more than a bit of congenial company whenever he cared to fit it in.

'What about children?' he asked, jolting her out of

her contemplation of what she wanted for herself, and hitting directly on a highly sensitive need.

'Children?' she echoed, unsure where this was leading.

'Do you see yourself as a mother some time in the future, or are babies a complication you don't want in your life?'

She sighed. It probably wasn't the smart answer but she simply couldn't pretend that missing out on having a family—at least one baby—wasn't any big deal to her.

'I would like to have a child one day…with the right father,' she added with a wry wistfulness.

'What would encompass *right* to you, Sunny?'

This was getting too close to the bone. Having envisaged *him* as the genetically ideal father, Sunny's comfort zone was being severely tested by his persistence on these points.

They had descended the staircase from the street overpass into the MGM casino area, and were now moving past a café with a jungle theme. Unfortunately Tarzan did not leap out and provide a distraction, and Bryce Templar's question was still hanging.

'What relevance does that have to my job?' she asked, deciding some challenge should be made on the grounds of purpose.

'It goes to character,' he answered smoothly. The green eyes locked onto hers, returning her challenge with an intimate undercurrent that flowed straight around her heart and squeezed it. 'I'm very particular about the character of anyone I bring into close association with me.'

Close.

The word pounded around her bloodstream, stirring up a buzz of sexual possibilities again.

'Some women's prime requirement of *right* would be a certain level of income. The child-price, one might say,' he said sardonically.

Sunny frowned. 'I could support a child myself. That's not the point.'

'What is?'

She rounded on him, not liking the cynical flavour of his comment, and hating the idea of him applying any shade of it to her. '*You* have a father. What was right for you as a child?'

His mouth curled with irony. 'For him to be there when I needed him.'

Which she could no longer trust Derek to do. The clanging casino noise around her drove that home again.

'You've just said it all, Mr. Templar,' she stated decisively.

Her eyes clashed with his, daring him to refute that this quality overrode everything else. It carried the acceptance of responsibility and commitment, displayed reliability and caring, and generated trust...all the things Derek had just demonstrated *wrong* about himself.

Bryce Templar didn't refute it. He stared back at her and the air between them sizzled with tense unspoken things. Sunny had the wild sense that he was scouring her soul for how *right* a mother she would be, judging on some scale which remained hidden to her but was vibrantly real in the context of mating.

'Let's make that Bryce,' he said quietly.

And she knew she had passed some critical test. They stood apart, yet she could feel him drawing her closer to the man he was, unleashing a magnetism that tugged on all that was female in her...deep primitive chords thrumming with anticipation.

He smiled...slowly, sensually, promisingly. 'You must be hungry by now. I am.'

'Yes,' she replied, almost mesmerised by the sensations he was evoking. She was hungry for so many, many things, and every day of this week in Las Vegas she had felt them slipping away from her, leaving an empty hole that even the most exciting career couldn't bridge. Maybe she was crazy, wanting this man to fill the emptiness so much, she was projecting her own desire onto him.

'This way,' he said, and proceeded to guide her around the casino area to the MGM reception desk.

Sunny was barely conscious of walking. She was moving with him, going with him, and he was taking her towards a *closer* togetherness. Dinner for two. On first-name terms. Sunny and Bryce.

She expected him to ask about restaurants at the desk, but he didn't.

'Bryce Templar,' he announced to the clerk. 'A suite has been booked for me.'

'Yes, Mr. Templar. The penthouse Patio Suite. Your luggage has been taken up. Your key?'

'Please.'

It was instantly produced. 'If there's anything else, sir...'

'Thank you. I'll call.'

He was steering Sunny towards the elevators before she recollected her stunned wits enough to say, 'I thought you were staying at the conference hotel.'

'I'd already checked out when I saw you in the lobby.'

She frowned, bewildered by this move. 'Couldn't you check in again?'

'I preferred to keep my business with you private.'

Private...in a private penthouse suite.

A penthouse for playboys?

The elevator doors opened and Bryce Templar swept her into the empty compartment...just the two of them...doors shutting off the crowded casino, closing them away from all the people who had surrounded them on their walk, and suddenly there was silence...except for the hum of the elevator and the thundering beat of Sunny's heart.

CHAPTER FIVE

SHE stood rigidly beside him. Bryce willed the elevator to go faster. He knew she had expected a public restaurant, not this, but he had to get her alone with him. Close the net. His mind worked double-time, producing a string of soothing words, ready to answer any protest she might make about the situation he'd set up.

He saw her hand clench. She took a deep breath. Her face turned to him, her stunning amber eyes swimming with questions. Her mouth moved, tremulous words slipping out. 'I don't think…'

'Don't think!'

The growled command came from nowhere. Before any sophisticated reasoning could stem the urge that exploded through him, Bryce scooped Sunny York into his embrace and kissed her with such devouring intensity, there was no possibility of any more words being uttered by either of them.

He was so hungry for her—for all that she was—the raging desire coursing through him directed all movement. The elevator stopped. The doors slid open. He swung his woman off her feet, hooking her legs over his arm, and it felt absolutely right as he carried her to his suite because her hands were linked around his neck and her breasts were pressed to his chest, and she was kissing him back as wildly as he was kissing her.

The slot-card in his hand opened the door. He kicked it shut. No bed in sight. The suite was a two-storey apartment. Catching sight of the staircase he charged up to the intimate rooms on the next level and straight into the bedroom. Seduction did not enter his head. There was no finesse at all in the need that had him put Sunny on her feet so he could get her clothes off. And his own.

He couldn't wait to have her naked with him, to feel every luscious curve of her, skin to skin, her lovely long legs in intimate entanglement around him. It excited him even more that she was as eager as he was to be rid of all barriers, her hands just as frantically busy with undressing, wanting to feel him and know everything there was to know.

Her eyes were a blaze of gold, burning him up. Her mouth was sensationally passionate in its hunger for his. Her hands were wildly erotic in their touch. Her glorious hair was pure sensual pleasure, its scent, its silky mass, its flashing colours. And fully naked, she was stunningly perfect, her whole body so lushly female, soft and supple, calling on him to perform as a man, and he was so ready to, the drive to take and possess was overwhelmingly immediate.

He laid her on the bed, kneeling over her for a moment, savouring the sight of her—all her sizzling warmth lying open to him, every inhibition abandoned in the sheer craving for this mating with him. Her arms lifted, winding around his neck, pulling him down, wanting him as much as he wanted her.

No foreplay. It wasn't needed by either of them. They were both poised for a completion that had to come. He drove forward, sheathing himself in her moist heat, revelling in her ecstatic welcome, loving the sense of being deep inside her. And her legs wrapped around him, holding him in, exulting in the sensation of feeling him there, then urging him to repeat the action, to move into the rhythm that would take them both on the upward climb to where they had to be...together.

It was an incredible feeling—this compulsive copulation with her—his intense arousal, the sense of being so aggressively male, primitively needful of having *this* woman. Somehow she embodied everything he had to have, and it drove him into a frenzy of possession.

The amazing, the wonderful, the totally exhilarating thing was, she was just as frenzied as he was in wanting what he was giving her, and when he could no longer stop himself from climaxing, she was right there with him, joining him in a fantastic meltdown that seemed to fuse them as one.

For a few moments he spread his body over hers, wanting to feel the whole imprint of her femininity as he kissed her again, sealing their oneness—all of him, all of her, together, as deeply and totally as they could be. The satisfaction of it was euphoric. He wished he could stay where he was, but it wasn't fair to subject her to his weight for long.

He rolled onto his side, scooping her with him to lie in the cradle of his arm, holding her snuggled close to him. He was swamped by a sense of tenderness for her, this woman who made him feel as a man should feel, wanted for what he was, not *who* he was…an instinctive, compulsive wanting.

His hands moved over her, gently caressing, loving the soft texture of her skin, soothing the endearing little tremors his stroking aroused. His fingers threaded through her hair, enjoying the winding spring of curls around them. The urge to bind her to him was so strong, he didn't even pause to wonder what she was thinking—or feeling—about what had happened between them. The words simply spilled straight out.

'Marry me!'

He didn't even realise he spoke in a command. Her head was resting just under his chin. He felt it jerk slightly, a startled little movement.

'What…' The question was choked with disbelief. He heard her sharply indrawn breath, then, '…what did you say?'

Bryce was not about to back off from having the advantage of their intimacy to press his suit. He rolled Sunny onto her back and propped himself up on his elbow beside her, meeting her stunned gaze with an intensity of purpose that was not to be shaken. He lightly traced the line of her full-lipped mouth with his finger as he delivered a clear and firm statement.

'I want you to marry me, Sunny York.'

Sunny could scarcely believe her ears. But he'd said it twice and his eyes were serious. Her sensitised lips were tingling and she couldn't get her mind thinking in any order at all. It didn't help when he lowered his head and grazed his mouth over hers, his tongue slid-ing seductively across the soft inner tissue, and the hand that had caressed her lips, moved down to cup her breast, gently kneading it as his thumb fanned her nipple with tantalising tenderness.

He knew how to do it right. Sunny's mind com-pletely glazed over again, mesmerised by the right-ness that had swamped it from the moment she had been seized by lustful madness in the elevator. He kissed her more deeply, re-igniting all the exciting sensations of previous kisses.

'I want you to be my wife,' he murmured against her lips, his breath still mingling with hers.

His wife.

Then he was trailing kisses down her throat, to the breast he hadn't touched yet, covering it with the hot excitement of his mouth, sucking it erotically, pump-ing pleasure through her in delicious spasms, building a craving for more and more.

'I want you to have my child,' he said, moving to her other breast, sliding his hand down to caress her stomach in circular sweeps, as his mouth played sweet havoc and her mind flashed images of…

His child.

His child in her womb, his child at her breast…the baby she'd love to have…with this man as the fa-ther…the man she'd secretly thought would be the *best* father.

And now he was kissing her stomach, as though he was imagining his baby in there, and his hand was between her thighs, stroking them apart, making room for him to come to her again, exciting the need to have him there. Such intense sensations of pleasure, demanding the fulfilment only he could bring, but when he moved again, it was to drive the need higher, his mouth closing over her sex, setting her on fire with the exquisite brushing of his tongue, the desire for him quickly reaching exploding point.

She heard herself cry out for him, begging, pleading, desperate for him to answer the ache inside her, and he responded immediately, filling her with a glorious rush of satisfaction as he plunged himself deeply into the quivering place that yearned for him.

It felt so good, so right, and she revelled in every stroke of him inside her, loving the hard fullness that kept pushing the pleasure of his possession higher and higher until she felt herself shattering around him, moving into a sea of bliss, and he rocked her there, bringing wave after wave of beautiful feelings that spread through her entire body. The spasms of euphoria kept coming even after he had climaxed and they were simply lying together, luxuriating in the intimate peace of needs fulfilled.

Feather-light fingers stroked the curve of her spine. His cheek rubbed over her hair. She felt his warm breath fan her temples as he spoke, gruffly demanding a reply from her. 'Say you'll marry me, Sunny.'

Marry him.

It was a huge step to take. Her still-floating mind struggled with the enormity of it, hardly believing it was real. It was still difficult to believe all she'd done with him was real. But here she was, lying naked on a bed with him, having been brought alive sexually to a fantastic extreme she had never imagined possible. Nevertheless, this…this hasty plunge into intimacy, did not warrant a hasty plunge into marriage!

'Bryce…'

She hadn't even called him by his first name before! The unfamiliarity of that alone had her hauling herself up to look at him, face to face…this man who seemed intent on marrying her…Bryce Templar, the CEO of Templar Resources, whom she had thought so far removed from her normal life, the idea of a marriage between them had been inconceivable.

His green eyes were simmering with pleasure in her. A sensual little smile curved his lips. 'You're even more beautiful with your hair all tousled,' he murmured.

He thought her *beautiful?* Her hair was probably a tangled mop with all the threshing around she'd done in the heat of passion. And that memory brought a flush to her face.

'We've barely met,' she rushed out, embarrassed by her terribly wanton behaviour.

'So?' He stroked her hot cheek, his eyes smiling reassurance. 'What has time got to do with anything? When something is right, it's right.'

The conviction in his voice eased her troubled sense of having acted out of character. This *was* different—what anybody could excuse as extraordinary circumstances.

'You might not feel it's so right tomorrow,' she said cautiously, still finding his proposal too stunning to really accept it could be genuine.

'Sunny, you said you wanted a partner. So do I, and *everything* about you feels right to me.' His eyes flashed absolute conviction as he added, 'And I don't believe you're the kind of woman who'd go to bed with a man *you* didn't feel right with.'

That was true. She'd never been promiscuous, and one-night stands were definitely not her scene. It was a relief to hear him reading her correctly. Although she'd never been hit by such overwhelming lust before. But lust wasn't love, more an instinctive thing running right out of control. She couldn't believe getting married should be based on *instinct*. There were many more factors involved in making a partnership work well.

'We're even in the same business,' he went on. 'All the more to share with each other, understanding what's involved in our lives.'

She'd thought she had that with Derek. It should be a plus in a relationship. But then she'd believed a lot of things about Derek—for months!—and only found out differently this past week. What seemed right could turn out very wrong indeed.

'And I want a child,' Bryce Templar pressed. 'A child who is wanted just as much by its mother. That's you, Sunny, isn't it? You want to be a mother.'

She couldn't deny it.

'We're not getting any younger,' he pointed out. 'How old are you?'

No harm in answering that question. 'Twenty-nine.'

'I'm thirty-four and I don't want to be an old father. The sooner we make a baby, the better.' He cocked a quizzical eyebrow. 'Any chance we might have already made one?'

It shocked her that protection had not entered either of their heads. Unsafe sex... 'I hope you're not a health risk,' she shot at him.

He laughed. 'No, I'm clean. And I have no doubt you are, too, Sunny York.'

She sighed her relief. 'Well, at least I'm on the pill.'

'Why not throw the pills away?' His eyes twinkled wickedly. 'We can try again. All night...'

Just like that? Plunge into pregnancy with him as the father? Her fantasy answered? Yet fantasies were one thing, realities quite another. People didn't make life commitments, virtually on the spur of the moment. She frowned at him, thinking that stopping contraception would be a very reckless decision, especially when she was feeling all at sea about what had already happened with him, let alone what he had in mind now.

'Do you really want that, Bryce?' she queried, uneasy with the way he seemed to be rushing decisions that shouldn't be hurried. It still sounded strange, using his first name, yet she could hardly call him Mr. Templar in this situation.

'Oh, yes,' he said decisively, a gleam of determination in his eyes. 'I wouldn't play you false about such serious things, Sunny. You're the woman I want as my wife, in every sense. Give me my way and we'll be married tomorrow.'

'Tomorrow!' She shook her head dazedly.

'Easily done in Las Vegas and I see no point in wasting time.'

'I'm on a flight home to Sydney in the morning.'

'You don't have to be on it. And I certainly don't want you on it. In fact...' He reached for the telephone on the bedside table. '...I'll make arrangements for your luggage to be packed and brought here.'

'Bryce!' she cried, grabbing his arm, totally rattled by how fast he was moving.

He shot her a piercing look. 'Do you *want* to go back to that hotel, Sunny?'

And break up what was happening here?

Run into Derek?

'No.' She withdrew her hand, fluttering a helpless gesture. 'It's just...'

'Leave it to me. I'll fix everything.' He grinned at her. 'How about running us a bath while I make the calls? I'll notify the Sydney manager that you're staying on and I'll get the hotel staff to pack everything for you and get it delivered here. Okay?'

Sunny took a deep breath.

It felt as though Bryce Templar was taking her on a wild roller-coaster ride and it was scary to think of where it would lead next, yet to get off...without knowing more...and the grin on his face made him *so* attractive, inviting her into his private and personal world, delighted to have her with him.

Besides, getting on the plane with Derek in the morning was not a happy prospect, seated next to him on the flight to L.A., then the long haul to Sydney. Arguments, stress, wondering what might have been if she'd stayed...

'Okay,' she echoed, the word torn out of her need to escape a miserable return to Sydney, as well as the strong temptation to stay right where she was with

Bryce Templar, at least long enough to see what the end of the ride might be like. 'But what about my ticket home if…'

'Do you imagine I wouldn't make good on that for you, should you want to go?' he cut in quietly.

Her heart cringed at her unwitting impugning of his integrity. 'I'm sorry. This is all so fast…'

'I promise I'll look after you. Whatever you need. Whatever you want. All you have to do is tell me, Sunny.'

She took another deep breath to steady her whirling mind. 'Okay. I'll stay on…for a while.'

His grin sparkled with triumph this time, putting a host of butterflies in her stomach. She had the wild sense that Bryce Templar had carried her into his cave and was now busily shutting off all exits until he had his way with her. Which clearly meant she needed some space to calm herself down and start thinking rationally about her immediate future with him.

'I'll go find the bathroom,' she said, remembering his suggestion of running a bath…*for both of them!*

'You do that,' he approved heartily, reaching for the telephone again. 'This won't take long.'

She slid off the bed, and very conscious of her naked state with his eyes watching her, headed straight for the most likely door to an adjoining bathroom. It proved to be precisely that and she shut it behind her to ensure at least a few moments' privacy.

As caves went, this was certainly a sumptuous one, Sunny couldn't help thinking as she noted the Italian marble accents, the positively decadent Roman tub, even a television set to watch while bathing. Life with

Bryce Templar could be very seductive with such luxuries. All the same, she was not going to be rushed into any rash decisions. The old saying—*marry in haste, repent at leisure*—was a good warning.

On the other hand, she might as well enjoy what was here. Having turned on the taps to fill the bath, she sprinkled in some scented grainy salts from a very elegant jar, then added a blue syrupy mixture that instantly frothed into bubbles. Satisfied that she wouldn't feel quite so naked with a mass of foam to hide behind, Sunny moved around the other facilities.

Beside the toilet was a European bidet—very civilised sophistication—and in a drawer of the vanity table she found a packet of hairpins which she proceeded to use, hoping not to get her hair wet in the bath. *Tousled* might look beautiful to Bryce but *wet* was definitely not her best look.

For a few moments she stared at her own face in the mirror. What did Bryce Templar see in her that he hadn't seen in the many many women who must have traipsed through his life? Why should he suddenly decide she was the one to marry?

She was passably attractive. Her eyes were probably her best feature. Her nose had that irritating tilt that always got sunburnt if she wasn't careful and her mouth was too wide. The hair he admired was the bane of her life. And she'd hated her legs in her teens, so long and gangly, though they did have more shape to them now she was older and her figure more mature.

Shaking her head, the puzzle of Bryce Templar's choice still unresolved in her mind, Sunny stepped over to the bath, which was now well filled. She turned off the taps and lowered herself gingerly into its warm foamy depths. A sigh of sheer pleasure relaxed the tension raised by too many uncertainties. Sinful pleasures, she thought, wondering if she would end up rueing her decision to stay.

A knock on the door preceded its being pushed slightly open. 'May I come in?' was courteously asked.

'Yes,' she answered, her heart jiggling nervously at the thought of sharing this bath with him. But since she'd already shared far more, it was way too late to start feeling shy.

The door swung wide open and Sunny's breath caught in her throat at the sight of him coming towards her. He had been naked on the bed, but she hadn't really seen him like this. They'd been too wrapped up in other things. His physique was stunningly male, magnificently proportioned and power-packed with just the right amount of masculine muscle.

He looked...fantastic.

And she could have *him* as her husband!

But there was more to marriage than the physical, Sunny hastily berated herself. This terribly strong desire he inspired was probably the most sinful pleasure of all.

'Brought the menus with me for us to choose dinner from,' he said with a smile, waving the large folders he held in his hand. 'I'm hoping your appetite will match mine. I think we should order a feast to celebrate our coming together.'

Dinner! She'd forgotten all about it.

'Yes. That would be good,' she agreed, trying to get her mind focused on an appetite for food instead of the very distracting appetite for him.

He laid one folder on the floor beside her, fetched a towel for her to dry her hands, then lowered himself into the bath, facing her from the other end. 'Your luggage should be here within the hour and I've let the Sydney people know you won't be on tomorrow's flight with them,' he tossed at her as he opened his menu to peruse its contents.

She wondered what reaction that announcement from Bryce Templar had caused amongst her colleagues. Had Derek been told? Her stomach suddenly clenched. What would Derek think? What would he do?

I don't care, she told herself on a surge of violent anger for the uncaring way he had treated her. She grabbed the towel, dried her hands, picked up the menu and opened it, determined on ordering a veritable feast.

The die was well and truly cast now.

One way or another, she'd thrown in her lot with Bryce Templar.

Dinner for two!

CHAPTER SIX

BRYCE saw the belligerent tilt of her chin and her mouth compressing into a line of determination as she reached for the menu. He had no difficulty in reading what those telltale expressions meant. The boats were burnt. There was no way back. Not tonight nor tomorrow. No point in not making the most of her time with him.

He smiled to himself. The net was closed. Not exactly how he'd meant to do it. In fact, he'd lost the plot completely in his somewhat intemperate need to have her, but he was now satisfied he hadn't hurt his end purpose by it. He may well have improved his chances of convincing her to marry him. Mutual desire was a strong persuader. And he had the rest of the night to capitalise on it.

He moved his legs to lie in tandem with hers, enjoying the long silky slide of her calves and thighs. She was certainly built perfectly for him. The way they fitted together was especially satisfying. He looked forward to much more of it.

'What are your favourite foods?' he asked, wanting eye contact with her.

Her lashes slowly lifted. From this distance the colour of her eyes looked darker, more a warm brown. They still lit up her face. She had a wonderful face. Not classically beautiful, like Kristen's, but Kristen's

61

was like a smooth mask in comparison. Sunny's was alive, projecting a wealth of fascinating expression.

'I *love* lobster,' she stated with open fervour. 'I see they've got Maine lobster on the menu, so I'm definitely having that.'

He laughed at the rich satisfaction in her voice. She truly was a delight in every sense. He would enjoy having her as his wife. 'What else?' he prompted.

She listed everything she found tempting, displaying a relish for food that whetted his own appetite. He couldn't remember ever having such fun, discussing a menu. They were discussing the merits of a selection of sweets when the telephone rang, interrupting the pleasurable anticipation of a superb meal.

'Probably announcing the arrival of your luggage,' Bryce commented, hauling himself out of the bath to deal with the call since the telephone, although in the bathroom, was out of his reach and he didn't want Sunny answering it.

She laughed at the foam flaking off him as he moved. 'You make a great snowstorm.'

'Maybe we should have the Bombe Alaska for sweets,' he tossed at her, grinning as he snatched up a towel.

'No. I really fancy the raspberry soufflé.'

'It'll probably sink before it gets here. Think about it.'

Her eyes chided him. 'Spoilsport.'

He laughed, loving the natural interplay between them. Sunny was much more relaxed with him now, not on guard at all. Which had to bring her closer to what he wanted.

Having wiped his hands, he picked up the receiver, expecting a quick communication. 'Templar here.'

'Ah, Mr. Templar. Miss York's luggage has arrived. And so has a Mr. Derek Marsden, demanding to see Miss York. He claims she is his fiancée.'

'No way,' Bryce returned tersely.

'He is being very insistent, sir. One could say threatening, if you take my meaning.'

Bryce tensed, a savage aggression instantly gripping him. The last thing he needed was Sunny's ex-fiancé hanging around, creating scenes, and possibly swaying Sunny off the course she had chosen. He had to protect the ground he'd won.

'I'll come down and deal with it. Give me a few minutes.'

'Thank you, sir. I'll hold the gentleman here. Should I send the luggage up?'

'No. Not yet. I'll deal with that, too.'

'As you wish, sir.'

He slammed the receiver down, startling Sunny. 'Something wrong?' she asked, wide-eyed at his change of mood.

He grimaced an apology. 'A business problem.'

'Not my luggage?'

'Still coming,' he answered, quickly towelling himself dry. 'I have to go and meet an associate in the lobby, Sunny. It should only take ten minutes or so. While I'm gone, call room service and order what we've decided upon.' He forced a smile to put her at ease with the situation. 'You get to choose the selection of sweets. Okay?'

She caught the undercurrent of urgency. 'Is it a bad problem?'

'No.' He relaxed his face into a wry expression. 'Just vexing that it's come up when I'd rather be with you.'

She smiled. 'Then I'll try not to miss you.'

'Think of great food,' he teased, and was off, striding for the bedroom and the clothes he had to put on before facing the rival he had to dismiss.

He couldn't allow this Derek Marsden any room for worming his way back into Sunny's affections. Bryce frowned, wondering how Marsden had picked up on where she was. He hadn't given out that information.

He dressed at lightning speed, his mind ticking over possibilities. Marsden had arrived at the same time as Sunny's luggage. Possibly he had gone to her hotel room, found her clothes and toiletries being packed by staff, then followed the trail, greasing palms with big tips to learn what was going on.

Dog in the manger stuff, Bryce decided. If Marsden had really valued Sunny, she wouldn't be here in this suite. No doubt it was *his name* being involved that was sticking in Marsden's craw. In any case, he had no claim on her. She had given him back his ring. The break was clear-cut and Bryce aimed to keep it that way. No second chance for Marsden.

Sunny was still in the bathroom, happily ignorant of her ex-fiancé's intrusion on the scene. Hoping to make his absence as brief as possible, Bryce made a fast exit from the suite, summoned the elevator, and waited impatiently for its arrival. His mind skated through his impression of the man he'd seen at the blackjack table this afternoon—about the same height as Sunny, fairish hair, clean-cut type of college-man looks, lean build.

Physically, Bryce knew he was the far more intimidating man. He didn't expect a fist-fight, but Marsden could turn ugly, faced with the frustration of losing out. The trick was to get him to accept defeat, and if possible, allow him some dignified retreat.

The elevator arrived. The descent to the lobby was uninterrupted. Bryce spotted Marsden near the reception desk but proceeded there without giving any sign of recognition. They had never personally met and Bryce had no intention of displaying any knowledge of him. He directed an inquiring gaze to the clerk who had handled his check-in.

Marsden stepped forward before an introduction was made. 'Mr. Templar,' he called aggressively.

Bryce paused, raising a challenging eyebrow at the man accosting him. His suit was crumpled, his eyes bloodshot, and he was clearly the worse for having imbibed too much alcohol. Possibly a belligerent drunk.

'I'm Derek Marsden,' he announced. 'Of the Sydney branch of Templar Resources.'

'Indeed?' Bryce returned frostily. 'I understand you're causing a problem here. What concern do you have?'

He rocked back on his heels, glaring at Bryce. 'I want to see Sunny.' His hand lifted, pointing an accusing finger. 'I know she's here. I know she's with you. And you have no right to stop me from seeing her. She's my fiancée.'

'Miss York is certainly with me,' Bryce acknowledged. 'We are negotiating her transfer to a new position in Los Angeles. As to her being your fiancée, Miss York has declared herself free of commitments and she is certainly not wearing an engagement ring.'

He flushed. 'We had an argument. She took it off. That's what I want to see her about. Fix it all up again.'

'Then I'd be obliged if you'd try doing so in your own time, Marsden. Not mine. This is a business meeting and you are interrupting without invitation.'

'So what is her luggage doing here if it's business?' he jeered, turning nasty.

'It was brought here at Miss York's request,' Bryce replied, keeping a cool calm. 'I understand she does not wish to return to the conference hotel. Perhaps you are the reason why, Marsden.'

The edge of contempt stung him into defence. 'I just want to talk to her. Get things straight. She's gone off half-cocked if she's discussing a transfer and that won't do *you* any good when she comes to her senses.'

'Miss York has presented herself to me as a free agent and I see no reason to give you the opportunity to harrass her. She is at liberty to contact you if she so wishes. Now if you'll excuse me...'

Bryce started to turn away.

'She's mine!' came the seething claim as Marsden grabbed him by the arm.

Bryce squared his shoulders and cast a quailing

look at the slighter man. 'You work for Templar Resources, Marsden?' he said quietly, threat embodied in every word.

The angry glaze in the bleary blue eyes wavered.

'You are not doing yourself any favours here,' Bryce continued quietly. 'I suggest you return to your hotel, sleep off this...unwise burst of aggression...and catch your flight back to Sydney in the morning...where you may still have a job.'

The hand dropped away.

Marsden stood slack-jawed, not having foreseen these consequences.

Bryce had no compunction whatsoever in using the power of his position to get this man out of Sunny's life. He signalled the concierge who instantly hurried over. 'Please get Mr. Marsden a taxi and see him into it,' he instructed and nodded towards a couple of security guards who could assist if necessary. 'Put the fare on my tab.'

'I'll pay for it myself,' Marsden blurted out in fierce resentment.

Bryce subjected him to one more icy look. 'As you wish. Goodnight, Marsden. I hope you have a safe trip home.'

He shouldered past the concierge and marched off towards the exit doors. Bryce watched him out, not quite sure he'd read the man correctly. Australians had a reputation for bucking authority, going their own way. Still, he'd given Marsden something to think about and he hoped it was enough to make him realise there was no chance of a reconciliation with Sunny.

He moved over to the clerk he'd dealt with at the reception desk. 'The bellhop can bring up Miss York's luggage now. If there's any more trouble from Mr. Marsden, let me know.'

'Certainly, Mr. Templar.'

He shared the elevator with the bellhop. Sunny's luggage comprised a medium-sized suitcase and a standard carry-on, obviously an economic travelling wardrobe, enough to suit what was required for a conference with its various functions, but not enough for a prolonged stay. Some shopping would need to be done.

He dismissed the bellhop at the door to the suite, carrying in the luggage himself. Seeing no sign of Sunny in the living room, he took the bags upstairs, expecting to find her there. She was not in the bedroom. Nor the bathroom. The yellow suit was gone from where it had been dropped on the floor. So were her other garments.

Bryce stared at the empty space that was no longer littered with her clothes. Unfamiliar feelings—fear, panic, an intolerable sense of loss—started screwing him up inside. His mind literally jammed over the thought she had gone…left him…was even now on her way back to Derek Marsden. He should not have given her any time alone to reconsider what she was doing.

Or maybe he was jumping the gun.

He hadn't searched the entire penthouse.

With his heart pounding harder than if he'd run a marathon, Bryce made a fast sweep through the other

upstairs rooms. Nothing! No sign of her presence anywhere!

'Sunny!' he roared as he reached the staircase and
started down it.

'Yes?'

He stopped dead, his head swivelling to her voice.
She was there, standing in the opened doorway to the
outside patio. Her hair spilled in glorious disarray
around the huge collar of an oversized white bathrobe. She hadn't dressed. Her feet were bare.

For several moments they stared at each other. It
hit Bryce that she looked very vulnerable, caught in
a time-warp between the past and the future, not
knowing quite where she was or what she was doing
here. He was her only focus right now.

Was he being fair to her?

Would she take Marsden back if the guy cleaned
up his act and grovelled enough?

'Is everything all right?' she asked, seeking guid-
ance.

'Yes,' he asserted, determination sweeping back.
He'd be a better husband for her than Marsden.
'Everything settled,' he assured her, walking down
the rest of the stairs. 'I took your bags up. They came
when I was in the lobby.'

'Thank you.' She looked discomforted by that information, half turning back to the patio as she added,
'I was out looking at the view. All the neon lights
along *The Strip*...'

'You're the best sight of all, Sunny,' he said
warmly, crossing the living room to reach her. 'I was

just thinking how much I'd like to come home to you every night. Exactly like this.'

Her gaze veered back to his and he caught the sense she wanted to believe him, but was uncertain of filling that role. He smiled, wanting to convince her of his pleasure in her. It was no lie.

'Did you get onto room service and order our dinner?'

She smiled back. 'I did. And I hope you're really hungry, Bryce.'

'I am.'

For you.

And that was no lie, either.

He drew her into his embrace. Her eyes were liquid amber, silently, eloquently asking if this was right, or was she hopelessly astray in being here with him.

He kissed her to burn away the doubt.

There was no doubt in his mind.

He wanted her as his wife and she was going to be his wife. Whatever he had to do to win her, he'd do.

CHAPTER SEVEN

SUNNY woke slowly, savouring the sense of a warm delicious languor…before she remembered why her body felt so replete and relaxed. A little electric jolt went through her brain. She sucked in a deep breath and carefully, quietly turned her head.

Her breath whooshed out on a relieved sigh. She didn't have to face him yet. The rest of the bed was empty. He'd obviously wakened before her and left her to sleep on. She resettled herself and started thinking.

Bryce Templar…

Her hand drifted over her naked body…remembering. He was certainly a fantastic lover. She closed her eyes, recapturing the incredible sensations in her mind, the power of them, the intensity of the pleasure that had rolled on and on through so much of the night.

What time was it?

Her head jerked up, eyes flying open again. The clock-radio on the bedside table read 9:14. The flight she should have been on from Las Vegas to Los Angeles had already left. Panic galloped through her heart, stirring up the enormity of what she had done…cutting herself off from all she had known…Derek…

She struggled to get a grip on herself. It wasn't all

71

irreversible. She could still go home if she wanted to. Bryce had promised that decision was hers anytime she chose. As for Derek...

She dropped her head back onto the pillow. Unaccountably tears pricked her eyes. Derek hadn't even tried to change her mind when she'd handed him back her ring. All those months of planning to marry...and they'd had many good times together. Her family had liked him. She had really believed they would make a good marriage together.

But he hadn't even tried to get her back.

He could have tracked her to the MGM hotel if he'd wanted to. Gambling had obviously meant more to him than she did. And always would, now that he'd caught the bug for it, Sunny savagely reasoned. Her chin set with determination. She would not mourn his passing out of her life.

Which left her with...Bryce Templar.

And his proposal of marriage.

She heaved a huge sigh. He was definitely a marvellous lover but she couldn't marry him on that basis alone, however tempting it might be. As it was, plunging into this intimacy with him was probably going to complicate any career decisions she made. Nothing was clear-cut anymore.

But...he certainly made her feel good about herself. For him to desire her so much...to want her as his wife... It was quite mind-boggling.

How could *he* make up his mind so fast? Wasn't he taking a big risk in committing himself to a marriage with a woman he'd only known for a day? Not even a full day! Surely a man in his position should take more care in choosing a life partner.

Not that there was anything wrong with her, Sunny quickly reasoned, but how could he know that? On such short acquaintance? Was he so confident of reading her character correctly? Maybe that was a skill CEOs had to have—choosing the right people for the right positions.

Deciding that lying here by herself wouldn't give her any answers, Sunny rolled out of bed and headed for the bathroom. She took a quick shower, all the time wondering what Bryce was doing downstairs—reading the newspaper, making business calls, having breakfast, *waiting for her?*

Grateful to have her own toiletries, she brushed her teeth, applied a light make-up, and did what she could to get her hair in reasonable order without taking too much time with it. She hesitated over dressing, not knowing what plans Bryce might have. Easier just to wrap herself in the bathrobe until some decisions were made.

She heard Bryce speaking to someone as she started down the stairs and paused, not wanting to interrupt anything important.

'Just do your best to keep the cost to a minimum.'

It was a terse command, showing impatience with the caller.

'No, I won't change my mind.'

Even more terse. Whoever was on the phone to him was stirring Bryce's ire and whatever was put to him now evoked an icy reply.

'Understand me very clearly, Sherman. It's finished. We simply write this off. No more negotiation. Nothing—absolutely nothing—will get me to reconsider this decision. Now you take it from there, knowing my position on this is irreversible.'

The cut-off click created a pool of silence that seemed to echo with the ruthlessness with which Bryce had ended the deal that had been in negotiation. Someone had pushed too far, Sunny thought. All the same, it was an insight into the character of the man. He wielded command with an iron fist when the occasion demanded it.

She couldn't imagine him ever being seduced by gambling. He would make a limit and stick to it. Yet he was gambling on her with his proposal of marriage, wasn't he? Perhaps that, too, had a limit. He'd give so much time to her, then...

Shaking off the thought which only time could prove right or wrong, Sunny proceeded down the stairs. Bryce was pacing back and forth across the living room, a frown of deep concentration on his face. Then, either hearing her soft footsteps or sensing her presence, he stopped, his face clearing as his gaze zeroed in on her.

'Ah! Some morning sunshine!' he said warmly. 'You slept well?'

'Very well.' He was wearing his bathrobe, too, so Sunny didn't feel uncomfortable about not being dressed. 'Have you been up long?'

He shrugged. 'There were a few things I wanted to get out of the way so I could concentrate entirely on you.'

His eyes were eating her up and Sunny's heart was

doing cartwheels. It was so incredibly flattering to be desired by him, and she couldn't help remembering how magnificent he was, under that bathrobe.

'All done?' she asked, trying to sound matter-of-fact.

'All done.' He grinned as he swept her into his embrace, his eyes teasing her caution. 'So here it is—the next morning—and I still want to marry you, Sunny York.'

'Mmm…have you had breakfast?'

He laughed. 'I was waiting for you.' His mouth grazed over hers with tantalising sensuality. 'And you taste so good,' he murmured.

'Food is good, too,' she choked out, struggling to keep her mind clear of the seductive web he was weaving again.

'Then we shall order breakfast right now.'

Everything she wanted, when she wanted it… It was terribly difficult to keep her head on straight around Bryce. He swamped her with such tempting attractions, most of all himself.

Over a sumptuous breakfast, she finally managed to focus on addressing the question of business. 'We haven't settled on the kind of position you're offering me, Bryce.'

'First and foremost, the position of my wife,' he answered, his eyes unmistakably reflecting very determined purpose.

Sunny's heart skipped a beat. 'What if I say no to that?'

'You haven't said no yet. Until you do, Sunny, I'll

be doing everything within my power to persuade you to say yes.'

She could feel his power winding around her and wondered if it would prove irresistible in the end. 'I really don't know much about you, Bryce,' she stated defensively.

'What do you need to know?'

His heart, she thought, then doubted her own ability to judge that, given her terrible misreading of Derek's heart. Needing to start somewhere, she said, 'Well, I know you have a father. What about the rest of your family?'

'My mother died when I was three. I was her only child.'

No wonder he'd counted so much on his father being there for him! 'I'm sorry. That must have been hard…to be left without a mother,' she said with sincere sympathy.

His mouth twisted with irony. 'Oh, my father kept trying to provide me with mothers. He married four more times, resulting in four divorces. I have a half-brother and two half-sisters, but their respective mothers took their children with them. I was…am…the only constant in my father's life as far as family is concerned. We are…very attached to each other.'

'I see,' she murmured, thinking his father hadn't exactly set an example on how to make a marriage work.

'Do you see that I don't want an easy-come, easy-go marriage?' he countered as though he could read her thoughts. 'That I want a wife who is as committed to me and our children, as I would be to her?' he pressed on. 'Parents together, Sunny. A stable home.'

All that he felt he hadn't had himself? It was strong motivation, but was motivation enough when faced with a clash of needs? Sunny suspected Bryce was very used to getting his own way on most things.

His eyes glittered knowingly as he added, 'You've come from a stable home, haven't you? It means something to you.'

'Yes. It's why I don't want to rush into such a serious step as marriage.'

'What reservations do you have about me?'

Sunny frowned, not having any criticisms to make except... 'I don't understand why you're so keen, so quickly.'

Her eyes flicked to his in sharp challenge, determined on getting a reply that satisfied her sense of reality—a reality that was not wrapped in hothouse passion or persuasive patter.

He leaned back in his chair but it was not a move that held relaxation, more putting a weighing distance between them as he considered what answer to give her. She could almost feel the wheels clicking around in his mind, and there was no mistaking the tension emanating from him as he came to a decision.

'I'll tell you why, Sunny,' he said quietly, and she tensed, every intuitive instinct telling her that something important was about to be revealed, and he was counting on her understanding, counting on a positive response from her, as well.

'My father has a heart condition. Every day he lives is a medical miracle. For some time he has been agitating for me to marry, have a child. I know this is a symptom of his own rather immediate sense of his mortality, but it is his dearest wish and I would like to give him that sense of our bloodline going on before he dies.'

A bloodline! It sounded almost Medieval. Like feudal lords securing a succession. 'You want to marry me for your father's sake?' she asked incredulously.

'No. I could have married any number of women for my father's sake. I am considered…' His mouth took on a cynical curl. '…very eligible in the marriage stakes.'

Sunny did not doubt that truth.

'But I didn't want just any woman as my wife, Sunny. I wanted a woman who felt right to me. A true partner on many levels.' His eyes blazed with conviction. 'Every instinct I have is shouting that I've found her in you.'

Her heart jiggled with an intemperate burst of joy. It took a tremendous effort to override the wild response and keep boring in on her misgivings. 'You trust your instincts so much?'

'In every aspect, you shine with rightness. No other woman ever has. Not to me.'

'Then I'll still be right to you in a month's time,' she argued.

'And my father might be dead in a month's time.'

It was softly said, yet it hit Sunny hard, making her remember her own father's death. He'd been a volunteer fire-fighter, supervising a burn-off. The wind changed unexpectedly, trapping him and two others. No goodbyes. No chance to tell him how much he'd given her and what it had meant. Not even a few moments to show him she loved him.

Bryce leaned across the table and took her hand in his, pressing his sense of urgency, his *caring*. 'I want to marry you now, Sunny. Today. And present you to my father as my wife for him to see what I see...so he won't fret about the future anymore.'

What she saw was how much it meant to him to answer his father's need, and she remembered him saying his father had always *been there for him*.

She understood the urgency he felt, and was moved by his reasoning, honoured that he had chosen her to be the wife he took home to his father, yet she could not get over the uneasy sense of being an instrument to resolve a situation, rather than a woman who was loved for herself.

It was difficult, knowing where Bryce was coming from, to set his proposal aside. The impulse to give him what he wanted was strong. She'd always wanted a marriage based on the kind of values she believed in, and in a way, Bryce *was* offering that—solid family values—yet...

'I'm sorry. I...I need to think about this.' Her eyes eloquently pleaded his patience. 'I can't do it today, Bryce. I can't just...walk straight into it.'

He brushed his thumb over the back of her hand, as though wishing—willing—to get under her skin. 'What's troubling you most, Sunny?' he asked quietly, his eyes meeting her plea with a caring concern that stirred more emotional confusion.

She shook her head, thinking she was probably being a fool, putting what had proved to be an illusion with Derek over the substance Bryce probably represented.

'Tell me,' he softly pressed.

'I always thought I'd get married for love,' she blurted out. 'Not…not for convenience.'

'Convenience,' he repeated with a harsh edge, frowning over the accusation implied in it. 'If I'd wanted convenience…' He bit off the thought, shaking his head. His gaze flashed to hers, searing in its intensity. 'I swear to you this marriage is not a convenience to me, Sunny. I want you. I want you in my life. How can I make that more clear to you?'

'It's too fast!' she cried. 'It's just too fast!' She pulled away from him, pushing up from the table in her agitation, gesturing a helpless apology. 'You've made it clear and I…I know this must be frustrating to you, but…I need time to feel sure I'm doing the right thing for me, too. I'm sorry…'

'It's okay,' he quickly assured her, rising from the table and holding out his hands in an open gesture of giving. 'I didn't mean to make you feel pressured. I guess my own decision is so clear-cut to me…' He grimaced an apology. 'I'm not about to force you into marriage, Sunny. It has to be your choice, too, and if you're not ready to make it…'

'I'm not. Not yet,' she quickly added, acutely aware she didn't want to shut the door on his proposal, however many doubts were clouding it for her.

'Then we'll make other plans for today,' he offered, smiling to soothe her agitation. 'Simply spend time together. Are you happy to go along with that?'

She nodded, her chest feeling too constricted to

find breath for more words. He was the most stunningly attractive man she'd ever met and one side of her was clamouring it was madness not to accept him on face value alone. Only the painful thud in her heart argued that *want* wasn't love, and she craved real love from the man she married—the kind of love that lasted a lifetime.

'Have you seen the Grand Canyon?'

'No,' she whispered shakily.

'Would you enjoy a ground/air combination tour—a helicopter flight, as well as travelling around the rim by road, hiking where you want to?'

Sunny scooped in a quick breath. 'Yes. I'd like that very much.' Outside distraction…more time…

'Shall I book it for an hour's time? Can you be ready to go that soon?'

She nodded, grateful to seize on quick action. 'It won't take me long to get dressed. I'll start now.'

Eager to be on the move, she was already heading for the staircase when he paused her with the words…

'One last thing, Sunny…'

'Yes?'

He had stepped over to the telephone table and had picked up the receiver to make the booking. His head was cocked quizzically and she was anticipating a further question about the trip they had agreed upon.

'You said…*married for love.* What, in your mind, is love?'

Her mind went completely blank, then tripped into a welter of needs that Derek's defection had wounded, very badly. Out of the miserable emptiness of bitter disillusionment came the one thing love had most represented to her, and precisely what Derek had torn away.

'Emotional security,' she said, with all the passion of having been stripped of it.

'I see,' he murmured, as though weighing her answer against what he could balance it with.

'What is love to you, Bryce?' she shot at him, wanting him to feel some of the vulnerability he had stirred with his question, though she couldn't really imagine him feeling insecure about anything.

He seemed to consider his answer carefully before giving it, perhaps gearing it to her own. She didn't want that. She intinctively shied from thinking he would pursue his purpose relentlessly, calculating every word, every move.

'I think it's something that grows,' he said slowly, his eyes holding hers with hypnotic intensity. 'It begins with strong mutual attraction, and is fed by the caring each person demonstrates towards the other. It's a commitment to caring, and without that commitment it dies a quick death.'

Derek, she thought, not caring enough for her.

While Bryce…how much did he care? His answer sounded genuine, a deeply held personal belief, not a reply designed to win her over.

His mouth quirked into an appealing little smile. 'A fair assessment?'

'Fair enough,' she agreed. 'I'll think about it.'

He nodded and turned away to make telephone contact for the tour booking.

He cared a lot about his father, Sunny thought, and

as she continued on upstairs, she decided he would
care a lot about any child he fathered, too.

But how much for her?

Would love grow between them?

Could she take that gamble?

CHAPTER EIGHT

BRYCE clamped down on his impatience. Rushing
Sunny was not going to work. Marsden had obviously
caused too much emotional damage for her to trust
easily. Yet he was quite certain her instincts sided
with him. She would never have responded as she had
without feeling the same deep attraction he felt.

Or was it rebound stuff—an overwhelming need to
be desired?

That was one need he could certainly answer. Desire was simmering through him right now as they
waited for the arrival of the elevator to take them
down to the limousine which would transport them to
the helicopter base. The stretch jeans and T-shirt
Sunny had pulled on showed every delectable line and
curve of her. She'd crammed one of the conference
caps over her rioting curls, and it, too, seemed provocative on her, like a perky invitation to whip it off
and free her hair.

Free everything!

The elevator doors slid open. Sunny glanced nervously at him as she stepped into the empty compartment. Bryce's chest tightened as he followed and
hit the control panel for the ground floor. What good
was restraint? Pouncing on her the last time they had
been in this elevator together had propelled them into

an intimacy that was working for him. Why should he hold back now?

The doors closed.

Driven once more by the urge to claim her as his, Bryce reached out and wrapped her in his embrace. Her lovely amber eyes lit with alarm. 'No pressure,' he gruffly promised, lifting a hand to gently stroke the tension from her face. 'I just have a need to feel you with me.'

The amber softened into a golden glow as he bent his head to kiss her and there was no hint of resistance when his mouth touched hers. The hands that had rested warily on his shoulders, slid quickly to link around his neck, an eager signal of her desire to feel him with her, too.

It was more than enough to push Bryce into seeking all she would give him and her active response as he deepened the kiss instantly ignited a passionate drive to break the emotional barriers in her mind, to draw all her feelings towards him with such dominant force, nothing else existed for her but the two of them together.

He pressed her closer, exulting in the long, feminine legs clinging to his, the soft fullness of her breasts spreading across the hard muscle of his chest, the whole delicious pliancy of her body as it seemed to crave every contact with his. He was so strongly aroused, so exhilarated by the fervour of her response, he wasn't aware of the elevator having come to a halt at ground level.

The whirr of the doors opening did belatedly register in his consciousness, but by the time he'd lifted his mouth from Sunny's, the doors were closing again, which was fine by him. He didn't want to stop what he was doing. They could ride straight back up to his suite and…

'Bryce…' An urgent gasp.

'Mmm?'

'We're down!'

He sighed, swiftly deciding he had regained some ground with her and playing for more might be a bad idea. He swung aside, reached out and pressed the Open Doors button just as the elevator was being sealed shut again.

Her hands dropped from his neck as she turned to face the exit, but she made no move to distance herself from the arm he'd left around her waist. They stepped out to the lobby together, which was a far more satisfying situation to Bryce than the apartness she'd been subtly maintaining since their breakfast conversation. It was clear he had to keep stoking this very mutual desire and sweeping her along with him until she accepted he was the man for her.

'You slut!'

The ugly words sliced through Bryce's pleasurable mission-plan, and the sight of Derek Marsden advancing on them switched his mind to red alert! Beside him he felt Sunny's whole body jerk with shock and her feet came to an abrupt halt, which halted him, as well, since no way was he about to let go of her.

'Derek?'

The name spilled from Sunny's lips, even as her mind recoiled from the horrible name he had called her. The shock of seeing him was stunning enough, having expected him to fly out on the plane to Los Angeles, but to be so insultingly labelled in public...

'Yeah,' he jeered. 'Thought you'd neatly got rid of me, didn't you? Sneaky bitch!'

'That's more than enough!' Bryce rapped out in a steely voice.

Sunny felt the surge of aggressive tension whipping through him, his hand on her waist gripping harder, pulling her protectively closer.

'She's taking you for a ride, Templar,' Derek threw at him, his eyes shooting daggers. 'Want to see the ring she gave back to me yesterday so she could go after you?'

'That's not true, Derek!' Sunny cried, appalled by this attack on her integrity.

He ignored her, plucking the engagement ring out of his shirt pocket, holding it in his clenched fist with the diamond pointing at Bryce, shaking it at him as he poured out more venom. 'No doubt you can buy one bigger than this.'

'That has nothing to do with why I broke with you, Derek, and you know it!' Sunny fiercely protested.

He turned on her in vicious accusation. 'You left me and went straight off with him.'

Sunny shook her head, bewildered by the totally unfair interpretation of the situation.

'At my instigation,' Bryce sliced in. 'You are mistaken. It was I who approached Miss York, not the other way around.'

'Miss York...huh!' Derek snorted derisively.

'Think I didn't see you in a clinch in the elevator just now?'

'I have asked her to marry me,' Bryce stated with icy dignity.

'*Marry* you?' Sheer fury twisted Derek's face. 'Well, let me tell you she was marrying *me* this time yesterday.' His eyes blazed at Sunny. 'What did you do? Give him the eye all the time you were sitting in the front row of the conference room?'

'No! I didn't do anything!' she cried, flushing with the guilt of having nursed lustful thoughts. But only in a fantasy way, not aimed to draw Bryce's attention to her.

'Like hell you didn't!' came the bitter rebuttal. 'You got your eye on the main chance and goodbye Derek.'

The sheer injustice of his slurs on her character whipped up Sunny's fury. 'It was goodbye Derek because all you could think about was gambling!'

'Well, it's you who's gambling now, you scheming little gold-digger! And I hope Templar sees you for what you are before he's fool enough to marry you.'

'I am not a gold-digger! It's you who wanted easy money.'

'At least I earn what I spend. I don't trade in sex for it.'

'Oh! Oh!' Sunny gasped, reduced to speechlessness.

'That is too offensive!' Bryce growled, his whole body clenching, ready to spring.

But it wasn't his fight, Sunny thought frantically. It was hers. And she had to fight back.

'Offensive!' Derek hurled at Bryce, too aroused to be intimidated. 'I track her here and discover there's no room in the name of Sunny York. She spent the night with you, sleeping her way to the top. That's *offensive.*'

'You're right!' Sunny snapped, leaping in to defend herself. 'I did sleep with him. *He* found me more attractive than a roulette wheel.'

'Well, you just keep spinning for him. I don't want a whore as my wife.'

'You insult Sunny once more and I'll ram the words down your throat,' Bryce bit out, violence shimmering in the air.

'No!' Sunny instantly swung towards him, slamming a hand on his chest, desperate to prevent any movement towards Derek who was shaping up to slug it out.

Fists wouldn't resolve anything. It would only make the whole scene uglier and more public than it already was.

She glared at her ex-fiancé over her shoulder. 'We have nothing more to say to each other. Please go, Derek.'

He glowered at Bryce to prove he wasn't intimidated, then sliced a look of contempt at Sunny. 'Screw you! I'll have plenty to say to everyone else about why you ditched me.'

'You keep your filthy mouth shut or I'll shut it for you,' Bryce threatened, his chest swelling against Sunny's hand.

'You don't have that much power, sucker!' Derek challenged, and on that jeering note, turned his back on both of them and strutted off as though he was cock-of-the-walk.

'Don't do anything, Bryce,' Sunny pleaded, frightened by the aggressive jut of his chin and the fighting strength that was teetering on the edge of exploding.

His gaze lowered reluctantly to hers, eyes glittering. 'You want me to let him get away with that slimy slander?' he demanded, rage clipping every word.

'It's true I broke my engagement to him yesterday,' she said, trying to excuse some of the offence.

'And none too soon,' Bryce ground out. 'There was no *love* for you in that outburst, Sunny.'

No…no love…just wounded ego and vile nastiness. Her stomach felt sick with it. 'Did you believe…' She anxiously scanned the glittering green eyes. 'Did you believe anything of what he said about me?'

The question brought a beetling frown. 'You know I don't. How could I? I've been with you every step we've taken together.'

But her staying with him as she had *was* open to misinterpretation. 'You don't think I'm a…a gold-digger? Out for what I can get?'

'Not you, Sunny,' he declared with ringing certainty.

She felt intensely grateful for his belief in her. Into her distressed mind flashed the image of Bryce always standing by her, ready to defend, to protect, caring with the kind of strength Derek had never had.

'Do you still want to marry me?' she asked.

'You think *he* could change what I feel?' came the incredulous challenge.

'No. Not you,' she answered, somehow knowing that very deeply. Bryce Templar trod his own path, and suddenly she wanted very much to share that path with him. It looked safe. It looked secure.

He cupped her face in his hands, commanding her full attention as his eyes blazed into hers. 'I want you, Sunny York. I'd marry you right this minute if I could.'

The warmth of his skin took away the dead coldness left by Derek's emotional kicks in the face. Bryce's desire for her sizzled into her bloodstream, bringing a vibrancy that re-energised her whole body.

'Then I will...I will marry you, Bryce,' she heard herself say, as though the words were drawn from a place she was barely conscious of, yet she knew even as she said them, she wouldn't take them back.

Bryce knew instantly it was a rebound decision. Her eyes were focused on him but they had a calm, almost distant expression in them, not one sparkle of happiness or even warm pleasure in the thought of being his wife. He should have felt an exhilarating zing of triumph, having achieved his goal so quickly, but the achievement wasn't his. It was Marsden's. Nevertheless, the prize was there to take, and Bryce was not about to let it slip away.

'Today?' he pressed.

'Yes.' Her mouth quivered into a challenging little smile. 'Right this minute if you like.'

He grinned, determined on being cheerful. 'We do have to get a wedding licence first.'

'Is that a problem?'

'A quick trip to the courthouse. No problem at all.'

'Then let's do it.'

As simple as that! Except Bryce was acutely aware of the complex undercurrents to this apparent simplicity. As he linked Sunny's arm around his and steered her out of the hotel to the waiting limousine, he asked himself if it was wise to take advantage of a decision she may well think better of, given a few hours' distance from Marsden's backlash.

Which reminded him that Marsden had to be dealt with before he caused more damage. He'd call Sherman as soon as he had a free minute. His crafty lawyer could speak to Marsden in L.A., pound home enough unpleasant legalities to demonstrate that silence held the greater good.

'Mr. Templar and Miss York,' the chauffeur greeted them affably, holding the passenger door open. 'Lovely day for a trip to the Grand Canyon.'

Bryce paused, hit by an unaccustomed sense of wrongness. It was a rare moment of indecision for him, yet this choice did involve Sunny very intimately and he did not want her to be unhappy as his wife. He lightly squeezed the hand resting passively on his arm, drawing her gaze to his and watching intently for any hesitation on her part.

'Are you sure about marrying me, Sunny?'

'Yes, I'm sure,' she stated decisively.

'You don't want to go to the Grand Canyon and take some time to think it over?'

'No.' Her chin was set in determination. 'I want to marry you today.' Her eyes sparked into vehement life. 'If it's right for you, it's right for me!'

It snapped Bryce straight into positive action. He turned to the chauffeur. 'Use your car phone to cancel the tour and take us straight to the courthouse.'

'Yes, sir.'

Bryce handed Sunny into the limousine and followed to settle beside her.

'The courthouse,' the chauffeur repeated, grinning happily at the change of plan as he closed the door.

It has to be right, Bryce fiercely told himself, taking Sunny's hand and lacing their fingers in a grip of togetherness.

I'll make it right.

CHAPTER NINE

SUNNY was amazed how easy it was to get a wedding licence. All she had to do was produce her passport, fill out a form and sign her name. No wonder Las Vegas was called the marriage capital of the world, she wryly reflected. Here it was a totally hassle-free procedure—no other certificates required, absolute minimal red tape, no enforced waiting time.

Her mind quickly flitted over that last considera-tion. Waiting was not good in this case. Bryce's father wanted to see him married. Not that Will Templar would actually be at the ceremony, but the *fait ac-compli* would ease his mind and hopefully be bene-ficial to his heart condition. And then…no waiting any longer to have a baby. No more waiting at all.

As they emerged from the courthouse, the licence safely tucked in Sunny's handbag, Bryce took out his cell phone and made a call, asking to speak to a wed-ding consultant. Sunny frowned at him, not wanting any delay, not wanting some hypocritical fuss, either. This was a straight-out marriage of convenience, not a love affair to be celebrated in the traditional way.

'Don't we just go to one of the wedding chapels?' she said bruskly, much preferring to get it over and done with.

He shook his head, determination flashing from his

eyes as he answered, 'We do it right. Down to every detail.'

Sunny listened incredulously as he spoke to the consultant, listing off the kind of detail she would have thought important...if she'd gone ahead and married Derek. But that would have taken months of planning and scheduling and decision-making— chapel, flowers, kind of ceremony, photographer. Bryce was taking it upon himself to organise the whole wedding deal in a matter of minutes, *without even consulting her!*

Sunny burned with resentment. Wasn't her consent enough for him? Why did he have to make a production out of a wedding based on mutual purpose?

Having completed the call to his satisfaction, he put the phone away, tucked her arm around his and grinned, clearly delighted with his planning. 'Next stop,' he said, hurrying her towards the waiting limousine.

'What stop?' she demanded to know, beginning to feel truculent.

He addressed the chauffeur who was once again holding the door open for them. 'The Top of the Town Bridal Boutique.'

'A bridal boutique!' Sunny gasped.

Bryce bundled her into the limousine, still grinning from ear to ear. 'Going to get you the wedding dress of your dreams.'

'It's not necessary,' she gritted out, rebellion stirring.

'Yes, it is.'

'There's just the two of us getting married,' she

argued, turning to face him, to hammer home the truth as she saw it. 'It's not as if we're doing it in front of a whole pile of guests.'

It wiped the grin off his face. With a far more serious expression, he quietly asked, 'Aren't we the most important two, Sunny?'

Somehow that point steadied the angry whirl of protest in her mind. 'Yes, we are,' she conceded, though this was not the wedding of her dreams and she didn't want to pretend it was.

'Do you want to look back on our wedding and think of it as some hole-and-corner ceremony?'

She frowned, not having thought of what they were doing in *those terms.* 'It…it means the same,' she argued, still feeling out of step with his grand plan.

His green eyes seemed to glow like emerald fire as he softly said, 'I want my bride feeling beautiful, and knowing she is beautiful to me.'

Sunny's heart turned over.

'And I want you to be proud of the photos of our wedding when you show them to our children—their mother and father on the day they were married.'

Their children? They swirled in the mists of Sunny's imagination—a little boy and girl, examining their parents' wedding photos.

'We owe it to ourselves and them to do it right, Sunny,' Bryce pressed.

She hadn't been looking ahead. The blind need for positive action had seized her, and nothing else had really entered the equation. Selfishly blind, Sunny suddenly realised. This was Bryce's wedding, too.

And the intent of their marriage was to have a child...children.

As he said, love could grow out of caring for each other. He wanted her to feel like a beautiful bride, and why shouldn't she? She would have wanted that with Derek, and Bryce was better husband material than Derek had ever been.

She could send a wedding photo to her family. That would make her marriage to Bryce more right for them, as well. And shift any nasty cracks from Derek into the sour grapes category. A *fait accompli* would certainly help to put a stop to criticism.

'Okay. We'll go for all the trimmings,' she agreed, glad now that he had thought of them for her. 'But I pay for my own wedding gown, Bryce.'

He laughed. 'One last stroke of independence?'

It was more a matter of pride. 'I'm not coming to you on a free ride.'

He instantly sobered, his eyes flashing darkly. 'Wipe that guy and everything he said out of your mind, Sunny. This is our day. I know what you're worth to me and in that context, counting money is meaningless. I'm not buying you.'

Shame wormed around inside her, raising a flood of heat to her cheeks. 'I'm sorry, Bryce. I...I guess that really stung me.'

'Let it go,' he advised quietly. 'Don't let it spoil what we can have together.'

'I won't,' she promised fervently, her eyes begging his forgiveness. It was Derek who had humiliated her, not this man. Bryce made her feel good about herself.

He smiled, chasing the painful shadows of Derek away.

She smiled back, determined that she *would* feel beautiful as his bride. And she wouldn't count the cost of anything because that was how Bryce wanted it. Pleasing her husband-to-be was important.

When they arrived at the bridal boutique, he instantly commandeered a saleslady, instructing her to show Miss York the very best stock she had, and he expected to see the selection of gowns paraded in front of him so he could judge for himself which one most suited her very unique style of beauty. He then settled himself on a white satin sofa and waved them on to the business of looking at what was available.

'Now there is a guy I could really take to,' the saleslady remarked to Sunny, rolling her eyes in maxi-appreciation. 'You sure have won yourself a prize in him.'

'Yes. Yes, I have,' Sunny agreed, determined to believe it.

'Hmm...' The woman eyed her up and down. 'With your height and legs, we certainly don't want a crinoline-style skirt. Too much. Slim and elegant with a fabulous train, I'd say. Shall we start with that?'

Sunny nodded. 'Sounds good.'

'Perhaps something off the shoulder to frame that gorgeous mass of hair.'

Sunny barely stopped herself from rolling her own eyes at this description of her unruly mop. Reminding herself that Bryce liked her hair, just as it was, she simply said, 'Let's see.'

Maybe because it all seemed rather unreal, it was actually fun, parading the gowns for Bryce, striking poses for his studied opinion. His running commentary on the detail of everything made her laugh and he scored each showing out of ten. Oddly enough, his scores matched her own judgment, demonstrating like minds, which also helped to push any misgivings about her decision aside.

The fifth gown, however, brought the sense of fun to an abrupt halt. It wasn't exactly a *traditional* bridal dress, not silk nor satin nor even white, and it didn't have a train, either. But Sunny loved it and to her eye it looked perfect on her, nothing to be fixed or altered. It also made her feel more...*female*...than anything she'd ever worn before.

This time she didn't prance out of the dressing-room to show it off to Bryce. She walked self-consciously, knowing the slinky ankle-length gown in cream garter lace was moulded to her every curve. The long sheer sleeves added an elegant grace and the scooped neckline was just low enough to reveal the uppermost swell of her breasts. The image of a sexy swan floated into her mind and she couldn't help thinking this was how she would have wanted to look—to feel—if she was marrying for love.

Bryce was not alone on the sofa. Another man had joined him, apparently showing off the contents of an attaché case. They both turned to look at her. Bryce's face instantly lit up with pleasure.

'That one!' he said, almost on a note of awe, his eyes drinking in the whole lovely flow of it on her.

It mightn't be love but the blaze of desire in his

eyes was warming. Sunny slowly twirled around to give him the benefit of every angle, basking in the heat of his approval and the sexual response he stirred in her...needing to take the chill off her heart.

'Ten out of ten?' she asked.

'About ten thousand out of ten!'

'Good! Then I'll buy it.'

'You do that,' he fervently approved. 'But first come and have your finger sized for the wedding ring so our jeweler here can get moving on it.'

A wedding ring! A convulsive little shiver ran down Sunny's spine. This wasn't a game of fantasy dress-ups. They really were doing this...getting married!

It only took a few moments to get her finger sized. Then she was swept into choosing a bouquet from a book of photographs. There were so many pictures, they became a blur to her. When a bridal nosegay was suggested as the ideal accompaniment to her dress—complimenting it rather than distracting from it, Sunny simply let herself be guided.

It was also suggested that a pretty coronet of flowers matching those in the bouquet, would look better than a veil. Sunny instantly agreed. No veil. Somehow a veil was going too far, a mockery of what a wedding should stand for. Not even for her future children would she wear a veil. She simply couldn't bear it...Bryce lifting it off her face as though she were a true bride.

No!

She would pledge herself to him bare-faced.

Let there be at least that honesty between them.

With everything decided upon, delivery to the hotel was promised within the hour.

Back at the hotel, Bryce had lined up a hairdresser, a beautician and a manicurist to give Sunny every bit of pampering a bride could possibly want. Although the whole process felt more and more like a charade, since it all took place in their suite, it was easy enough to submit to it.

Trays of tempting finger food were brought to her, meant to satisfy any hunger pangs. Champagne was served. Sunny forced herself to nibble a few delicacies since fainting at the altar was hardly a good start to any marriage. The champagne was a good nerve-soother, but she was careful only to sip it occasionally. Being a drunk bride wasn't a good start, either.

The whirl of activity centred on her kept Sunny from thinking too much. She had to make more choices about her fingernails, her hair, her make-up, how the coronet of flowers was to sit. Only when all the preparations had been completed, and a fully dressed and meticulously groomed bride looked back at her from the mirror, did her nerves stage a revolt against any possible soothing. They plunged straight into an agitated tangle.

All the helpers had retired from setting the scene. The show was about to go on, except it wasn't a show. It was real, and the lines she would speak—the vows she would take—would affect the rest of her life.

'You take my breath away.'

Bryce...standing in the doorway...shaking his head as though she were a miracle he couldn't quite believe in. He took her breath away, too, looking utterly superb in a formal grey morning suit, a touch of cream in his silk cravat and a cream boutonniere to match the exquisite little flowers in her bouquet.

'Time for our photo call in the chapel studio,' he said huskily, pushing forward to collect her and take her with him.

Sunny took a deep breath and turned towards him, managing a somewhat shaky smile as she said, 'I'm ready.'

'Not quite.' His smile was a warm caress, driving off the rush of goose bumps on her skin. He took her left hand and slowly slid a magnificent emerald ring onto her third finger. 'I chose this for you. I hope you like it.'

'Bryce...' She could barely choke out his name.

Not a bigger diamond than Derek's. An emerald...and she felt his green eyes burning into her heart, willing her to take it without question, and wear it because it was *his* gift to her, *his* promise which would not be shabbily broken as Derek's had.

She swallowed hard to remove the constricting lump in her throat. 'It's...it's wonderful. Thank you.'

He wrapped his hand around hers and heaved a satisfied sigh. 'Let's go and get married.'

The final act.

Somehow his ring and his hand sealed it for Sunny. The decision was made...the outcome inevitable.

The half-hour photographic session in the chapel studio seemed to pass in a matter of minutes. Bryce was there with her every second, showing his pleasure in her, making her feel beautiful, making her feel…*loved.*

And the brilliance of the ring he'd placed on her finger kept dazzling her whenever she rested her hand on his chest or shoulder or next to her bouquet…a pear-shaped emerald—almost a heart—its vivid green hue emphasised by a border of white diamonds set in yellow gold. She had never seen anything like it…so very special, unique…and he'd chosen it for *her.*

For Bryce to value her so much…*she did want to marry him!*

It felt right.

They moved on to the chapel.

It was decorated with sumptuous floral arrangements.

A pianist sat at a grand piano, playing Celine Dion's song—'I've Finally Found Someone.'

A marriage celebrant smilingly beckoned them forward.

Somehow it didn't matter that the chairs on either side of the aisle were empty. Sunny thought fleetingly of her mother and sisters, but they had had their weddings. This was hers and Bryce's, and it belonged to them, no one else.

The civil ceremony performed was a simple one. There was no sermon, no gushy sentiments. To Sunny, the words seemed all the more meaningful for their straightforward simplicity.

When Bryce spoke his vows, his gaze remained steadfast on hers, and his voice carried a quiet solemnity that seemed to seep into her soul, spreading a sense of peace and dispelling any worries about a future with him.

She spoke hers just as solemnly, meaning every word of her commitment to him and their marriage. It was very real now. There was no going back from this moment. They would go forward together and make the best of whatever life served out to them.

Bryce had bought two gold wedding rings, one for her, one for him. It touched her that he wanted to display the fact that he was married—a bachelor no more—a husband who cared about his commitment to her.

'With this ring, I thee wed...'

He had to take off the emerald ring to slide the gold band into place, but the removal was only momentary. Sunny stared down at the dual rings on her finger, fitting perfectly, brightly shining proof that she now belonged to him.

'I now pronounce you husband and wife.'

Such fateful words...

Sunny poured all her hope for a good future with Bryce into the kiss that followed, and from him flowed a fervent eagerness to get on with it.

The wedding certificate was filled out, placed in a special holder, and given to Sunny—a lasting memento of a momentous day. The pianist was playing 'All The Way' as they thanked the marriage celebrant and the official witnesses.

They turned as a wedded couple to walk back down the aisle, and the words of the song were running through Sunny's mind, echoing what she hoped would prove true. At least she wasn't carrying any false illusions about this marriage. It was a matter of making it right, not expecting it to just turn out that way without having to work at it.

'Where is the Bryce Templar wedding?' a woman's voice shrieked, blowing the music right out of Sunny's ears.

Her step faltered as Bryce squeezed her hand hard, having come to a halt himself. Not only was tension ripping through him but any trace of a benign expression was gone, replaced by grim anger.

'Too late? Just finishing?' the woman's voice shrilled, then broke into furious determination. 'We'll see about that!'

Sunny jerked her gaze from the startling reaction from Bryce, just in time to see the woman burst through the entrance to the chapel, charging at battle pace before coming to a heaving halt at the start of the aisle, her gaze ripping Sunny up and down, then stabbing at Bryce.

'How could you?' she screamed at him.

The wild intrusion and the ear-piercing outrage was a total show-stopper. Sunny could only stare at the woman in a tumult of confusion. Who was she and why was she on the attack?

'How could you do this to me?' the woman demanded fiercely of Bryce, apparently deciding to ignore the bride beside him as though Sunny were nothing.

'Very easily, Kristen,' Bryce answered coldly.

Kristen? He knew her, then? It wasn't some complete madwoman on the loose?

'You ruthless, callous pig!' came the blistering indictment. Her face screwed into vicious fury. 'You'll pay for this!'

'Oh, I expect to,' Bryce drawled, a fine edge of contempt in every word. 'But not as much as I would have paid... *had I married you.*'

CHAPTER TEN

MARRIED!

Bryce had been going to marry *this woman?*

Even as Sunny's mind jammed with shock, her eyes swiftly took in everything there was to take in about his first choice—very, very classy with her polished blond hair falling in smooth perfection to her shoulders and cut to feather inwards from her ears to her throat, a stylishly artful frame for a face that was classic model material.

So was her body, though she wasn't quite as tall, nor as long-legged as Sunny. In fact, she was much better proportioned, her figure looking very sexy in a straw linen wrap-around dress and lots of gold accessories—chain belt, sandals, bag, bangles, necklace— all shouting the kind of money Sunny had never had at her disposal.

Bryce's contemptuous comment had acted like a smack on the face, but the jolt of it only lasted a few seconds. The pent-up fury was unleashed again, propelling the woman forward, her arm upraised to deliver a very physical slap to Bryce's face.

He caught her wrist before violent contact was made, holding it in a vice-like grip. 'Back off, Kristen!' he commanded in his steely voice, lowering her arm and slowly releasing it as he emphatically

107

asserted, 'It's over. I told you it was finished this morning.'

This morning? Sunny glanced sharply at Bryce. Before or after she had agreed to marry him? There was a very disturbing question of integrity here.

He sensed her glance, caught the worry in it, and instantly answered, 'Before you woke up, Sunny.'

Even so, he had gone to bed with her first. Had he been testing her out before giving up Kristen?

'Damn you, Bryce!' his ex-fiancée stormed. 'I would have backed down if you'd given me the chance.'

'No chance.' He released Sunny's hand to put his arm around her shoulders in a very possessive and reassuring hug. 'I now have the wife I want.'

'A bargain basement bride, no doubt,' Kristen jeered, switching her gaze to Sunny, her grey eyes blazing scorn. 'You didn't even have the sense to marry him in the State of California.'

Which totally bewildered Sunny. What did California have to do with getting married?

'I'm sure it's beyond your comprehension, Kristen,' Bryce bit out coldly, 'but Sunny didn't marry me with an eye to a divorce settlement. Nor did she put a price on having a child.'

Money? Was that the currency of marriage in California?

'Then more fool her, with your record of using women as you please. Sucked her right in, did you, Bryce?' Kristen mocked savagely.

Sunny's mind whirled around this hasty marriage in Nevada—all Bryce's doing...except for her consent...which he'd started working for as soon as he'd had sex with her!

'I think women tend to draw from men what they put out themselves,' Bryce commented coldly. 'Users do get used, Kristen. It so happens Sunny is a different breed to you.'

'And such a convenient windfall *for you*,' she flashed back at him. 'Except this cheap move of yours is going to cost you, Bryce. Cost you big!'

A windfall...Derek's blow-up...her hasty consent...

'Go ahead and sue me, Kristen. Buying you out of my life will be worth every cent I have to pay.'

She bared her teeth, hissing, 'I'll take you down for as much as I can.'

'Your demonstration of greed in the prenuptial agreement leaves me in no doubt you'll money-grub as far as you can.'

Sunny's mind boggled over a prenuptial agreement. She'd always thought such things horribly cynical with their implication that the marriage commitment was inevitably a transitory thing and a division of property had to be worked out beforehand. If Bryce had even mentioned one, she would have backed off so fast...yes, she was a different breed. A *convenient windfall?*

'It's a straight breach of promise,' Kristen argued in fierce resentment, again sneering at Sunny as she added, 'throwing me over for her.'

'Oh, I think any judge would find good reason for that,' Bryce drawled, hugging Sunny even closer. 'My wife is such a warm contrast to you, Kristen...'

'I'm a Parrish!' she declared with belligerent arrogance. 'That name *means* something. I'll be listened to, Bryce Templar!'

'Yes, you undoubtedly will be,' he agreed uncaringly. 'The media will gobble up every bit of it as you prove you've been badly done by, revealing your avaricious little soul to the whole world in a public courtroom. You think you'll win their sympathy?'

Angry heat speared across her cheekbones. 'So…you figure you've got all the angles covered so you can cheat me.'

The words were flying so fast and furiously, Sunny was only catching the fact that Kristen was a gold-digger. Big time! Despite the name she set such store by.

'No agreement was reached, Kristen,' Bryce stated bitingly. 'You weren't content with what was offered.'

'What about *this agreement?*' She thrust her left hand up in a clenched fist, showing off the huge diamond ring on her engagement finger. '*It* shows something.'

'Yes. It shows my good will, which you proceeded to flout.'

She tossed her head defiantly. 'Well, don't think you're getting it back!'

'I don't want it back. I don't want anything remotely associated with you. We have nothing left to say to each other.'

'Except through our lawyers!'

'Agreed. Now if you don't mind…'

Sunny was subjected to a scathing look. 'Congratulations! You've got yourself a cold, calculating pig and you're welcome to him!'

Having delivered her best exit line, Kristen Parrish flounced a quick about-turn and strode out of the chapel, her stiff back eloquently denying any wounds whatsoever.

Just like Derek, Sunny couldn't help thinking. Rejection was never a palatable situation, but rejection in favour of someone else...that could definitely bring out the worst in some people.

Both she and Bryce had been badly misled in choosing their first partners for marriage. The question was...had they made the right choice now?

Sunny hoped so. With all her heart she hoped so. Yet she couldn't shake the feeling they had both been driven into this choice by a rebound effect...Bryce seemed to be everything Derek wasn't...and she was a *warm contrast* to Kristen Parrish.

A windfall marriage...

She shivered.

Bryce's arm instantly tightened around her. 'I'm sorry you were subjected to that, Sunny,' he said ruefully. 'My big mistake...'

She sighed, lifting her gaze to his in anxious query. 'Am I a windfall, Bryce?'

'Yes.' His eyes simmered with hot possessiveness. 'The best windfall that's ever come my way and I consider myself the luckiest man alive to have you as my wife, Sunny.'

Instead of Kristen, she thought.

'And I need, very much, to be alone with you,' he added softly.

He drew her with him, out of the chapel, into the elevator, back to their suite, and while Sunny took comfort from his desire for her, she couldn't stop the questions whirling around in her mind.

When had he calculated the difference between her and Kristen?

When had he decided to marry her instead?

And the bottom line—marrying to please his father—was she simply a better candidate? A cheaper candidate? *The bargain basement bride?*

CHAPTER ELEVEN

THE moment they were in their suite with the rest of the world shut out, Bryce turned her into his embrace. Sunny didn't mean to stiffen up, but she couldn't quite feel right, pretending nothing had happened to colour things differently. Her hands pressed nervously against Bryce's chest, holding her bouquet between them, her heart thumping painfully instead of happily.

'It's worrying you, isn't it...all that Kristen said?' Bryce quietly probed.

'Not...not all of it.' She fiddled with his bouton-niere, wishing Kristen hadn't turned up. But there was no joy in hiding her head in the sand, now that she was more aware of circumstances.

'Tell me what's preying on your mind, Sunny. Let me fix it.'

'You didn't tell me about her.'

'She was irrelevant to us.'

No, she wasn't irrelevant, Sunny thought, and such a ruthless wipe-out of a woman he'd planned to marry—without any second chance offered—did not sit well with her. It was too...too uncaring.

'You were still engaged to her until this morning,' she reminded him, shying away from Kristen's ac-cusation of him being a cold, calculating pig, yet cal-culation had to have come into his actions, given his need for a wife and the time pressure involved. To give up Kristen before he had secured Sunny's consent…had he? Had he really?

'Technically I was still engaged to her, yes,' he answered. 'In my heart, no.'

'In your heart, Bryce?' She lifted her eyes to scan his, to see how much he meant by that.

'When I asked you to marry me last night, *you* had completely obliterated any possibility of my ever marrying Kristen. I could never have gone back to her after you, Sunny.'

He looked and sounded genuinely sincere.

His grimace held a wealth of distaste as he added, 'I called Kristen at seven o'clock this morning, making it absolutely clear that everything was ended.'

She frowned, remembering similar words he'd spoken much later. 'I heard you talking on the phone to someone just as I was coming downstairs.'

'My lawyer. He had to be notified.'

'Because of the…the prenuptial agreement?'

'Yes.'

'Why did you do that with her? Was it the only way for you to get a wife and child…to buy them?'

His mouth twisted in a fleeting expression of bitter self-mockery. Then his whole face seemed to harden, his eyes reflecting a deep inner cynicism as he replied, 'Prenuptial agreements are quite common in the States, Sunny, especially since divorce has become a national pastime and a boon to lawyers who are out to get their cut. In a financial sense, such agreements offer both protection and security.'

They weren't common in Australia. Or perhaps

they were amongst the very wealthy. Not having ever moved in those circles, she simply didn't know.

'If that is your practice here, Bryce, why didn't you offer one to me?' she queried, *the bargain basement bride* tag nagging at her sense of self-worth.

He didn't have a ready reply. Sunny had the disturbing impression that the wheels had just fallen off his train. The silence reeked of a massive re-calculation being made. It totally unnerved her. She broke away from him, frightened now of this marriage she had entered into, feeling hopelessly alienated by an attitude of mind she could never be sympathetic to.

She dropped the pretty bridal nosegay onto an arm-chair. The rings he'd placed on her finger glinted up at her, mocking the 'forever' sentiments she'd given them. Her heart bled for the dream he wasn't giving her and she cursed herself for having been so hasty in choosing this man to be her husband.

'Do you want a financial agreement, Sunny?' he asked in a flat, weary tone. 'I'll see to it right now if it will make you feel more secure.'

Secure! That was such a black joke she might have laughed if it had involved anyone but herself. 'No!' she exploded, wheeling on him as a turbulent rush of emotion demanded he at least understand where *she* was coming from. 'I would be the whore Derek said I was if I let myself be bought like that, and don't you dare treat me like one, Bryce Templar.'

He frowned. His hands lifted in appeal. 'I thought...you seemed upset that I hadn't brought it up with you.'

'If you had, I would never have married you,' she shot back at him in towering contempt. 'It's looking for the out before you're even in. It makes a mockery of the commitment that marriage is supposed to stand for. Especially when children are planned. Especially!' she repeated with passionate conviction.

'That's precisely why I didn't bring it up, Sunny,' he declared, his concern clearing.

'Is it?' she hotly challenged. 'Or am I the windfall that won't cost you as much as Kristen Parrish would have? *The bargain basement bride!*'

He flinched.

For one heart-cramping moment, Sunny thought she had hit the nail right on the head.

Then he exploded into violent rebuttal, his arms slicing the air in scissor-like dismissal. 'I will not have you thinking that of yourself! Nor of me!'

Sunny quivered in shock as he came at her, not having expected to stir such a storm of emotion in him. A calculating man surely stayed in control, but there was nothing at all controlled about his wild gesticulations or the passion pouring from his voice.

'Money didn't once enter into my wanting you. *You,* for yourself, Sunny. I sat there in that conference room yesterday morning, watching you give your presentation, and the whole vibrant warmth of you called to me so strongly...'

'Then?' she squeaked. 'You wanted me then?'

'Yes! So much I was planning to ask you to join me for lunch! Anything to have more of you!'

'But you didn't.'

'No. Because when you stepped off that podium I

saw the engagement ring on your finger. Which meant you belonged to someone else. And I didn't think you were the kind of woman I could *buy* away from a man you were committed to.'

She shook her head, stunned by these revelations.

'You made me hate the thought of marrying Kristen.' His mouth curled around the name in savage disgust. 'Kristen, who kept putting a higher and higher price on having a child in the prenuptial agreement she insisted upon.'

He tore off the silk cravat and unbuttoned his collar as though it were choking him. 'Then…then I was on my way out of the hotel and I saw you confronting some guy at a blackjack table. I saw you take off your ring and hand it back to him.'

'You saw?'

'It stopped me in my tracks. I watched you come towards the lobby and all I could think of was…I *can* have her. I *will* have her.'

She hadn't been mad for thinking what she had in the lobby—Bryce Templar determined on claiming her as his woman.

'If that feels wrong to you, I'm sorry, but it felt very right to me. And I acted on it. What's more…' He hurled off his coat and his fingers attacked the buttons of his vest with speedy efficiency. '…I'll keep acting on it.'

The vest went flying. In an instant he was right in front of her, grasping her upper arms, his eyes blazing with the need to burn away anything standing between them. 'You came with me, Sunny. You wanted me last night. You wanted me this morning. You agreed to marry me. You're my wife.'

It was all true. She stared back at him, overwhelmed by the passion he was emitting. Somehow it didn't matter that there had been ruthless calculation behind everything he'd done, because it was for her...because he wanted her.

'My wife,' he repeated, his voice throbbing with fierce possessiveness. 'And that's how it's going to be.'

He kissed her, and his need poured from his mouth to hers, igniting her own need to have all the worries of this day obliterated, to simply lose herself in the primitive heat of being one with him, as she had been last night, as she could be now...

With a low, animal growl, he scooped her off her feet, carrying her with him, clutching her to his chest, raining kisses on her face and muttering, 'I'll make it right. I'll make it right.'

The frenzied refrain pounded through Sunny's heart, making it swell with a wild kind of joy. She clung to him, kissing him back as feverishly as he kissed her. Nothing had to make sense. This frantic desire had a momentum all its own.

Beside the bed they had shared before, Bryce stood her on her feet to peel off her clothes, and he slowed himself down, taking care, his eyes glittering over her as he removed each garment. 'You are so beautiful to me. Do you know that? Have I told you?'

His hands caressed, sending delicious quivers of anticipation through her. He knew how to touch. He knew how to do everything.

'Yes,' she said. 'Yes. You're beautiful to me, too, Bryce.'

And she did the same to him, stripping off the rest of his clothes, taking the time to glide her hands over his marvellous male body, revelling in his perfect musculature, the gleaming tautness of his skin. She exulted when she felt little tremors running under it, knowing he was as excited by her touch as she was by his. It was especially wonderful to run her finger-tips up the impressive strength of his thighs, to hold and stroke and feel the power of his sexuality.

'Sunny...' It was a furred breathing of her name, threaded with barely contained longing. His hands spanned her waist, lifting her up, sliding her body against his. 'Wrap your legs around my hips. I want to feel you hugging me, wanting me...'

She did, with both her arms and her legs, holding his head to the soft cushion of her breasts as he dropped an arm to support her where she was, instinc-tively balancing both their bodies so he could join them, the insertion so slickly smooth, so incredibly satisfying, so intensely *right,* Sunny closed her eyes and breathed a sigh of utter bliss.

His arms slid up on either side of her spine. 'Lean back. I won't let you fall.'

There was no question of not trusting his strength to hold her wherever he wanted to hold her. She leaned back and his penetration went deeper, increas-ing the sense of intimate union so exquisitely, Sunny was unaware that angling away from him left her bare breasts tilted perfectly to be reached by his mouth. The heightening of pleasure was enormous when he started kissing them, swinging her body from side to side as he moved from one to the other, creating arcs of intense sensation and building such a rapid escalation of excitement, she was swamped in huge rolling waves of it.

'Oh...oh...oh...' she heard herself gasping, totally beyond doing anything active herself. It felt as though she were absolutely possessed by him, enthralled by the sweet havoc he wrought inside her, and wanting more and more and more of every fantastic sensation he imparted.

He lowered her wildly palpitating body onto the side of the bed, still holding her pinioned to him, and the voluptuous roll of him inside her changed to a fast plummeting rhythm that brought surges of sheer ecstacy, a fierce tumbling of pleasure that engulfed her, and the deep inner beat of him went on and on until suddenly it ebbed into a delicious sea of peace.

She was hopelessly limp when Bryce gathered her to him and moved them both fully onto the bed, turning to lie on his back with Sunny half sprawled on top of him. She could feel his heart thumping under her cheek and it seemed to pulse through her own bloodstream. Into the haze of her mind slid the thought...*This is my husband*...and a sweet contentment accompanied it and lingered.

Sexually, what more could she ask for in a partner? He excited her beyond anything she had ever felt before. And she loved his physique. It was such a pleasure to look at him, feel him, and he was now hers to have and to hold—a fantasy come true—so she had every reason to feel content.

'I think, if you want to save this bridal coronet of flowers, I'd better unpin it,' Bryce gruffly remarked.

'Mmm…'

'It's got a bit bruised, but it did look fantastic on you with the rest of you naked, Sunny. Still like a bride.'

Sexy pleasure in his voice—visual satisfaction as well as physical. Sunny smiled as she felt his fingers move gently through her hair, removing pins. She must have looked like some kind of pagan bride. Which led her to the thought that probably in primitive times, mating for life was all physical. The choice of instinct. Survival.

She certainly would have picked *him* out of any bunch of men. Why should it be any different now? The saleslady at the bridal boutique had it right. She'd won the prize.

Though, in a way, she'd won it because the sleekly glamorous status-holder, Kristen Parrish, had defaulted in the marriage stakes, demanding too big a bride-price. A child-price, as well. Which was particularly offensive to Sunny's way of thinking. In fact, it was a cold, callous calculating thing to say—I won't have your baby unless you pay me big bucks.

If anyone was 'the pig' in this agreement, Sunny decided it was Kristen.

Which raised a niggly little question.

'Bryce?'

'Mmm?' Having removed the coronet of flowers, he was busy gently massaging her scalp where the pins had been.

'Would you have married Kristen if you hadn't met me?'

His chest rose and fell as he deeply inhaled and breathed out a heavy sigh. 'She's gone, Sunny. This is us,' he said emphatically.

She hitched herself up to assure him she wasn't being jealous or going down some negative path. 'I know. And I'm glad it's us. Truly I am.'

'Good!' He looked and sounded relieved.

'I just want to know if you would have gone through with it, lacking me to replace her?'

His face tightened. She saw a flash of grim ruthlessness in his eyes. 'Yes, I would have married her. But given the fortune she was demanding, I would have insisted on getting uncontested custody of any child we had.'

His child. Sunny believed him. In his world, his father's marriages had come and gone, so Bryce probably didn't set much store by them, but a child—*his child*—meant a great deal. And she understood he much preferred a wife who *wanted* to be a mother to his child, simply because being a mother was important to her, having a value beyond money.

His expression softened as he lifted a hand to her face, gently stroking the contours of it. 'I know you'd never hold a child to ransom, Sunny. You want to share. You care what happens. You want what's best. You'd ensure our child has...' He smiled. '...emotional security.'

'Money doesn't give that, Bryce.'

'I know. I want to give our child emotional security, too. Are you willing to throw your pills away now, Sunny?'

Decision time.

It had been a whole day of decisions.

There seemed no point in hesitating over this last one now.

'Yes,' she answered firmly. 'It's what we both got married for, isn't it? To be parents.'

He laughed, his eyes twinkling wickedly. 'Well, there are some fringe benefits, wife of mine.' And he rolled her onto her back, exuding happiness as he began kissing her again. 'I'm going to love every minute of every effort needed for us to make a baby.'

Sunny had no doubt she would revel in the process, too.

'Though the sooner I get you pregnant, the better,' Bryce murmured. 'I want to take that load off my father's mind. And give him a grandchild.'

His father… Bryce's whole motivation for marrying.

A dark concern sliced into Sunny's mind.

What if she didn't get pregnant?

What if she couldn't have children at all?

Everything hung on it.

Everything!

CHAPTER TWELVE

BRYCE was smiling as he picked up the telephone to call his father. *His wife* was still upstairs, getting ready for their flight to Sedona, and he'd left her smiling, too.

No problems left unresolved.

Everything was on track, just as he wanted it.

He dialled the number and Rosita Perez, the resident housekeeper, picked up at the other end.

'Bryce Templar, here. How is my father this morning?'

'A bit poorly, Señor Bryce, but I'd say it's more grumpy humour than anything else. Do you want to speak to him?'

'Yes, I do.'

Bryce waited, happily anticipating improving his father's humour. Good news, it was said, was the best medicine of all.

'About time you called,' came the curt and typical greeting.

Bryce grinned to himself. 'I'm flying to Sedona to have lunch with you. Does that suit?'

'Of course, it suits. Darned carers won't let me get up to anything myself. Doctors meddling all the time. Pack of quacks, if you ask me.'

'I'm bringing my wife with me.'

'Wife? Did you say *wife?*'

'I did. We got married yesterday.'

'Well, now…'

Bryce could hear his father smiling through the mellowed tone. Without a doubt, being presented with what he wanted was a fine lift to his heart.

'…a done deed, eh!' He actually chuckled. 'Smart move, talking Kristen out of the big showcase wedding she was planning. Lot of nonsense.'

'I didn't marry Kristen.'

'What?'

'I said…*I didn't marry Kristen.* I broke off my engagement to her and married a much better choice for me—Sunny York.'

'What? Who?' His voice rose several decibels.

'Calm down, Dad. You wanted me married. I'm married. To a woman who not only has beauty and brains, but also a warm heart. Even her name is warm—Sunny. Please remember it when we visit.'

'Sunny who?'

'Sunny York. Now Sunny Templar.'

'I don't know any Yorks.' His tone had dropped to querulous.

'You'll get to know her if you treat her nicely.'

'Where'd you meet her?'

'Here in Las Vegas.'

'She's not a showgirl, is she?' Dark suspicion winging in.

'No. Sunny actually works for our company. From the Sydney branch. An Australian.'

'That's going a bit far afield, isn't it? What's wrong with a good American woman?'

'There's nothing wrong with a good American

woman. It just so happens that this Australian woman has more appeal to me than any other female inhabitant of this planet.'

'This sounds too impetuous.' A muttered grumble. 'Good stock, the Parrishes. What do you know about this York family? Do they breed well?'

'Sunny has two sisters with children. Satisfied?'

'Better to have tests done.'

'Did you get *my* mother to have a fertility test?'

'Different times then. You said so yourself. Besides, I was younger than you. How old is this wife of yours?'

'Plenty young enough to have children. And so am I.'

'Huh! Grey in your hair already. Better get started.'

'We intend to.'

'Good!'

'I'm glad you approve,' Bryce said very dryly.

'Don't come that tone with me, boy. You needed pushing into doing the right thing. You just bring this wife along to me and I'll see if you've done it.'

'Her name is Sunny, Dad. You'd better get it right, too, or we won't be staying long.'

'Are you threatening me?'

'No. Just telling you how it is.'

'I hope you're not being led around by the brain below your belt, Bryce.'

'Oh, I think both brains are in fine operation.'

His father snorted. 'When can I expect you?'

'Around noon.'

'I'll be looking forward to it.'

'That was the idea.'

He heard his father chuckling as he put the receiver down.

It gave Bryce's heart a lift.

It *was* good that he'd got married. All the better that he was married to Sunny—a wife worth having in every sense. Producing a grandchild for his father would be no hardship. The trick was to get Sunny pregnant immediately. He'd wasted three months on Kristen. His father was counting his life in terms of one year, which meant there were only nine months left.

Bryce decided he could afford to take a week off work for a honeymoon. Making a baby with Sunny was more important than anything else.

Sunny was all packed and ready to leave for Sedona. Meeting and having lunch with Bryce's father—Will Templar himself—was scary enough without getting her nerves into more of a twist. She didn't have to check her laptop computer for e-mail. It was probably better not to.

Back home in Sydney it was still the middle of the night, so if there was some response from her family about her marriage to Bryce, they wouldn't be looking for any reply from her for many hours yet. Although she'd sent the announcement and the scanned wedding photograph over twelve hours ago, there was no guarantee that her sister, Alyssa, or her husband, John, had even turned on their home computer since then.

Better not to look.

She checked the bathroom once more in case she'd

left something behind. She re-checked her appearance, hoping Will Templar would not find any fault in his new daughter-in-law. Her hair hadn't moved too much out of yesterday's styling for the wedding. Her make-up looked good, if anything understated, but that would probably meet more approval than overstated.

She was wearing one of her conference suits—not the yellow one which she considered too business-like for such a personal meeting. This was a pantsuit in a terracotta gaberdine mixture that didn't crush. Smart casual. The cream silk blouse with its geometric print in green and gold and terracotta gave it a classy touch. She hoped she looked right as Bryce's wife.

Bryce Templar's wife…

Her mind flitted to the e-mail she had sent to her family—short and to the point.

'Today I married Bryce Templar, CEO of Templar Resources. See attached wedding photograph. Will explain everything when I see you. Bryce simply swept me off my feet. As soon as we can he'll be flying home with me to meet the family and help me settle everything there. We'll see you then.'

She walked back into the bedroom and stared at the laptop computer again. What could they say, anyway? A whole pile of recriminations wasn't going to change anything. It was a done deed. Maybe they'd congratulate her.

The laptop stared back—Pandora's box.

Sunny took a deep breath. Not looking was really cowardly. Besides, her nerves couldn't get into much more of a twist. She acted fast, slinging the laptop onto the dressing-table, plugging it in, opening up, switching on, her fingers moving like lightning over the keyboard. The dialling tone seemed to mock her impatience, playing its infuriating little ditty.

Checking incoming messages.

One clicking across the screen.

From Alyssa!

Sunny's heart skipped all over the place as her eyes skated over the words.

Wow! Some bombshell! I called Mum and she cried over missing the wedding but she says to tell you if you're happy she's happy for you and she'll look forward to meeting your new husband.

I called Nadine and she thinks you're crazy for rushing into it. You should have brought him home first. But she wishes you all the best and hopes you haven't made a *big* mistake.

I took one look at the wedding photograph and thought, If I didn't have John—that guy you've married could sweep me off my feet any day. Or night. And that sure is some ring on your finger! Good for you, Sunny.

Lots of love and I can't wait to see him in the flesh!

Sunny breathed a sigh of huge relief. It was okay. They accepted it. And after a while her mother may well be relieved not to have had the expense of an-other wedding. Paying for her sisters' weddings had been a struggle financially. Sunny had helped out as much as her mother would let her.

She smiled down at the fabulous emerald ring on her finger. It was certainly a statement that none of her family would miss, with its obvious message that Sunny had done very well for herself with the CEO of Templar Resources. Not that money was any yard-stick for a successful marriage. It bought things but it couldn't buy happiness.

As for Nadine's hope that she hadn't made a big mistake, well, Sunny hoped that, too, but she wasn't going to let her mind drift down that negative path. She and Bryce had a lot of positive things going for them and they both wanted the marriage to work, es-pecially with becoming parents. Rather than hoping she hadn't made a big mistake, Sunny hoped she'd made the best decision she'd ever made in her life.

She quickly typed a reply—'Thanks, Alyssa. I'll be in touch with details before Bryce and I fly home. 'Bye for now. Love, Sunny.'

Having sent it off, she packed up the laptop again and was just setting it down with the rest of her lug-gage when she heard Bryce coming up the stairs. She swung to face him as he came through the doorway and was instantly hit anew by his strong sexual im-pact. Dressed in fawn slacks and a clingy green sports shirt, his magnificent physique seemed to leap out at her, and the grin on his handsome face gave it a mag-netic attraction.

Alyssa's words zipped through her mind—*he could sweep me off my feet any day. Or night.*

He'd done just that, Sunny thought, and she didn't

regret a second of it. In fact, if he wanted to do it right now...

'I've called for a bellboy. Are you all packed, ready to leave?'

Her hands fluttered, appealing for his opinion. 'Do I look right to meet your father?'

His eyes simmered over her, causing her breasts to peak into hard nubs and sending tremulous little ripples down her thighs.

'Perfect!' he declared huskily, his gaze finally lifting to sear away any doubts or fears in hers. 'Don't worry about what my father thinks, Sunny. You're *the wife* I want. He'll see that fast enough.'

He walked towards her, emanating a ruthless determination that she was coming to recognise. Nothing was going to shake Bryce from what *he* wanted. Her heart quivered with the knowledge that he'd wanted her from the moment she'd come to his notice, and now she was his.

But would she stay his if she couldn't give him the child he wanted?

No negative thoughts, she savagely berated herself as he drew her into his embrace, the green eyes warmly smiling at her, promising there was no possible conflict of interests in this meeting with his father.

'He's looking forward to our visit.'

'Yes...well...it will be interesting.' She managed a teasing little smile in response. 'Father and son.'

Bryce laughed. 'Always a testing ground.' He raised quizzing brows. 'Any reply from your family?'

'Shock/surprise, but best wishes and looking forward to meeting you.'

'So...no problems there.' His eyes glittered satisfaction. 'I've booked us into the L'Auberge Inn at Sedona for tonight.'

This was startling news. 'We're not staying with your father?'

'What? On our honeymoon?'

'We're having a honeymoon?'

'After the wedding comes a honeymoon,' Bryce asserted. 'We are going to do everything right, Sunny.'

And as he bent to kiss her, Sunny was thinking, surely nothing could go wrong when Bryce was so intent on making everything right.

CHAPTER THIRTEEN

THE fantastic red rock formations around Sedona just seemed to suddenly rise out of the Arizona desert, as startling and as stunning as The Olgas rising out of the desert in the red centre of Australia. Sunny was amazed by what was wrought by time and nature, and the likeness to parts of the Outback.

She had a marvellous view of it all from the plane before it set down at the airport, which was surprisingly situated on top of a hill overlooking the township. They were met by Will Templar's chauffeur who loaded both them and their luggage into a very plush Cadillac. It was a very scenic drive, down the hill, through the town which seemed to be spread around a T-junction, then up another hill and finally into the driveway of a huge sprawling house built of stone and wood.

It commanded a spectacular view in every direction, and there were big windows and furnished porches to take advantage of it from both inside and out of doors. A large swimming pool occupied one side of the grounds with what looked like sophisticated barbecue facilities under a roofed area nearby. Everything projected a casual lifestyle, not a formal one, which set Sunny more at ease.

They were met at the front door by a middle-aged

Mexican woman whom Bryce introduced as Rosita Perez, adding that Rosita ran the household.

She beamed at Sunny. 'You are very welcome. *Very* welcome. Such wonderful news!' Her dark eyes twinkled at Bryce. 'Señor Will wants fajitas for lunch. It is a good sign.'

Sunny smiled and nodded. She didn't know about fajitas but the warmth of the greeting helped to calm the butterflies in her stomach.

'Where is he?' Bryce asked.

'On his favourite balcony. I have set out drinks and dips there. Go on....' Rosita shooed them forward. '...he is waiting.'

They walked through a huge living room; big stone fireplace, big furniture in wood and black leather, brightly patterned scatter cushions and rugs featuring Indian motifs.

'What are fajitas?' Sunny whispered.

Bryce grinned. 'Dad's favourite dish. Spicy meat and vegetables wrapped in a kind of tortilla.'

'How spicy?'

'Not too spicy.' His eyes teased her concern. 'There'll be other dishes for you to choose from, so don't worry. You'll get fed.'

'Being nervous makes me hungry.'

'The avocado dip Rosita makes is great. So is the corn one. Get stuck into them,' he advised, his eyes positively laughing as he opened one of the glass doors to the designated balcony.

Sunny took a deep breath and stepped out.

It was a very wide, spacious balcony, holding a dark green wrought-iron-and-glass dining table, with six matching chairs cushioned in green and white. There were occasional tables, as well, serving groups of sun loungers upholstered in the same colours. However, the drinks and food Rosita had mentioned were set out on the dining table.

The rustle of a newspaper being put down was the first indication of Will Templar's presence. She swung her gaze towards the sound and caught the movement of legs being swung off one of the loungers…long legs encased in light grey trousers. Behind her the door closed and she sensed Bryce stepping to her side as the man on the lounger rose to his feet.

Her first thought was, this will be Bryce thirty years from now. The likeness between father and son was striking, despite the older man's white hair and the illness that had stripped him of extra weight that would have normally filled out his face and powerful frame.

They shared the same impressive height and strong facial features, as well as the air of being in command of their world. Will Templar's heart condition certainly hadn't diminished that, Sunny thought, and fancied these father and son meetings could sometimes develop into the clash of the Titans.

'Sunny, this is my father,' Bryce said casually. 'Dad, this is my wife.'

In the face of such an intimidating authority figure, all her sales training leapt to the fore, pushing her into taking the initiative. 'Hi,' she said warmly, smiling as she moved forward to offer her hand and focusing directly on his eyes, which to her surprise were a silvery grey, different to Bryce's. 'I've been looking forward to meeting you, Mr. Templar.'

He took her hand and held it, seemingly amused by her brashly open approach. 'Impressive. A sunny disposition...' His gaze flicked to Bryce, one brow lifting. '...and the legs of a showgirl.'

'Ignore that, Sunny,' Bryce returned dryly. 'My father has a fixation on showgirls.'

Will Templar laughed and pressed her hand reassuringly. 'My son made the claim of beauty and brains. Since both are in evidence, I just thought I'd add my observations to the list. A very great pleasure to meet you, Sunny.'

The feeling of being patronised instantly raised Sunny's hackles. 'Is this a case of let the fun begin between you two?' she challenged. 'Shall I just sit down and eat while you get on with it?'

'Sassy, too.' Will Templar grinned, patting her hand in approval. 'I think I'll let you entertain me instead.'

'If you're not careful, Dad, Sunny may very well eat you for lunch.'

'I did notice her teeth, my boy,' he retorted good-humouredly. 'A smile to dazzle you with before chomping.'

'Beware the bite,' Bryce tossed back at him. 'Mine, too.'

'I do love a good fight,' Will Templar confided to Sunny, wrapping her arm around his as he drew her towards the table. 'Especially when I win.'

'I'm the winner here,' Bryce declared, his eyes hotly assuring Sunny she was the top prize to him.

'I can see that,' his father conceded. 'But who spurred you on to take a wife?'

Again the feeling of being a mere cipher between them goaded Sunny into further speech. 'Actually, Mr. Templar, I took Bryce as my husband.'

'What?' He looked flabbergasted at her temerity.

Sunny smiled. 'You could call it a mutual taking. I did have equal say in it, you know.'

Bryce laughed.

His father looked askance at her. 'You have a very smart tongue.'

'Smart brain, too,' Bryce chimed in. 'What would you like to drink, Dad?'

'I've got to stick to juice.'

'Sunny?'

'I'll have juice, too, thanks, Bryce.'

'I had Rosita bring out a bottle of Krug champagne,' his father pointed out.

'Lovely,' Sunny warmly approved, 'but not on an empty stomach.'

He pulled out a chair from the table and waved her to it. 'Then sit down and eat,' he commanded, put out at not having everything go his way.

Sunny grinned at him. 'Thank you.'

He shook a finger at her. 'You...are a very provocative young woman.'

'You mean...not a yes-woman?' Sunny tilted at him before reaching for a corn chip and the avocado dip. 'Having a mind of my own has always worked better for me, Mr. Templar. I see no reason to give it up just because I married your son.'

She coated the chip with dip and popped it in her

mouth, feeling highly invigorated for having stood up for herself.

'Here's your juice, Sunny.' Bryce set a filled glass in front of her.

'What about mine?' his father growled. 'I'm the invalid around here.'

'I thought you were fighting fit, Dad.'

'Two against one is not a fair fight.'

'You asked for it. Now if you'll stop assuming Sunny is a walkover, we could have a really pleasant lunch together.'

'Just testing her out.' He settled himself on the chair at the head of the table, gesticulating at Bryce. 'You bring a stranger into the family. How am I supposed to know her mettle if I don't test her out?'

'You could try trusting my judgment,' came the ready advice as Bryce set a glass of juice in front of his father.

'Huh! Men can get blinded by a woman's beauty.'

Bryce raised an eyebrow at Sunny. 'Am I blind?'

She grinned at him, having just tried the corn dip and found it as delicious as the avocado one. 'No. Just besotted. But that's okay because I'm besotted, too.'

Will Templar barked with laughter, vastly amused by the exchange. 'Oh, that's good! Very good! If you're not careful, Bryce, she'll be giving you the rounds of the kitchen.'

'A novel thought,' he retorted, pulling out the chair at the foot of the table and relaxing onto it.

'Novelty wears off,' came the sardonic reply. 'She might be compliant now, but...'

'You know, Mr. Templar,' Sunny cut in sweetly. 'Where I come from, it's rude to talk over a person as though she's not there.'

His silvery grey eyes narrowed on her. 'No respect for authority. I've heard that about Australians.'

'Then you've heard wrong. We do respect an authority who shows us respect.'

'Just what position do you hold in our company, young woman?'

'I do sales presentations. And I work hard at commanding respect, Mr. Templar. I do not lie down and let people steamroll over me.'

'But you're married to Bryce now,' he said sharply. 'Do you expect to keep on working?'

'Do you have a problem with that, Mr. Templar?'

'What about children? Do you figure on having any?'

She flashed a look at Bryce who smiled back at her, confident of her reply and perfectly content to let the conversation run without his interference. His eyes said she was doing fine with his father.

'Yes, we do,' she said, smiling her own pleasure in the prospect of having a family with Bryce.

'Do you intend on working then?'

'Being a mother will have priority, but it does take nine months to make a baby, Mr. Templar. Do you think I should twiddle my thumbs until one arrives?'

He frowned. 'Got to take care of yourself during pregnancy,' he said bruskly. 'My first wife—Bryce's mother—had a hard time of it. Kidney problems. Shouldn't have had a child at all. Died when Bryce was only a toddler.'

The brusk tone carried shades of old pain, instantly cooling Sunny's fighting instincts and stirring her sympathy. 'I'm sorry,' she said softly. 'I really want to have a baby, so you can be sure I'll take every care when I do fall pregnant, Mr. Templar.'

'Yes, well, no time to waste,' he said gruffly. 'Bryce isn't getting any younger. He's thirty-four, you know. Should have started a family years ago.'

'A bit difficult when I only met Sunny this week,' Bryce drawled, his eyes mocking his father's contention. 'And you can hardly accuse me of wasting time once I met the right woman.'

His gaze shifted to Sunny and she basked in the warmth of it, feeling more and more that she truly was right for him, and he was right for her. A hasty marriage it might be, but she certainly didn't repent her decision…yet.

'Got an answer for everything,' Will Templar grumbled. 'Sunny, you're hogging those dips. While I'm happy to see you have a healthy appetite, I like them, too.'

'Would you like me to spread some on the chips for you?' Sunny immediately offered.

'I can help myself if you'll kindly pass them up.'

'Not thinking of yourself as an invalid anymore?' Bryce archly commented as Sunny obliged.

'I can handle a bit of finger food.' He glowered at Bryce. 'I see you're feeling on top of things, just because you got married.'

'I generally am on top of things, Dad. I work at it. Which is why you made me CEO, remember?'

'Well, don't be getting too cocky about

it…counting chickens before they hatch. Damian called me yesterday.'

'Nice for you that he keeps in touch.' Bryce slanted a wry smile at Sunny. 'Damian is my half-brother. Dad's son by his third wife.'

'A very caring son, too,' Will Templar declared, pausing to give the statement weight, and eyeing Bryce with a very definite glint of challenge. 'Told me his wife's pregnant.'

Bryce nodded affably. 'I must call and congratulate them.'

'Giving me a grandchild before you do.'

Sunny sensed the threat behind the words and instantly felt uneasy. Was Will Templar playing one son off against another, with the position of CEO as the prize? If so, there was a factor in his marriage decision that Bryce hadn't told her about. She looked sharply at him but discerned no rise of tension in his demeanour.

He smiled, maintaining an affable front. 'I'm glad you'll be getting in some practice as a grandfather before Sunny and I have a child. In fact, maybe we should wait a while, simply enjoy having each other before Sunny gets pregnant. I believe a baby needs to be welcomed and loved for itself…' His lips were still curved into a smile but his eyes hardened to green flint as he softly added, '…not used as a pawn.'

Suddenly the air between father and son was so thick with threat and counter-threat, it could have been cut with a knife.

Sunny knew intuitively Bryce would not back off. And she didn't want him to. What he'd stated was what she believed, as well, although she didn't really want to wait. Not long, anyway. All the same, she understood that pleasing his father was one thing, being dictated to was quite another. Bryce would not be the man he was if he tamely succumbed to his father's string-pulling.

She was startled when Will Templar abruptly switched his focus to her. 'Do you want to wait a while, Sunny?' he demanded rather than asked.

'I think husband and wife should be in total agreement on when they have a baby and it's no one else's business but theirs,' she said slowly, keeping her wits alert to the undercurrents. 'I'm sure Bryce would consider what I want, every bit as much as I would consider what he wants.'

Will Templar leaned forward, boring in. 'Do you realise I still have the power to strip Bryce of his position in the company?'

Sunny felt her spine bristling. Her eyes locked onto the older man's and fought fire with fire. 'I didn't marry Bryce for *his position,* Mr. Templar.'

'What did you marry him for?'

'I fancied him rotten and I thought he'd make a great father for the children I want.'

'You fancied him *rotten?*'

Either he was unfamiliar with the term or she'd knocked him off his power perch. Sunny decided to play her hand to the hilt.

'Mmm...' She gave Bryce a smouldering look. 'He has a way of inspiring the most terrible lust in me.'

He smouldered right back. 'The inspiration goes both ways.'

'Enough!' Will Templar snapped. 'You don't have to prove you're *besotted* with each other at my table!'

Bryce shrugged. 'Actually, we don't have to prove anything, Dad. We just came to visit.'

'Fine visit this is…not even opening the bottle of champagne.'

'I'll be happy to open it,' Bryce said, lifting the bottle out of the ice bucket. 'Ready for a glass now, Sunny?'

'Yes. Thank you. These dips really are delicious.'

'Are you always so direct?' his father demanded of her.

Sunny frowned quizzically at him. 'Weren't you being direct with me, Mr. Templar?'

He looked somewhat disgruntled. 'Just testing your mettle.'

'Did I pass the test?'

He snorted. 'It's plain you and Bryce are two of a kind.'

'Is that good or bad?' Sunny queried.

For the first time she saw a flash of respect in his eyes. 'You can call me Will.'

'Thank you.' She smiled warmly. 'I take that as a real compliment.'

'So you should.' He visibly thawed. 'Just see that boy of mine starts fathering real soon. Can't wait forever for a grandchild, you know.'

From which Sunny deduced it was Bryce's child he most wanted to see, not Damian's.

That thought stayed with her long after the lunch visit was over and Will Templar had conveyed his rather crotchety blessing on the marriage and expressed his pointed hope that their honeymoon would be *productive*.

The chauffeur transported them to the L'Auberge Inn which was nestled along the bank of a pretty, tree-lined creek and surrounded by towering red cliffs. It had a European-style lodge, supplying luxurious amenities for resident guests, and the secluded cottage Bryce had booked for the night was very romantically furnished in a rich, French provincial style.

'May I say how delighted I am that you fancy me rotten,' Bryce tossed at her the moment they were alone.

She laughed and repeated her smouldering look. 'Your father clearly does not see you through the eyes of a woman.'

'I'm only interested in your eyes, Sunny,' he said seriously, enfolding her in his embrace. 'You handled my father brilliantly, but...can I believe every word you said?'

'You know the wanting is real, Bryce. How could it not be when...' She blushed at the memories of her deeply primitive response to him.

He reached up and ran his fingertips over the self-conscious heat, his eyes burning into hers as he softly asked, 'Did you fancy me rotten before you broke with Derek?'

Her skin became even hotter under his questing touch. The intensity he was projecting seeded a wild thought. Was he jealous of the relationship she'd had with her ex-fiancé?

'You must be aware of how attractive you are physically, Bryce. I think any woman would fancy you. The saleslady who sold me my wedding dress certainly did. But I didn't know you in any personal sense...'

'And now that you do?'

'Derek belongs in the past. It's you I want.'

She wound her arms around his neck and kissed him to prove there was no looking back on her part. He was her husband now and she wanted no other.

Bryce stormed her mouth with a passionate possessiveness that swiftly moved into much more than a kiss. They made love in a frenzy of desire for each other, craving an affirmation that their marriage was right and always would be.

It was hours later, when they were dressing for dinner—Bryce insisting she wear the cream lace gown again for the six-course 'wedding feast' he planned to order at the gourmet restaurant in the lodge—that Sunny recalled the question raised at lunch with Will Templar.

'Are you in competition with your half-brother, Bryce?' she asked bluntly, wanting to know the truth.

'Damian?' He looked amused, his eyes mocking the suggestion as he answered, 'My father cares too much for Templar Resources to ever put Damian in control of it, Sunny. He knows it. I know it. It's not an option.'

'Then why did he threaten it?'

Bryce shrugged. 'It's simply a measure of how much he wants me to have a child.'

She frowned. 'You played it like a power game, saying we might wait.'

'A gift is one thing, a pressured demand quite another.'

'What would you do if he did give the CEO position to Damian?'

'Go into opposition. In effect, my father would lose me.'

And you would lose him, she thought.

'He won't go that far, Sunny. Don't worry about it.'

All the same, she couldn't help thinking it would be best—easier all around—if they did have a child straight away. And Bryce had to be thinking that, too.

A productive honeymoon...

CHAPTER FOURTEEN

SUNNY was not the least bit nervous about introducing Bryce to her family. She was happily looking forward to it as she settled herself to sleep away some of the hours on the long flight from Los Angeles to Sydney. Travelling first class gave her much more leg room to make herself comfortable and the wider seat took away the sense of feeling cramped. She tucked the airline blanket around her, sighed contentedly and closed her eyes.

'Sweet dreams,' Bryce murmured indulgently, leaning over from the seat beside her to drop a kiss on her forehead.

She smiled. He made her feel loved. During their whole honeymoon, which Bryce had extended to ten days, he had made her feel loved, and she knew now that she loved him. The words had not been spoken but that didn't matter. The feeling was there, which meant nothing was missing from their marriage...except a baby...and since she may well have conceived already, Sunny was not going to let that concern weigh on her mind.

She had such good memories to dwell on; action-packed days, touring the rim of the awesome Grand Canyon, cruising Lake Powell, hiking the trails through the breathtaking beauty of the hoodoos at Bryce Canyon—well named, her husband had jokingly declared—and absolutely blissful nights, revelling in the sensual pleasures of intimacy.

Her sleep on the plane was deep and untroubled. She awoke with a sense of well-being that stayed with her until the plane circled over Sydney before landing. The view of the harbour, the great Coat-hanger bridge, the gleaming white sails of the opera house, the sparkling blue of the water…it suddenly grabbed her heart and gave it a twist. *This was home.* What had she done, abandoning it for a host of unknowns?

A rush of strong emotion brought tears to her eyes. She blinked rapidly to drive them back. It was silly to let a familiar view get to her like this. People were more important than places. She had Bryce. And right on that thought, he reached across, took her hand, and gently squeezed it.

'A touch homesick?'

'It's just so beautiful,' she excused.

'Yes, it is. One of the most beautiful cities in the world,' he said warmly. 'We will be back, many times, Sunny.'

She flashed him a watery smile. 'It's okay. I do want to be with you, Bryce.'

He nodded and interlaced his fingers with hers, reinforcing their togetherness. There were times when he seemed ruthlessly intent on not allowing anything to shadow it.

He had arbitrarily dismissed the idea of staying in her Sydney apartment, booking an executive suite at the Regent Hotel for the duration of their visit. Sunny suspected he didn't care to be anywhere Derek had been, but he argued comfort and the fact that it would complicate her task of clearing everything out and ending the lease. Which was true enough.

She was thankful she and Derek had maintained separate apartments, never actually living together. At least she didn't have the complication of dividing up possessions. That would have been really messy. They had never swapped door keys, either, which was probably just as well, given their bitter parting. Sunny saw no problems in doing what had to be done today.

Although they had left Los Angeles on Wednesday night, crossing the dateline meant they were arriving in Sydney on Friday morning, and they'd be flying out again on Sunday. A packing company had already been lined up to help her at the apartment. Bryce wanted to spend the day in the Sydney headquarters of Templar Resources and he offered to collect her personal belongings from the office where she had worked.

This, Sunny realised, neatly avoided any unpleasant encounter between her and Derek, so she had agreed to the plan, but she did regret missing the opportunity to say goodbye to the people she had been friendly with. Though they were mostly men who would prob-ably side with Derek, she argued to herself. Since her life was now with Bryce, it seemed wiser to simply stay out of the situation.

The plane landed safely at Mascot Airport. A lim-ousine took them to the Regent Hotel. They had time to freshen up, eat a light second breakfast, and go over their plans for the day in case something had not been thought of. Satisfied that everything was in hand, Bryce left for head office and Sunny took a taxi to her old neighbourhood in the suburb of Drummoyne, only a short trip from the centre of the city.

It was strange, moving around the apartment she had occupied for the past four years, wondering what to do with everything she had collected here. There was no point in taking anything but clothes, photo albums and those personal possessions which were especially dear to her. Having spent the last day before their flight to Sydney at Bryce's home in Santa Monica, Sunny was only too aware that it wanted for nothing.

Bryce had advised sending her surplus stuff to a charity but she didn't feel right about that now. It was like irrevocably sweeping out her past—everything that had made up her life before she had gone to Las Vegas. It seemed like saying none of it had any value anymore—all she'd worked for over many years. To just get rid of it because Bryce could provide more and better...it simply didn't sit well with her.

While she waited for the packing people to arrive, she telephoned her mother, letting her know what was happening and asking if there was anything she would like from the apartment. To Sunny's intense relief, her mother suggested sending everything to her. It could be stored in the garage and the whole family could pick and choose what they could use.

'Better we keep it for you,' her mother added. 'You never know, dear. You might not be happy living so far away in another country.'

'Mum, I'm married,' Sunny protested.

'Yes, and I'm sure you're wildly in love. I truly hope this marriage works out wonderfully for you,

Sunny, but…it was rather hasty, dear. And he is an
American, not…well, not what you're used to. If
sometime in the future you want to come back
home…'

'I'm not thinking like that, Mum.'

'I understand, dear. I'd just feel better about it if
we keep things for you.'

Insurance against some unforeseen future?

Sunny frowned. Did she herself feel that? The idea
warred with her sense of commitment, yet…who
could really know what the future held? All she knew
was that keeping her things did make her feel more
comfortable.

'Okay, Mum. The boxes should arrive this afternoon.' Her mother and sisters lived at Quakers Hill,
on the western outskirts of Sydney, not more than an
hour away if the truck went there directly. 'Will you
be home to direct where they're to be stored?'

'Yes, I'll be home. What time can I expect you and
Bryce tomorrow?'

'What time do you want us there?'

'In time for morning tea. Say ten-thirty? I'm cooking your favourite carrot cake this afternoon.'

'Thanks, Mum. That's great! We'll be there soon
after ten.'

'If you've got the time, Sunny, call your sisters,
too. They're dying to chat to you.'

'I'll try. 'Bye for now.'

With the storage decision made, Sunny threw herself into sorting out what clothes she should take with
her now, and what was to be boxed up and sent to
her. As arranged, two men from the packing company

turned up at ten o'clock and were amazingly efficient at their job; wrapping breakables, grouping things for easy labelling, even boxing the furniture in thick cardboard so nothing could be damaged.

By one o'clock the apartment was completely cleared. The men even carried the suitcases she'd packed down to her car for her. She drove to the local shopping centre, had a quick lunch, then dropped into the real estate agency which handled the lease of her apartment. After handing in her keys there, arranging for cleaning and settling what was owing, Sunny only had one item left on her business agenda—returning the company car which had been part of her salary package.

It was easy, at this point, to simply follow Bryce's advice. She returned to the hotel, had her luggage sent up to the suite, and instructed the concierge that the car was to be picked up by the Templar Resources company. Having now completely dismantled her previous life in Sydney, Sunny suddenly felt drained. Jetlag, she told herself, and retired to their suite to sleep it off.

Except sleep eluded her and she remembered she hadn't yet called her sisters. Or any of her old girlfriends! She started with Alyssa who wanted to hear all about her honeymoon and bubbled on about how marvellous it must be to have a really wealthy husband who could just do what he wanted without counting the cost.

'Bryce does work, too, you know,' Sunny said dryly. 'A CEO doesn't have a lot of leisure time. This was our honeymoon, Alyssa.'

'Yes, but let's face it, Sunny. Derek couldn't have given you all that. And talking of work, did you know he'd resigned from Templar Resources?'

Sunny frowned over that piece of information. 'How could I know when I've been out of the country? And how do you know, Alyssa?'

'Nadine found out. She felt sorry for him and called him.'

'I wish she hadn't done that.'

'Well, you were engaged to him for months, Sunny. Your whirlwind marriage to Bryce was a bit of a shock.'

'Derek spent every spare minute in Las Vegas gambling. Plus time he should have spent at the conference, too. Did he tell Nadine that?' Sunny demanded sharply, annoyed that her youngest sister had gone behind her back to Derek, instead of waiting for her to come home.

'Hey! I didn't do it,' Alyssa protested. 'I just thought you might want to know Derek had left your husband's company. Pride, I guess.'

A niggle of concern made Sunny ask, 'Has he got a job somewhere else?'

'He said he was going to work for the opposition. Beat Templar Resources at their own game. He was angry. You can't exactly blame him.'

Yes, I can, Sunny thought, remembering how he had ignored and neglected her in favour of roulette and blackjack and whatever other games he'd played.

'After what he did in Vegas, resigning was probably the best move he could make. He was well on the way to inviting being sacked, in my opinion,' she remarked stonily.

'That bad, huh?'

'Yes. I just hope he can stay out of casinos and get his life together again.'

'You still care for him?'

'No. Derek killed off any caring when...' She stopped, shying away from the ugly memory of the confrontation in the MGM lobby. She took a deep breath before firmly stating, 'I really don't want to talk about Derek, Alyssa. That's over.'

'Okay. That's fine with me,' came the quick reply. 'I'm really looking forward to meeting Bryce tomorrow.'

'Good. We'll be at Mum's about ten. See you then, Alyssa.'

Still vexed over Nadine's action, Sunny had no inclination whatsoever to call her other sister. Nadine could wait for tomorrow for whatever fuel she wanted for more gossip. She spent a couple of happy hours telephoning her long-time girlfriends, telling them her news, giving them her new address in Santa Monica and promising to keep in touch. The contact lifted her spirits. She wasn't cut off from her old life. It was simply a matter of making adjustments.

Bryce came back from the office in good spirits, too, pleased with the meeting he'd had with the managing director, and the business being done in this branch of Templar Resources. They had an early dinner and talked over what position Sunny could take on in the Los Angeles office, discussing various exciting options.

All in all, Sunny went to bed that night a happy woman, and her happiness with her new husband was shiningly evident at the family gathering the next day. Bryce's personal charisma was so powerful, doubts about *her* hasty marriage were obviously squashed within minutes, wariness switching almost instantly to pleasure in his company. Even her brothers-in-law were impressed, keen to ask Bryce's opinion on anything and everything.

He was especially good with her sisters' children, paying kind attention to the toddlers when they demanded it. Sunny was highly gratified that he fitted in as one of the family, though she doubted Bryce was used to sitting in an ordinary middle-class home, nor having the kind of rowdy lunch her family engaged in.

'Well, he's certainly something,' her mother acknowledged, when the four women were in the kitchen cleaning up after a very elaborate and celebratory meal. Her eyes twinkled delighted approval as she gave Sunny a hug.

'A hunk plus!' Alyssa agreed, rolling her eyes appreciatively.

'Yes, I can see why Derek got his nose out of joint when Bryce stopped him from seeing you,' Nadine dryly commented.

Sunny gave her an exasperated look. 'Bryce didn't *stop* Derek from seeing me. Derek waylaid us and did his nasty best to turn Bryce against me. Which, I'm thankful to say he failed to do.'

Nadine grimaced. 'I meant the night before when Derek followed your luggage to the MGM Hotel. He wanted to make up with you, and Bryce blocked him out.'

Sunny's mind whirled, remembering Bryce had left her in the bath, saying he'd been called down to the lobby to deal with an urgent problem. Derek... demanding to see her? Wanting to right the wrongs between them?

What had Bryce said to him?

Was this why Derek had been so virulent the next morning? So virulent, she had agreed to marry Bryce then and there!

'To be faced with Bryce...' Nadine went on with a shrug. '...poor Derek simply wasn't a match for him.'

'No, he's not,' Sunny grated. 'And I wish you'd drop the subject of *poor* Derek, Nadine. I was running a very *poor* second to his gambling addiction before I even met Bryce.'

'Sorry. I just meant...well, I'd choose Bryce, too.' She grinned to smooth over her gaffe. 'Who wouldn't?'

It was a question Sunny kept asking all afternoon— *who wouldn't?*—but the sparkle had gone out of the day for her. Bryce hadn't exactly lied about Derek's first foray to the MGM Hotel, but he had certainly omitted telling her. She might not have chosen to see Derek that night, but Bryce had clearly removed any choice, ruthlessly removed it, intent on keeping her with him until...until she married him.

Why?

Not out of love for her.

He needed a wife to please his father.

Kristen was demanding too much.

He preferred Sunny...*the bargain basement bride!*

It was difficult to keep up a facade of happily wedded bliss while this inner torment churned through her, but Sunny managed it. Pride made her keep pretending everything was perfect, though she barely kept her own tears at bay when her mother got teary at their leave-taking. It was an enormous relief when the chauffeured limousine pulled away from her cheerfully waving family and she could relax back in the plushly cushioned seat and close her eyes.

'Exhausted?' Bryce asked sympathetically.

'Yes,' she muttered, keeping her eyes shut, not wanting to look at him.

As he had in the plane, he took her hand, interlacing their fingers in a possessive grip. Sunny raised her lashes a little to stare down at the linked hands, at the emerald ring glinting up at her. She was married to this man, committed to having a family with him. If she didn't have his love, at the very least she needed honesty from him.

'I thought the day went well,' he commented.

'Yes, you handled my family brilliantly.'

It was what he'd said of her meeting with his father. He'd probably handled *her* brilliantly, too, all along, from the moment he decided she should be his wife instead of Kristen.

'It wasn't hard. They're nice people.'

'I'm glad you think so.'

'Need some quiet time now?'

'Yes.'

He said nothing more until they walked into their

hotel suite and the door was closed behind them. Sunny was working herself up to confront him with what Nadine had told her when he softly asked, 'Want to tell me what's wrong?'

The question hit all the raw places in Sunny's heart. She swung on him, words shooting out of her mouth in a bitter spurt. 'What? So you can fix it, Bryce?' Her eyes hotly accused as her tongue ran on. 'You're very good at that, aren't you? Fixing things to be how *you* want them.'

'And you, Sunny,' he said in a calm, quiet tone. 'I care very much about how you want them, too.'

'You have no right to decide that for me, Bryce,' she retorted fiercely, inflamed by his air of unshakeable control.

He lifted his hands in appeal. 'What have I decided without discussing it with you?'

'Derek! You stopped him from seeing me and didn't even tell me he'd come to try for a reconciliation.'

His face visibly tightened. The green eyes flared with violent feeling. 'You throw him up at me? A man who knew you so little he could abuse you in terms that I knew were false on just one day's acquaintance with you?'

'How do I know you didn't give him reason to think those things, Bryce? To get rid of him so you'd have a clear running track for what you wanted.'

'Your relationship with him was finished.' He hurled an arm out in savage dismissal. 'You acted on that. Why wouldn't I act on it?'

'He came to see me. Not you. You had no right to…'

'You gave me the right by being in *my* suite, *my* bath...' His eyes glittered with angry possessiveness as they raked her up and down. '...*my* bed!'

Sunny clenched her hands, fighting the sexual power he projected. 'You didn't *own* me, Bryce.'

'You were with me,' he asserted, his eyes burning that undeniable truth straight through her defences. 'Why would I let a drunken fool whom you had rejected, violate the intimacy you were sharing with me?'

Her mind spun on one point she hadn't known. 'He was drunk?'

'And creating trouble.'

'Trouble because you wouldn't let him see me,' she shot at him, determined not to get distracted from the main issue here.

'He had lost the right to demand anything of you, Sunny.'

The mention of *rights* exploded any gain he'd made with his picture of a drunken Derek. She stormed around the suite, putting distance between them, seething at his arrogance in making that judgment. Which he'd clearly made to suit *his purpose*.

Never mind that she'd been hurt by her belief that Derek seemingly hadn't even noticed her absence that night. Bryce hadn't cared about her feelings, except in so far as making them more positive towards him. She swung around to accuse him of it, noting he hadn't moved. He stood tautly watching her, channelling all his energy into working out how to achieve his ends this time.

'The truth is...you weren't going to give him any second chance, were you, Bryce?'

'He'd had his chance with you and blew it,' he grated.

'That was for me to decide.'

She saw him gather himself, shoulders straightening, his formidable chest lifting, strength of mind emanating powerfully from him as he stepped towards her, his gaze holding hers with mesmerising intensity.

'What are you telling me, Sunny? You would have had him back?'

It was a pertinent question, challenging where she stood as he closed on her. Sunny's chin lifted defiantly. Just because she had married him didn't mean she would overlook how he had dealt with possible opposition.

'I'll never know now, will I?' she flung at him. 'I didn't hear what he had to say.'

Bryce kept coming, relentlessly determined on his will prevailing. 'You heard him the next morning,' he pointedly reminded her.

'Yes, I heard him.' Her heart was pounding. He was so big, so indomitable, and one perverse side of her liked the fact he wouldn't be beaten. Yet he shouldn't have taken her choice out of her hands. 'And I wonder now what you said to him the night before.'

'I told him we were negotiating a new position for you in Los Angeles and I didn't care to have our discussion interrupted,' came the imperturbable reply.

'Did he fight that?' she instantly queried, knowing she would have fought, as she was fighting now for integrity in her relationship with Bryce.

'Yes.' Contempt flashed into his eyes. 'He lied, claiming you were his fiancée, which I knew you no

longer were. I faced him with the lie and told him
you were free to contact him at any time...*if* you
wanted to.' His hands curled around her upper arms,
pressing his truth. 'But you didn't want to, Sunny.
You wanted to be with me.'

'I thought there was nothing left with Derek,' she
argued, resenting the way he was boxing her into a
corner.

'He's not worth the candle you're burning for him,
and you know it,' he insisted. 'You liked what you
had with me. You wanted it.'

Her eyes warred with the blazing certainty in his,
yet she couldn't deny the wanton desire he stirred in
her. 'What I've learnt from this, Bryce, is that you
play to win,' she bit out angrily. 'Whatever it takes,
you play to win.'

'You're right. I do play to win,' he conceded with
ruthless intent. One hand slid up and tangled in her
hair at the nape of her neck. 'That's the kind of man
you married, Sunny.'

She couldn't bring herself to move or even protest.
Her mind screamed it was wrong to feel excited by
the electric energy swirling from him, yet her whole
body was tingling, and when he spoke again, his
voice seemed to throb through her bloodstream.

'I wanted you as my wife. I got you as my wife.
And I'll do everything in my power to keep you as
my wife.'

Then he kissed her.

CHAPTER FIFTEEN

BRYCE lay awake in the darkness long after Sunny had fallen asleep in his arms. She had responded to him as she always did, caught up in the storm of desire that raged through them, demanding every possible satisfaction. His mind kept hotly buzzing *she was his*. But a more chilling section of his brain acknowledged he had *made* her his.

He had blocked Marsden out and seized the advantage of the rebound effect, refusing to believe that such a stupid loser could possibly be the better man for Sunny. He still didn't believe it. Yet why relationships worked for the people involved was often perplexing to an outside viewpoint. Needs could go right back to a person's roots and seem totally illogical to anyone who hadn't lived that life.

Yes, he'd won the play. Sunny was *his* wife. Yet if her emotions were still tied up with that guy…what did he have? The use of her body. Not long ago he might have thought that was enough. Certainly he'd expected no more from Kristen. But Sunny…

Somehow everything was different with Sunny. He wanted the whole package—heart, body and soul. Why she inspired this craving for all of her he didn't know, but he knew he wouldn't be content until he had it.

The black irony was he'd felt their honeymoon had

moved her much closer to him. It had been a risk coming to Sydney so soon, but it was the appropriate course to take—meeting Sunny's family and collecting what she wanted of her clothes and other possessions—and he'd thought he had the risk covered.

Sherman had straightened Marsden out about the legal consequences of malicious slander and damage during his stopover in Los Angeles. There'd been no loose talk at the Sydney office when he'd resigned—of his own free will, no pressure involved on that front. Bryce hadn't been anticipating any comebacks.

Careful questioning of the managing director had assured him the resignation was interpreted as a matter of pride. And given Marsden's lack of career interest at the conference, he wasn't considered a loss to the company. On the business side, the field had been cleared. It was the personal side that had slipped past him.

Marsden had mouthed off to one of the family.

So who had been tactless enough to face Sunny with her ex-fiancé's rantings? Her mother? No. Too kind-hearted. Alyssa? No. She'd been happily positive about the marriage. He doubted Alyssa would have done anything to take the shine off it. Which left Nadine. Little flashes of envy there. She was the most likely candidate, though she probably hadn't meant to undermine Sunny's confidence in her decision to marry him.

The critical question was how much harm had been done. Certainly Marsden had been brought right back to the forefront of Sunny's mind, and what had been clear-cut on the morning of their wedding day, was now muddied. Somehow he had to get Sunny positive about their marriage again. Wipe Marsden right out of the picture.

She was quiet the next morning. Bryce sensed she was both mentally and emotionally withdrawn from him as she moved about the suite, getting ready for their departure. He controlled his frustration as best he could, but when they sat down to the breakfast delivered by room service, and Sunny persistently evaded his gaze, the urge to confront came thundering into prominence.

'Would you prefer to be married to Marsden?' he growled.

That lifted her eyelashes. It probably wasn't the smartest question to ask but at least it got her attention.

'I'm married to you, Bryce,' she stated flatly, making it an incontravertible fact that was not up for question.

It goaded him into saying, 'Maybe I don't care for the idea of being married to a woman who's hankering after someone else.'

Her eyes flared to an intense gold. 'I'm not *hankering* after Derek. That would be really stupid, wouldn't it? Given the circumstances.'

'I would have thought so, yes,' he answered tersely.

'Do you consider me stupid?'

'No.'

'Then why do you imagine I'm hankering after him?'

'You're angry with me because I didn't allow him a second chance with you. Which suggests you would have liked that.'

She reached for a piece of toast and buttered it with

slow deliberation, her face completely closed to him. 'I might have given Derek a hearing at the time, but that time has gone,' she said, adding strawberry conserve to the toast. 'I chose to marry you and that's where I am...married to you.'

'You were happy about it until yesterday,' he reminded her.

'I didn't understand that it was about winning.' Her gaze flicked up to meet his. 'I'm sorry to report a setback in your winning play this morning.'

He frowned, completely missing what she meant. 'What do you find wrong in my wanting you as my wife?'

Her mouth curled into a wry little smile. 'Possibly the fact that I'm slow off the mark delivering the rest of what you want, Bryce.'

'Which is?' he prompted, still puzzled by her words and needing more insight on where she was coming from.

'I didn't get pregnant on our honeymoon.'

The blunt statement caught him by surprise. His entire thought process had been focused on her feelings for Marsden. He shook his head, his brain whirling to accommodate this new parameter, to fit it into her behaviour and make a different sense of it.

'Believe it, Bryce,' she said dryly, misinterpreting his confusion. 'My period came this morning.'

He watched her bite into the strawberry-laden toast as though she needed a sweetener for the sour taste that piece of news had left in her mouth.

'You're upset because you're not pregnant?' he blurted out, relieved that *this* was the problem.

'It *is* why we got married…to have a child,' she reminded him, her eyes flashing bleak irony.

'That's what you've been holding in from me this morning? You didn't want to tell me?'

'It is…' she grimaced, her eyes dulling further as she added, '…disappointing.'

Bryce instantly reached across the table and took her free hand in his, gently fondling it. 'I'm sorry you're disappointed, Sunny. But it is only early days in our marriage,' he pressed, wanting to console her. 'I'm sure it will happen. It's probably better that you're not pregnant straight off, what with having to settle into a new home and a new job.'

She stared at him in stunned disbelief. 'Aren't *you* disappointed?'

Bryce hadn't stopped to think about it. He paused for a moment, remembering the motivations he'd spelled out to her. Somehow they didn't seem quite so important now. But having a child *was* important to Sunny, he reminded himself before answering.

'We'll make a baby soon enough,' he warmly assured her.

'But…you wanted this for your father,' she said in obvious bewilderment.

'I don't see that you can force nature for anyone,' he answered reasonably.

'You wanted to give him a grandchild before…before…'

'My father is happy that I've married, Sunny. He's seen for himself we're a good match. He knows we intend to have children. It would be good to give him the news that we're expecting a baby, but it doesn't have to be immediate. Another month or two...' He shrugged, wanting to remove her anxiety.

She shook her head, still disturbed. 'I don't understand why I didn't fall pregnant. We...' She flushed, obviously recalling their intense sexual activity.

'Maybe the pills had some lingering influence. Don't worry about it, Sunny.'

'You're not worried by it?' she queried uncertainly.

'No.' He smiled. 'I'm very happy just having you as my wife.'

Sunny searched his eyes, disbelief warring with the sincerity he was projecting. Was this the truth? He wanted her as his wife first, and his father's needs came second?

'Forget about it. Enjoy your breakfast,' he urged, withdrawing his hand to continue his own meal, his whole demeanour beaming good humour. His eyes twinkled wickedly as he added, 'We have a month of high-level energy business ahead of us.'

He *was* happy. There could be no doubting it. The tense silence, which Sunny had to acknowledge causing herself as she'd battled with the emotional conflict of failing to conceive, was completely banished by a stream of plans from Bryce—plans that were clearly coated with pleasurable anticipation.

She was almost giddy with relief. When they finally left for the airport, she didn't mind at all when Bryce took her hand in the now familiar, possessive grip. It felt more like a symbol of togetherness, a warm, secure promise of his commitment to her.

His wife...

Her heart went all mushy at the memory of how

wildly he'd wanted her last night. He'd driven any thought of Derek right out of her mind. Besides, there had been fair reasoning in his argument for having denied Derek a reconciliation bid. Why should he let a potential rival break into the intimacy she had willingly shared with him?

That would have been stupid.

As stupid as her hankering after Derek now.

No way!

She smiled to herself over the realisation that Bryce had been nursing jealous feelings over her supposed lingering attachment to Derek. It wasn't just her body he wanted. Desire was certainly a driving force but there was also a passion for more than sex in their relationship.

A sigh of contentment whispered from her lips, bringing a swift look of concern from Bryce.

'Are you okay, Sunny? If you're in some discomfort from…'

'No.' She smiled to erase any doubt. 'Just glad you're not disappointed.'

He slanted his eyebrows ruefully. 'Well, it does curtail some rather basic pleasures but we'll probably need the rest after this trip anyhow.'

She laughed, happy that he was thinking of just the two of them and not the baby she wasn't having yet.

Next month, she thought.

Next month they would surely have good news to give to his father.

CHAPTER SIXTEEN

FORTUNATELY there was a dispenser carrying sanitary napkins in the ladies' room. Sunny hadn't come to work prepared for such an unwelcome and demoralising eventuality. She had felt absolutely certain she would fall pregnant this month, even buying a pregnancy test kit ready to confirm the fact, counting the days to when it could be used.

Now this...

She hated her body for betraying her. Why couldn't it co-operate with her dearest wish? And how was she going to tell Bryce they had failed again?

A wave of sickening depression rolled through her. It made no sense that she hadn't conceived when they'd been making love every night. Over and over again she had lain in Bryce's arms, smiling, wondering if it was happening...the miracle of life beginning. Happy dreams...

Except they weren't coming true!

Feeling totally wretched, Sunny walked slowly back to the office Bryce had set up for her in the Los Angeles headquarters of Templar Resources. It was a wonderful office. Normally it gave her pleasure to enter this room, knowing Bryce had every confidence in her ability to carry off her new position as head of sales presentations, advising the team under her and monitoring their results. She had enjoyed the challenge of being in charge.

But she wasn't in charge of her body.

The fear of being infertile started hovering. She sat down at her desk and stared blankly at the printout of figures in front of her. Her womb ached with the draining of hope. It was impossible to concentrate on work. All she could think of was not measuring up to motherhood.

If there was something wrong with her...if she couldn't have a baby...what was this marriage worth? She loved Bryce with all her heart, but if she couldn't give him a child...it just wouldn't be right to even try to hang on to him. He wanted children, and not only to satisfy his father.

As it was, time was slipping away on giving his father a grandchild. Would Bryce start thinking Kristen Parrish might have been the better choice of wife? Sunny shuddered at the unbearable thought. He was *her* man, *her* husband. Yet if she couldn't deliver what he wanted...and he had spelled it out before he'd married her...

A hasty marriage.

Repent at leisure.

The words were coming back to haunt her now.

They should have waited. She should have had tests done first. No doubt Bryce would have insisted on tests during his premarital wrangle with his first choice of wife. Sunny couldn't bring herself to question his potency. She was sure it was beyond question. The fault had to lie with her.

Somehow she dragged herself through the rest of

the working day, though she did cancel a meeting
she'd scheduled, too aware of not being able to give
her best to it. Her head was pounding by the time
Bryce came by her office to collect her for the trip
home. She looked at him—this man amongst men—
and it was totally heart-ravaging to think she couldn't
give him the progeny he deserved.

'Something wrong?' he asked, frowning at her, the
perceptive green eyes sharply scanning.

She grimaced. 'Raging headache.'

'Have you taken some pain-killers for it?'

'Yes.'

'Let's get you home then. You don't look at all
well.' He took her bag from her, ushered her out of
the office, then tucked her arm around his, keeping
her close to him for support on the walk to the basement car park. 'Do you suffer from migraines,
Sunny?' he asked gently.

'Not as a rule,' she muttered, feeling horribly guilty
for letting his sympathy flow over her instead of telling him the cause of her pain.

'I guess you don't feel like talking,' he said, his
understanding making the guilt even worse.

She had to tell him. He had the right to know. It
couldn't be hidden anyhow. Sheer misery made her
hold her tongue until they were in his car and heading
for home, but her sense of fairness forced her to speak
at the first long traffic stoppage on the freeway.

'I've got my period again,' she blurted out.

She sensed more than saw his head jerk towards
her. Her own gaze was fixed on the road ahead. Her

hands were clenched in her lap. She could barely stop herself from bursting into tears.

Then a big warm hand covered hers. 'I'm sorry, Sunny,' came the soft, gruff words. 'I know how much you were counting on being pregnant this time.'

The tears welled and spilled over. She had to bite her lips against breaking into sobs. Speech was impossible. The traffic started moving again and Bryce returned his hand to the driving wheel. She heard him heave a deep sigh and that was the worst thing of all...knowing how he must be feeling now.

Overlooking her first failure was one thing. They'd only been married two weeks and the contraceptive pills she'd been using might have messed up any chance of getting pregnant. There simply wasn't any reason for failing this month. If she was fertile, there should be a baby growing inside her right now. Bryce had to know that as certainly as she did.

She swiped the stream of tears from her cheeks and leaned forward, fumbling in the bag at her feet for some tissues. Her make-up was probably running everywhere. Not only was she a mess inside, she was fast becoming a mess outside, as well. She grabbed the little packet of tissues she always carried with her and sat back again, removing a couple to mop up her face.

'Please don't take it so much to heart, Sunny,' Bryce said quietly. 'It's not unusual for many couples to try for months before...'

'We're not just any couple!' she cried. 'You know we're not.'

He sighed again.

She closed her eyes and willed the tears to dry up.

'I'm sorry,' Bryce murmured. 'If you're worrying about my father…I just wish you'd stop. I hate seeing you in this state.'

She took a deep breath, trying to ease the tightness in her chest. Nothing could ease the pain in her heart. She understood that Bryce didn't want to see her weeping. Men were invariably uncomfortable with displays of deep emotional stress. Apart from which, he undoubtedly had his own inner dismay to deal with. He'd married her to have a child, the child was not forthcoming, and it was certainly not from any slack performance on his part.

Sunny had no idea how long it took to drive to their home in Santa Monica. Bryce remained silent and her mind was in a total ferment. Only the rolling open of the garage door, triggered by the remote device in the car, alerted her to the fact that the journey was over and facing up to the situation with Bryce was now imminent.

Her legs were hopelessly shaky as she walked ahead of him along the short hallway that led from the garage to the space-age kitchen with its gleaming stainless steel surfaces. Her churning stomach refuted any idea of food. Preparing any dinner for them was beyond her tonight. She went past the kitchen, wishing she could make a bolt for the staircase and a bed where she could curl up and quietly die, but there really was no hiding place.

'Sunny…'

The concern and soft appeal in Bryce's voice forced her to stop halfway across the open-plan living area. She took a deep breath, straightened her spine, and swung to look back at him. He'd halted by the kitchen serving bench. He gestured towards the refrigerator.

'Can I get you anything?'

Her heart turned over. He wanted to do something for her...help...but there was no help for this.

'A cup of tea?' he suggested, knowing she preferred it to coffee.

'Do you know where I should go to have a fertility test, Bryce?' she asked, determined on not evading the issue.

'Yes, but...' He looked pained by the question.

'I'll go next week. If it turns out that I'm...I'm barren...' What a terrible word that was, so redolent of empty devastation!

'You don't need to put yourself through this, Sunny,' he protested.

'Yes, I do. Both of us need to know if I can or can't have a baby.'

He shook his head.

'If I can't, Bryce, we get a divorce as soon as possible.'

'No!' The negative was harsh and explosive.

Sunny ignored it. 'I won't take you for anything. What's yours will remain yours. You can trust me on that. I'll just go back to Australia and get on with my life.'

'Money has nothing to do with it!' he fiercely claimed.

'I'm glad you understand that,' Sunny shot back at him, undeterred by his vehemence. 'It never did for me,' she continued flatly. 'But a child matters, Bryce. If I can't give you one, it's best we part now.'

'No!' he repeated strongly.

She looked at him with deadly calm washed out eyes. 'You know it. I know it. That's how it is.'

He stared back, his black brows beetled down over eyes burning with the need to wipe out all she'd said. But he couldn't. The equation was irrefutable.

Sunny turned away, forcing her tremulous legs to take one step after another, increasing the distance between them as she made her way up the stairs to the bedroom where their mating had been a delusion. It had not borne fruit. An empty bed…but a soft pillow to bury her misery in.

Bryce watched her walk away from him, too stunned by the bald words she had spoken to make any move. All he could think of was…*did he mean so little to her?*

He didn't want a divorce. Not for any reason. They'd been married almost two months and it had been the best two months of his entire life. He'd felt…truly not alone anymore. Not that he had ever really dwelled on loneliness. He'd considered himself self-sufficient.

But Sunny had filled all the empty spaces that he hadn't even recognised before she came into his life…filled them with warmth and joy, giving him a sheer pleasure in being, in having her with him, in sharing all the things he'd never really shared with anyone.

Divorce!

For the sake of some theoretical child he might have with a Kristen-like replacement?

Could such a child make up for a *barren* marriage?

Everything within Bryce shouted *no!*

He'd just paid out a fortune to be rid of Kristen Parrish and her self-righteous claims, a costly mistake for choosing her in the first place. But choosing Sunny was no mistake. Child or no child, he couldn't bear to even think of living the rest of his life without her.

She was his wife.

His wife in every sense.

He'd won her and nothing was going to stop him from keeping her.

Nothing!

His feet started moving. The adrenaline rush of going into battle carried him up the stairs at a pace that brooked no opposition. He was going to smash any barriers Sunny put up. He would hold her to him, no matter what! His whole body bristled with the ferocity of his feeling. He strode into their bedroom, intent on fighting with everything he could fight with, his heart thundering with the need to win.

One look at Sunny and his intent was instantly blown to pieces. She was scrunched up on the bed, her back turned to him, a back that was heaving with sobs, muffled by the pillow her face was pushed into. She was hugging another pillow for comfort. She'd kicked off her shoes and there was something terribly vulnerable about her stockinged feet, tucked up and rubbing against each other as though they were cold.

It struck him forcefully that this was grief. Heart-breaking grief. Was it possible that she didn't want their marriage to end any more than he did? Maybe she just couldn't see over the hump of not having a child. He couldn't say it didn't matter because it did to her. She wanted to be a mother. But if she couldn't be, he was still her husband and she was still his wife and he had to show her that what they had together was still worth having.

Quietly he took off his suitcoat and tie and dropped them on a chair, freeing himself of constriction. He moved over to the bed, resting one knee on the side of it to get his balance right, then slid his arms under Sunny, scooping her up against his chest, then swinging around to sit and cradle her on his lap.

'Bryce...' she choked out shakily.

'Hush now,' he soothed, pressing her head onto his shoulder and stroking her hair, trying to impart warmth and comfort. 'I want to hold you. I need to hold you, Sunny.'

She shuddered and sagged limply into the cocoon of his embrace, her strength all spent in trying to play straight with him. He simply held her for a while, stroking away the little tremors that shook her, thinking of all she meant to him.

He loved the rare integrity of her heart and mind—her whole character—the way she threw all of herself into whatever she took on, her openness and her honesty. He loved her innate decency, her caring, her sharing. He loved the feel of her, the scent of her, the wonderful sexuality of her. She was his wife.

'I want you to listen to me, Sunny,' he appealed softly. 'Just hear me out...'

* * *

She simply didn't have the energy to argue anymore. It was easier to let his words float over her because they couldn't really mean anything. It felt bittersweet being held like this, kindly, protectively, but for a little while she wanted to wallow in the sense of closeness, of Bryce caring for her.

'I know you want to be a mother,' he started slowly. 'I think you should go and have a fertility test next week so you'll know beyond any doubt if motherhood is on the cards for you. This fear you have…you're letting it eat you up, Sunny, letting it take over as though you're not worth anything if you can't have a baby. And that's not true.'

He wasn't getting it right, she thought wearily. It wasn't the end of the world for her if she had to be childless, but it would be the end of her world with him. Why was he holding off from seeing that?

'You're worth a great deal to me,' he continued gruffly. 'You've given me more than I ever imagined any one person could give another. You've shown me…what a woman in a man's life can mean to him…in so many ways…and on so many levels…'

His voice seemed to throb into her mind, his words like slow, deep heartbeats, pulsing with the very essence of *his* life. She was stirred out of the apathy she had fallen into. Her ears prickled with the need to listen, to hear every shade of what he was saying.

His chest rose and fell as he gathered more of his thoughts. 'My father…'

A sick tension gripped Sunny again at the mention of Will Templar.

'My father...is my father.'

He spoke as if searching for a truth he needed to communicate. She found herself holding her breath, listening with every atom of energy she had.

'He's been the only real constant in my life...all my life. And I do feel...an undeniable bond with him. He's my father...'

And they were very alike, very much father and son...a bond that would never be broken, she thought, and one she couldn't fight.

'But you're my wife, Sunny...and I love you. I love you as I've never loved any other person.'

He *loved* her?

'I didn't know what love was...how it could be...'

He swept his mouth over her hair, pressing warm, lingering kisses as though wanting, needing to imprint his feeling on her, and Sunny started tingling with the sweet joy of it, unable to cling to any fearful caution.

'But I do now with you,' he went on fervently. 'And I don't want to lose it. Ever...'

She didn't, either.

'If we can't have a child...believe me, Sunny...I don't want a child with any other woman. You are more important to me than any child could ever be. Having *you* sharing my life...that comes first. I promise you...it will always come first.'

She was swamped by his caring...caring for her...only her...

His hand threaded through her hair and cradled her head, his fingers gently kneading as he made his last bid for the marriage he wanted.

'You said love to you was emotional security. I

don't know what more to do…to prove you have that with me, Sunny.' He took a deep breath and poured out his heart. 'Please…I love you so much. Can you let this pregnancy issue go, and just…*be* with me?'

How could she not?

She loved him.

CHAPTER SEVENTEEN

SUNNY gazed in adoring fascination at the baby snuggled in the crook of her arm. Her baby. Hers and Bryce's. He was so beautiful, she couldn't stop smiling.

It was possible to look back now and be glad she hadn't fallen pregnant in those first couple of months of their marriage. To Sunny's mind, it was so much better having their child a true child of love and not the result of a marriage bargain. And that was how it had happened in the end.

The most probable cause of her initial infertility was anxiety, the doctor had told her—wanting to get it right for Bryce and his father. There'd been nothing physically wrong with her. Once she had felt emotionally secure in her marriage, she had fallen pregnant the very next month. And here she was...a mother at last.

The footsteps coming along the hospital corridor heralded Bryce's return from the airport. A glance at her watch assured her the time was about right. The clacking heels undoubtedly belonged to her mother who had flown from Sydney to see her new grandchild and stay for a while to give Sunny any help she might need in getting used to motherhood. Voices became more decipherable and she heard Will Templar giving forth.

'Oh, I knew it would be a boy. No surprise at all.'

Sunny rolled her eyes at her father-in-law's smug confidence. His flight from Sedona must have come in at approximately the same time as her mother's for them to have all met up together.

'Bryce was bound to have sons,' he went on proudly.

Sunny almost wished she'd had a daughter. Will Templar was far too fond of getting his own way. Not that she'd swap her darling little boy for any other baby. He had his tiny hand curled around her little finger, and while he might be too young to focus properly, he seemed to be looking straight into her eyes, loving her right back.

Bryce popped his head around the door and grinned at her. 'Ready for visitors?'

'It's showtime,' she said, grinning back at him.

In came her mother, beaming excitement and carrying a big bunch of irises and daffodils. 'Sunny... you look wonderful! And here he is...' She set the flowers on the bed, gave Sunny a kiss, and swept the baby up to cradle him herself. 'Oh, what a bonny boy!'

'Looks just like Bryce,' Will declared, peering over her shoulder.

'Nonsense!' her mother chided indulgently. 'See those curls? He's got Sunny's hair.'

'But it's black, like Bryce's,' Will pointed out, sticking to his judgment.

'Will, your son does not have curls,' her mother said firmly.

'Chip off the old block anyway,' Will muttered.

'Lucky your daughter's got brains as well as beauty, Marion. What we have here is a fine set of genes.'

'There's no luck involved at all, Will. Sunny married a man who matched her.'

'Well, can't go wrong with that combination,' he conceded. 'They're a good pairing. Saw it straight away.'

'Yes. They struck me that way, too. Very much in love.'

It was clear Will Templar considered this a soppy sentiment. 'What's love got to do with it?'

Her mother gave him an archly knowing look. 'Everything.' Then she smiled her perfect understanding at her daughter. 'What are you calling him, Sunny?'

'Adam,' she answered, giving Bryce a quizzical glance that encompassed their separate parents.

He rolled his eyes back at her, indicating there'd been a running altercation between them all the way here.

'Good strong name,' Will approved.

'Yes. It goes well with Templar,' her mother agreed.

'He's my grandson, too, you know,' Will reminded her mother. 'How about letting me hold him?'

'I think you'd better sit down first,' Marion York advised him. 'Sunny told me you had a heart condition.'

'Doctors are fixing that up. Gave me a whole heap of new drugs and they're working,' he declared. 'Do I look like a man with a heart condition?'

In truth, Bryce's father was looking surprisingly well, Sunny thought. He'd put on some weight and his face was a much better colour.

'Well, I must say you look like a man in his prime, Will,' Marion said admiringly, and Will Templar instantly puffed out his chest. She smiled winningly as she added, 'But why not sit down anyway? Much easier to handle a baby sitting down. You haven't had as much practice at it as I have.'

'True. But I'll have you know this grandchild is giving me a new lease on life.' He settled himself in one of the armchairs. 'Give him here.'

Sunny and Bryce exchanged highly amused looks as her mother carefully handed their baby son over to his grandfather who immediately started rocking him to show he knew exactly what a baby liked.

'Isn't he lovely?' her mother cooed.

'A real boy,' Will declared.

Her mother straightened up, positively glowing. She was wearing a plum-coloured pantsuit, a skivvy in a soft shade of wheat, a pretty scarf with a swirl of purple and plum and gold. The colours looked wonderful on her, and her eyes were sparkling, no sign at all that she'd just endured a long flight from Sydney.

'I'll go and find a vase for these flowers, Sunny. Though I don't know where we're going to put them,' she added ruefully, gazing around at the flower-filled room. 'Did Bryce buy out all the florist shops in Los Angeles?'

'Only the red roses are from me,' Bryce told her. 'Sunny has a knack of making lots of friends.'

'We can move something, Mum,' Sunny assured her. 'I love the irises and daffodils.'

'Good!' She gathered up the bouquet. 'I won't be long, dear.'

Off she went with Will Templar gazing after her admiringly before commenting to Sunny, 'Fine-looking woman, your mother. Think I'll stay on in L.A. and make sure she enjoys herself here.'

'Dad, you do have to take care with that heart of yours,' Bryce quietly reminded him.

It earned a flash of proud defiance. 'I'm not dead yet, boy.' He looked down at his new grandson. 'He's the future but I'm still very much alive,' he muttered. 'No reason I can't take a sixth wife.'

Bryce and Sunny burst into laughter.

The new grandfather didn't understand their amusement.

'You wouldn't want to be doing anything hasty, Dad,' Bryce advised with mock solemnity.

'No,' said Sunny. 'A hasty marriage might not work.'

'Did for you,' Will Templar argued. 'I don't see you two repenting at leisure.'

'No repentance at all,' Bryce agreed.

'And not likely to be,' Sunny chimed in.

Whereupon, Bryce sat on the bed next to her and drew her into his embrace. 'Hi, new Mom,' he murmured.

'Hi, new Dad,' she answered, winding her arms around his neck. 'I love you Bryce Templar, and I still fancy you rotten.'

'Likewise.'

Then he kissed her.

Queens of Romance

Were these sisters destined to be wives?

To Have a Husband

Harriet found enigmatic stranger Quinn McBride incredibly attractive, but she wasn't sure she could believe or trust him. Could she really be falling for the enemy?

To Become a Bride

Right from the beginning Danie crossed swords with Jonas Noble, but the secretive, handsome male was still unwittingly tempting her to imagine herself as his blushing bride!

To Make a Marriage

Her unborn baby had been conceived in a moment of irresistible passionate madness. But how much longer could she keep her secret? How was Adam Munroe going to react to impending fatherhood?

Available 20th April 2007

Collect all 4 superb books in the collection!

**In 1875, a row
of tiny cottages
stands by the
tracks of the
newly built
York – Doncaster
railway…**

Railwayman Tom Swales, with his wife and five
daughters, takes the end cottage. But with no room to
spare in the loving Swales household, eldest daughter
Mary accepts a position as housemaid to the nearby
stationmaster. There she battles the daily grime from
the passing trains – and the stationmaster's brutal, lustful
nature. In the end, it's a fight she cannot win.

In shame and despair, Mary flees to York. But the pious
couple who take her in know nothing of true Christian
charity. They work Mary like a slave – despite her heavy
pregnancy. Can she find the strength to return home to
her family? Will they accept her? And what of her first
love, farmer's son Nathaniel? Mary hopes with all her
heart that he will still be waiting…

Available 16th March 2007

*Victorian London is brought to vibrant
life in this mesmeric new novel!*

London, 1876

All her life, Olivia Moreland has denied her clairvoyant
abilities, working instead to disprove the mediums that
flock to London. But when Stephen, Lord St Leger,
requests her help in investigating an alleged psychic, she
can't ignore the ominous presence she feels within the
walls of his ancient estate. Nor can she ignore the
intimate connection she feels to Stephen, as if she has
somehow known him before…

Available 20th April 2007